THE
SEASIDE
SISTERS

Pamela Kelley

ST. MARTIN'S GRIFFIN
NEW YORK

First published in the United States by St. Martin's Griffin, an imprint of St. Martin's Publishing Group

THE SEASIDE SISTERS. Copyright © 2024 by Pamela Kelley. All rights reserved. Printed in the United States of America. For information, address St. Martin's Publishing Group, 120 Broadway, New York, NY 10271.

www.stmartins.com

Library of Congress Cataloging-in-Publication Data

Names: Kelley, Pamela M., author.
Title: The seaside sisters / Pamela Kelley.
Description: First edition. | New York : St. Martin's Griffin, 2024.
Identifiers: LCCN 2024003552 | ISBN 9781250861627 (trade paperback) | ISBN 9781250283597 (hardcover) | ISBN 9781250283603 (ebook)
Subjects: LCSH: Sisters—Fiction. | Self-realization in women—Fiction. | Books and reading—Fiction. | Summer—Fiction. | LCGFT: Novels.
Classification: LCC PS3611.E4432528 S43 2024 | DDC 813/.6—dc23/eng/20240129
LC record available at https://lccn.loc.gov/2024003552

Our books may be purchased in bulk for promotional, educational, or business use. Please contact your local bookseller or the Macmillan Corporate and Premium Sales Department at 1-800-221-7945, extension 5442, or by email at MacmillanSpecialMarkets@macmillan.com.

First Edition: 2024

10 9 8 7 6 5 4 3 2 1

THE SEASIDE SISTERS

Also by Pamela Kelley

The Bookshop by the Bay

Nashville Dreams

The Wedding Photo

Gilded Girl

The Hotel

Court Street Investigations series

The Nantucket Restaurant series

Nantucket Beach Plum Cove series

Montana Sweet Western Romance series

River's End Ranch series

Quinn Valley Ranch series

Waverly Beach Mystery series

Indigo Bay Sweet Romance series

*Dedicated to my sister
and best friend, Jane Barbagallo.
I feel lucky and grateful that
you are my sister.*

THE SEASIDE SISTERS

Chapter 1

"Good news. You're not having a heart attack."

Hannah Brewster felt equally embarrassed and relieved. At the age of thirty, she'd doubted she was having a heart attack, but her friend Lucy had insisted that she go to the ER and get checked out.

They'd been sitting in Hannah's Brooklyn apartment, drinking tea and chatting, when Hannah's literary agent, who was also her aunt, had called to let her know that Hannah had hit the *New York Times* list. Her first book, a beachy romantic comedy, had been out for a few months and it was selling reasonably well for a debut book, but over the past two weeks word of mouth had kicked in and it went viral on TikTok. That sent sales soaring.

After she and Lucy were done screaming, Hannah's first impulse was to call her mother and share the news. But that wasn't possible. And just like that, her mood deflated like a balloon that someone had stepped on. Her mother had died six weeks ago and even though they'd known the lung cancer would take her, it was still hard to believe she was gone. And she and Hannah had been so close.

As Hannah sat in her tiny Brooklyn kitchen, sipping her tea, she'd felt her chest tighten so much that it was hard to catch her breath. Her chest ached and when she turned she felt a sharp pain under her ribs. She'd also felt a little dizzy and light-headed. She ate a cookie, hoping that might settle things. Eating was generally her solution to every problem—they called it *comfort food* for a reason.

But Lucy could tell something was wrong. When Hannah described her symptoms, Lucy immediately tried to get her to go to the ER.

"I'm too young for a heart attack," Hannah had protested.

"Probably, but it happens. Let's go get you checked out. You don't mess around with chest pain."

Hannah insisted on waiting for a half hour to see if the pain calmed down. But the more she focused on it, the more anxious she felt, and her mind went to her deadline, which she'd been stressing about all day as well. She was so behind on this book. It was supposed to be a spin-off, another romantic comedy with the heroine's best friend, but Hannah couldn't figure out what to do with her. Her mind and her page were a blank and as she thought about it another wave of pain tightened across her chest as she breathed in. Lucy saw her face, stood and grabbed her car keys, and this time Hannah didn't protest. She let Lucy drive her to the nearest hospital.

In the ER, as soon as Hannah muttered the words "chest pain," they brought her in immediately and did an EKG and checked her vital signs. An hour later she was brought into a room, had blood drawn, and was sent for a chest X-ray.

An hour and a half later, the doctor came in and asked what had brought her into the ER. Hannah told him her symptoms and he nodded.

"Your EKG, blood work, and X-ray all came back fine. Have you been under any stress lately?" The doctor was about her age, and his eyes were sympathetic as he asked his questions.

Hannah nodded. "My mother passed away recently, I just ended a two-year relationship, and I have a publishing deadline hanging over me and I can't seem to write."

He smiled and his eyes were kind as he spoke calmly, his tone immediately reassuring. "That sounds like the kind of perfect stress storm that can lead to a panic attack. And to costochondritis—that's the chest pain you are feeling. It's from stress and the tightening of your chest muscles. It can mimic the feeling of a heart attack. So, it's a good thing you came in. You should always be evaluated for any chest pain."

Hannah relaxed and some of her chest pain seemed to instantly ease. "Will this happen again? What do I do about it?"

"It's possible. The best way to make sure it doesn't happen is to alleviate your stress. Do whatever you can to lower your stress levels. I can write you a prescription for Ativan. It's a mild relaxer that will calm your anxiety and ease your muscles. You can use it as needed, and just take it when you're feeling more stressed than usual."

Forty-five minutes later, Hannah was discharged with a prescription for Ativan and Lucy took her to Duane Reade on the way home to get it filled.

"Do you want me to stay?" Lucy asked as she pulled up to Hannah's building.

Hannah shook her head. "No, thank you. I'm going to go crawl into bed and watch Netflix until I fall asleep. Thank you for making me go and for taking me there."

Lucy pulled her in for a hug. "Rest up and call me tomorrow. I'm so glad it was nothing serious."

Hannah made her way up to her third-floor apartment. Her place was small, like most apartments in the city, but it was cozy and it had high ceilings, which made it feel a bit more spacious. It also had a tiny deck, with just enough room for two small chairs and a table between them. In nice weather, she spent a lot of time on that deck. She'd been in Brooklyn for almost ten years and it was home.

When she'd gotten her advance for the first book, it was large enough that she'd quit her administrative job so she could write full-time, and she'd gone shopping at Pottery Barn for furniture to replace her eclectic collection of thrift shop finds. Now everything in her apartment was creamy white, from the slipcovered sofa and chair to her bedding and plush area rug in the living room. She'd painted her walls a pale gray, which overall gave her home a spa-like feel that also reminded her of Cape Cod, specifically Chatham, where she'd grown up.

Once she was settled in bed, with her comfiest sweats and a pint of Ben & Jerry's almond milk Cherry Garcia ice cream, Hannah called her sister, Sara, who still lived in Chatham. Sara was five years older and had married Tom, her college boyfriend, right after graduation. Tom was a tech company executive and Sara was a stay-at-home mother with four boys under the age of twelve.

"Hannah, is everything okay?" Sara asked immediately. It was later than Hannah normally called and they'd already talked that morning. Sara often called after she'd gotten the boys off to school and had a few minutes to herself. But before Hannah could speak, Sara hollered at her oldest, "Cody, go ask your father, I am on the phone!" She turned her attention back to Hannah. "Sorry about that, I haven't seen Cody for an hour and the minute I answer the phone he comes running. It has been a day. What's up with you?"

Hannah told her what happened and the doctor's direction to lower her stress levels.

Sara immediately suggested that Hannah should come home to Chatham for a while. "We have a guest room you could use. And I'd love to see you. But I don't know that our house will be the most peaceful environment. I live with five loud, messy men."

Hannah laughed. "You do. I appreciate the offer though."

"You could always go to Mom's house. It's sitting there, empty."

Hannah sighed. That wasn't an option. The house she'd grown up in would definitely be quiet. But she wouldn't be able to relax or to focus there. They'd agreed not to sell their mother's house for a year. Neither one of them was ready to deal with it. Even though Sara was older and in many ways stronger, Hannah knew that her sister was having a hard time processing her grief, too. They'd both been close to their mother. Their parents had divorced twenty years ago and their father had remarried soon after. They rarely saw him.

"I can't do it. It would be too sad to be there, surrounded by all of her things. It's just too soon."

"I understand. I couldn't do it, either. What about Aunt Maddie? I bet she'd love the company."

"That's a thought. It would be great to spend some time in Chatham," Hannah said. Just the thought of it eased her tension a bit. She'd always felt energized and restored being near the ocean. And Chatham not only was a beautiful Cape Cod town—it was where she'd grown up. It was home.

"Call her," Sara said.

Hannah hung up the phone and was about to call her aunt when her phone beeped and it was her aunt calling. She answered the call and laughed. It had often happened with Hannah's mother— they'd be talking on the phone, and either Sara or Aunt Maddie would beep in. Hannah could picture Aunt Maddie sitting in her sunroom, which overlooked the ocean. Her aunt was always so put together. She'd been a top literary agent for years even though she mostly worked from home. She always looked so stylish with her wavy brown bob that just hit her collarbone and her beach-toned Eileen Fisher linen shirts and pants, and she almost always wore a gorgeous diamond necklace. It had been Uncle Richie's mother's engagement ring, which she left to Aunt Maddie. It was vintage and very delicate with an oval diamond surrounded by smaller ones. It made for a beautiful necklace.

"Your ears must have been ringing. Sara and I were just talking and I said I was going to call you."

"Is everything okay?" Her aunt immediately sounded worried. Hannah filled her in on the trip to the ER and the panic attack diagnosis.

Her aunt immediately sympathized. "I used to get panic attacks. Haven't had one in years, but they can be very scary. Totally brought on by stress, which you've had your share of. Why don't you come here for a few months? I'd love the company. The change of scenery might do you good."

"I think I'd like to do that, if you're sure it's no trouble?"

"Don't be ridiculous. You'll have plenty of room here and won't run into me unless you want to. The main guest room is at the opposite side of the house and it should be nice and peaceful for you. Come as soon as you want."

Hannah felt more of her tension ease as the decision was made. "How about a week from this Friday? I'll head down that weekend."

"Perfect! We'll relax on the deck and solve all of our problems with the help of a good chardonnay and some steamed lobster. Sound good?"

Hannah smiled. It sounded perfect. "I can't wait."

Chapter 2

"Mom! Dylan won't give me the remote!"

Sara Ellis had her hands in a bowl of ground beef, making meatballs for supper, when the latest fight started. She hollered at her sons for them to figure it out and finished what she was doing. Once the meatballs were baking in the oven, she washed her hands and headed into the living room to play referee.

Cody, her oldest, at twelve, was sitting in her husband's favorite chair, while Dylan, her ten-year-old, was sprawled on the leather sofa. Both of them were quiet now, watching *Stranger Things* on Netflix, which they both liked. Her younger two—Brad, who was eight, and Sam, the baby at six, were in the den playing a video game. The house was relatively calm for the moment.

She went back to the kitchen and started the spaghetti sauce, sautéing garlic and onions in a big pot, then added a can of crushed tomatoes, spices, and a splash of wine. When everything was just about ready, she poured a glass of wine, sat at the kitchen table, and opened her laptop, jumping online for a few minutes until her husband, Tom, got home.

Now that the kids were all in school full-time, Sara had been keeping her eye out for a part-time job. Before the kids came, she'd been a librarian and had loved it. But she'd been out of the workforce for so long that she didn't know anyone anymore at the local library. And she hadn't seen any openings posted online. She looked regularly and had even stopped in a few times over the past year to ask if they might know of anything coming up. But it seemed like no one ever left.

A quick search of the local job listings didn't turn up anything new. Tom had a good job, as a VP for a software company, so she didn't need to get just any job. She could hold out to make sure it was something interesting. Ideally she wanted something book or publishing related, but the local magazines and newspapers seemed to be cutting back instead of hiring. Sara couldn't help but worry that maybe she'd missed her window where she could easily get a similar job again. What if no one would hire her now? The thought made her anxious. She needed to find something soon.

Tom came through the door a moment later. Sara kissed him hello and went in the kitchen to bring the food to the table. Twenty minutes later, her hungry men had inhaled their dinner and resumed their positions in front of the TV. She didn't allow video games in the evening, so they were all in the living room, including Tom. By the time Sara cleaned up in the kitchen and joined them, Tom's eyes already looked heavy and she knew he'd be fast asleep on the sofa by seven.

Before he drifted off, she asked him if he wanted to go to dinner with friends Friday night.

"Courtney and Kevin invited us to meet them for dinner at the Squire. There's a band playing there that he likes. It could be fun."

Tom nodded. "Sure, if we can get a sitter?"

"I don't need a sitter," Cody said. He had a point. Sara had been babysitting at eleven. But boys were not as mature at that age and she didn't feel comfortable leaving him to watch the others. Not yet.

"Actually, that might not work out," Tom said. "I have to go into the office on Saturday. And I'll probably be working late on Friday to get ready for this presentation. It's a big one."

Sara sighed. She'd been so looking forward to going out for an evening and catching up with friends. She hadn't gone out in ages.

"You could still go," Tom offered. "I can bring my work home and lock myself in the den."

It wasn't exactly what she'd had in mind. She'd wanted a date night. But maybe she would go anyway.

❦

Maddie sat in her office, gazing out the window and watching the white-tipped waves crash against the shore as she took a call from one of her favorite editors.

"Do we have a chance of getting her? I don't want to jump through the approvals hoops and get everyone excited if she already knows she wants a different house," Alissa asked anxiously. She'd been a bridesmaid on the last three auctions that Maddie had set up for her authors.

"I can't promise anything. But you have as good a shot as anyone else. This is all new to her and she doesn't have any favorites. If you are up for a Zoom call, I think that could help." The video calls gave each house a chance to get to know the author and to share their excitement and hopes for the book. Usually several people from each publishing house would attend the call, an editor or two and often someone from marketing.

"Perfect. Let's do it. Thanks for your help." Alissa hung up and Maddie turned her attention back to her inbox, which was overflowing, as usual. She'd just opened her next message when her phone rang again. This time it was the main number of the literary agency in Manhattan where she worked.

"This is Madeline Sharp."

"Do you have a minute to chat, Maddie?" It was Kathryn, the head of the agency and Maddie's direct supervisor.

"I do. I just hung up with Alissa. Her imprint wants to offer on Shelley's book. We're going to set up a Zoom call."

"Oh, that's great. Are any others interested, do you think?"

"At least two more, possibly three. They were all excited to read it."

"It's a good book. I'm not surprised. And you did an excellent job creating anticipation for it."

"Thank you." Maddie had signed the author eight months ago and had been blown away by her manuscript, which was an edgy psychological thriller. She hadn't been able to put it down and got that sense as she read that others would feel the same way. Maddie had always been a big reader and had an instinct for what might go over in the market.

She'd started with the agency as an intern, the summer before she graduated. And she'd loved it from the moment she stepped through the doors over twenty years ago. Kathryn, the agency founder, was in her early seventies now. The agency was smaller then, just a few other agents, all women. Now the team was close to thirty people, half agents and half support staff and foreign rights specialists.

Maddie took to agenting immediately. She'd always had a knack for sales. Growing up in Chatham, she'd spent most of her summers working in the service industry and honed her people skills. As a waitress, she learned to deal with difficult personalities and she also learned that the more she hustled, the faster she turned her tables, and the more money she made.

That drive, combined with her love for books and ability to sense when something could be a commercial hit, had served her well. Over the years, her client roster grew from referrals of other happy authors and she was second only to Kathryn in total billing. Which meant that when Maddie wanted to spend more time in Chatham working remotely, she was allowed to do it and her sales continued to grow.

"How is Hannah doing with her book? Is she on track for her new deadline?" Kathryn asked.

Maddie took a deep breath. She'd only just hung up with Hannah and Maddie was concerned. She hoped that coming home to Chatham for the summer would help her niece to focus.

"Hannah's great. I'm going to be seeing her soon. She's going to spend the summer in Chatham. She is looking forward to writing by the beach."

"Hmm. Everything is okay with her? We can't push this deadline out again. That could slow her momentum. And her sales are increasing. There's a lot of buzz around her book. We need to bottle that and keep it going."

"She's struggling a little," Maddie admitted. "But I think she'll figure it out and finish on time," she assured her. "I'll keep you posted if there are any issues."

"Good! And we'll see you next week, then? We'll have to do dinner one night. There's a restaurant in the West Village I haven't been to yet, and their twenty-layer lasagna is apparently to die for." Maddie smiled. Kathryn was a foodie, too, and they always tried to go out to dinner at least once whenever Maddie was in Manhattan.

"That sounds great. I'm in."

Maddie ended the call and made a list for shopping later that day. She wanted to pick up some of Hannah's favorite foods, to help her settle in. And she would introduce her to her neighbors, Joy and Ben. They were a lovely older couple, and since Maddie would be heading to Manhattan for a week soon after Hannah arrived, she felt better knowing her niece could knock on their door.

✸

With the decision made to head to Chatham, Hannah felt lighter the following week. She still wasn't able to write much and felt anxious about it, but there were no additional panic attacks. She kept the bottle of Ativan in her purse, just in case she felt one coming on. She looked forward to going home to Chatham and just sitting in the sun, listening to the waves. The beach had always been her happy place. Something about the smell of the air and the breeze against her skin was so soothing. Hannah couldn't explain it, but she felt certain that going home might help her to get unstuck. She was in such a better mood that she let Lucy talk her into going to a party with her.

The party was Saturday night at the apartment of one of Lucy's coworkers and was right around the corner from where Hannah lived.

"If you're having a miserable time, you can just run home," Lucy said. It was impossible to argue with that. And Hannah was feeling a little stir-crazy and eager to get out. She was, however, a bit worried about running into Jeremy, her ex as of about two weeks ago. She'd met Jeremy through Lucy as they all had worked at the same marketing agency. Lucy handled event marketing while Jeremy worked in accounting.

"I don't think he'll be there. I thought I overheard him say he was heading out of town," Lucy had assured her.

So, it was fun to get dressed up and wear a new outfit. Especially when there was no pressure to try to meet anyone. Hannah wanted to visit with friends, have some wine, and maybe eat something delicious. Lucy was a foodie and most of her friends seemed to be, too.

The host of this gathering was one of the directors at Lucy's company. She lived in a huge apartment and had the food catered. There were all kinds of appetizers—cheeses, kabobs, sliders, dips. Hannah enjoyed a little of everything and sipped a very good glass of cabernet.

She was having a great time, until she heard a familiar voice.

"Hannah. I didn't expect to see you here." Jeremy, of course.

Lucy looked horrified. "I thought I heard you say you were heading out of town?"

"I was. But my plans changed. Hannah, can we talk for a minute?"

Lucy shot her an *I'm sorry* look and backed away.

"Sure."

Jeremy led her to a quiet area away from the crowd. Hannah cupped her glass of wine and took a sip.

"So, how've you been?" he asked. It had been two weeks since the breakup.

"I'm okay. I'm actually heading home next week. I'm going to spend a few months at my aunt's place on the Cape. I need to focus and get this book done, and as you know, I've been struggling with that."

He looked sympathetic. "With your mom and all, I know it's been hard. I just wondered how you were doing and if you've thought about us at all. You said you needed some time to figure out what you wanted. So I'm wondering if maybe you wanted to give it another shot? I've missed you."

Jeremy looked so sincere that it made Hannah feel like a terrible person. She wanted to like him more than she did. She'd tried, but after almost two years, she just couldn't see herself taking the next step and getting married. She knew she probably should have ended it long ago. But she liked Jeremy and thought maybe her feelings would grow. She just didn't love him enough to marry him and didn't see that changing.

"I've missed you, too," she said truthfully. But she'd also liked having some space and alone time. She'd wondered more than once if she was being too picky. Maybe missing someone that you liked meant you should be with them. In a weak moment, a week after the breakup, she'd run the idea by Lucy, who'd looked like she wanted to shake her.

"If you stay with Jeremy, you'll miss out on the kind of love that you dream about. Has Jeremy ever made your toes curl? Do you eagerly anticipate seeing him and hate to be apart?"

"Hmm. Not exactly. You may have a point."

Hannah tried to gather her thoughts to tell Jeremy that she didn't want to give it another shot. Before she could speak, he tried again.

"We could go to dinner tomorrow night. There's a new place that just opened that we could try."

Hannah shook her head, sadly. "I'm sorry, Jeremy. I think I really need to be by myself for a while. I need to focus on getting over my mother's passing and give all my energy to this new book. I think we should probably both try to move on."

Jeremy nodded sadly. "Okay. If anything changes, let me know." He turned and left and Hannah went in the opposite direction.

She found Lucy by the charcuterie board debating between salami and ham. "Go for the salami, it was good. Peppery."

"Thanks. How did it go with Jeremy?" Lucy asked.

Hannah sighed. "He wants to get back together. I told him we should both move on. Now I feel mean and think I should probably go. He's a nice guy. Am I making a big mistake?"

"Come with me." Lucy led her to the kitchen and topped off her wineglass before leading her onto an outside balcony. It was a warm night and there was a soft breeze that felt soothing as it brushed across Hannah's face.

"Do you regret breaking up with him?" Lucy asked.

"Not until I saw him," Hannah admitted.

"And when you ended things you felt more relieved than sad?"

"Yes. So, you're saying I made the right decision. I think I know that. But then seeing him. Jeremy is a nice guy. What if I never meet anyone better than him?" She paused for a moment, her thoughts swirling. "I could get married to Jeremy. He told me a month ago that he wanted to ask me, but wanted to make sure we were on the same page." And she'd instantly realized she had to break up with him, for his sake as well as hers.

"Clearly you're not. I think you will meet someone that you will fall madly in love with. And if you don't . . . well, at least you gave it your best shot. That's better than staying with someone just because you're afraid you'll never find that kind of love."

"You're right. I know you're right. Honestly, the last thing I feel like even thinking about right now is meeting someone anyway. I just want to feel better, not have any more panic attacks, and have my book start talking to me again."

Lucy laughed. "Is that how it is? You wait for your book to tell you what happens next?"

"Sort of. When I'm in the zone it's like everything falls away and I'm in the story and I see and feel what the characters do, and it just comes to me. Lately, nothing has been coming."

"Because you're so stressed?"

Hannah took a sip of her wine. "Yes. It is a creativity killer. But I have a feeling once I'm at my aunt's place I'll start to feel better and the words will come again."

"It won't be too sad for you, being in Chatham?"

"It would be if I stayed at my mother's house. And I'm sure when I go to the places she used to go, in town, it will hit me. But my aunt's home is so beautiful. It's right on the water and she and my uncle never had kids, so it's just a big, quiet house."

"That sounds perfect," Lucy said.

"Once I get caught up, you'll have to come and visit. I'd love to show you around." They'd been talking about doing that for years but one summer passed after another and they were always so busy that it had never happened.

"I'd really like that. I can take a week or so off later this summer. If things are going well for you then, we can make a plan."

Chapter 3

Sara sipped her chardonnay as she gazed around the Chatham Squire restaurant. She was sitting at the horseshoe-shaped bar with Courtney and Kevin. A band was setting up nearby and the place was busy, with people of all ages having dinner. Servers rushed by carrying plates of fried clams and lobster rolls. The clams smelled amazing.

"Tom's missing out," Kevin said as the bartender set down steamed lobster dinners for each of them. Sara had debated whether to go out with them without Tom and finally decided to do it. And she was glad that she did. They all had steamers, corn on the cob, and baked potatoes with their lobster and melted butter, and it was delicious.

Sara laughed. "He definitely is."

"I'm so glad you decided to come out," Courtney said.

It was nice to just get out and talk to adults for a change. It had been months since they'd had a night out with their friends, so Sara hated to skip it, especially if Tom was just going to be in his home office working.

After they finished eating, they ordered another round of drinks and listened to the first set of the band that was playing. The music was good, a mix of new and old rock. When the band took a break,

Sara checked the time on her phone. It was still early. And there had been no urgent messages to come home, which was nice. Tom was handling things.

"Are you excited for your sister to come home for the summer?" Courtney asked.

"I'm looking forward to seeing her. We talk often, but she hasn't come home much in recent years. Except at the end, of course, but we were focused on my mom then."

"It will be nice for her to enjoy the summer and relax," Courtney said.

Sara agreed. "I hope it helps. She's been having a hard time focusing since our mother passed."

"How are you doing?" Courtney's eyes radiated sympathy.

"I'm okay. I have my moments still when the sadness takes me by surprise. The holidays are the hardest."

"They say the first year is especially hard. It supposedly gets a little easier after that." Courtney shared the wisdom that Sara had heard many times, but it was true.

"I think it's the first time that she's not with us for each milestone—birthdays, holidays—that we feel it the most. I'm hoping it will get easier."

Sara took a sip of her chardonnay and felt the familiar wave of sadness at the mention of her mother. She'd loved the Chatham Squire, too. On the rare occasions that Sara had been able to sneak out for lunch or dinner with her mother, it was usually where they went and her mother almost always got the lobster roll.

"Any possibilities job-wise?" Courtney asked a bit later.

Sara sighed. "Not yet. I keep looking but there's not much out there. I was about to send a résumé in to the Chatham magazine just to keep me in mind for anything that might open up, but then I heard they just had another round of layoffs and are mostly working with freelancers now."

"Oh, I hadn't heard that. Could you freelance maybe?"

Sara had wondered about that, too. "I'm not sure. I think they usually hire people with recent experience for those kinds of things."

"Something will turn up." Courtney sounded so certain of it that it made Sara smile.

"I'm sure it will."

❦

Hannah flew on JetBlue to Hyannis the following week. Flying was the easiest and quickest way for her to get to Cape Cod. The flight was just over an hour to the Hyannis airport. Aunt Maddie met her there and they drove to Chatham in her white Volvo SUV.

It was just after five on a Friday and they hit a little rush hour traffic, but the forty-minute drive to Chatham went by quickly as her aunt chatted with Hannah the whole way.

"You'll meet my neighbors tomorrow. Joy and Ben have become good friends over the past few years. They're coming by midmorning for coffee. I'll be gone the following week. I have a bunch of meetings with publishers. I know you'll be fine by yourself, but I wanted you to meet them. It's quiet this time of year, as you know, and I'll feel better knowing you can go to Joy and Ben if you need anything."

Hannah smiled. Sometimes she thought her aunt still thought of her as a child. "I'm sure I won't need anything."

"Well, you never know. We've exchanged keys, so if you happen to lock yourself out, for instance, Joy can let you in."

Hannah didn't say anything and her aunt continued. "We've both done it more than once! So it's worked out well having each other's keys."

"That is a good idea, actually. I've locked myself out before," Hannah admitted. And no one else had a key, so she'd had to track down the building manager, who hadn't been pleased to have her day interrupted.

"We'll have the house to ourselves. Your uncle is in Manhattan." Her aunt's tone was bright but Hannah noticed something seemed off.

"When is Uncle Richie coming home?"

Her aunt sighed. "I'm not sure. I didn't say anything earlier because you have enough going on, but we've actually separated. Not officially, just temporarily. I'm not sure for how long."

"Oh! I didn't know."

"No one does. Neither one of us wanted to make a fuss about it. We've just had some issues recently and I thought some time apart might be good for us both."

"I'm sorry. I hope you work things out." Hannah was stunned. Her aunt and uncle always seemed to have such a solid relationship. She didn't want to pry by asking too many questions, but there was one she couldn't help but ask.

"Is Uncle Richie at the Manhattan apartment? Will you stay somewhere else next week then?"

Her aunt shook her head. "No, I'll stay there, too. The apartment has three bedrooms and an office. There's plenty of room for us to avoid each other. Your uncle has been going to the office, so he won't be around during the day." Uncle Richie did something in finance. Hannah had never understood exactly what, but knew it involved lots of number crunching and huge sums of money.

Hannah couldn't quite wrap her head around this news and decided to change the subject.

"Have you been to the Impudent Oyster lately?" It was one of their favorite year-round restaurants in Chatham.

Aunt Maddie replied, "I was just there last week with some friends. Delicious as usual. We'll have to go soon. Maybe tomorrow night if you don't have plans?"

Hannah laughed at the thought. "I have no plans."

"Well, I didn't know if you might be seeing Sara. She's welcome to join us, too. It would be fun to all go out."

"I'll give her a call and see if she can get away." Hannah doubted it. Sara had mentioned how difficult it was to find babysitters and how rarely she and Tom went out because of it.

Her aunt turned the car onto Shore Road and they drove past the gorgeous Chatham Bars Inn. It was a beautiful resort right on the ocean in Chatham with sprawling lawns and a feeling of understated elegance. They came around a corner and Hannah saw her aunt's house straight ahead. It was a large, all-white home with its own beach. Her aunt pulled onto the long, winding driveway and into the garage.

Hannah got her suitcase out of the back seat and followed her aunt into the house. She stopped short when she stepped into the kitchen to admire the view. It always took her breath away. There were floor-to-ceiling glass windows that ran the whole length of the house and looked out over the beach and ocean.

"You know where your bedroom is, honey. Drop your luggage there and let's have a glass of wine in the sunroom. We can watch the sun set. You still prefer chardonnay?"

Hannah nodded. "Yes, but I like all wine."

"I picked up a good one for us, La Crema. I had it at a friend's house and loved it."

Hanna wheeled her suitcase into the guest room and set it by the bed. It was a pretty room, spacious, with windows on all sides, one with a gorgeous ocean view. There was an attached bathroom and a big closet. The bed was a sleigh bed, made of polished dark pine, and the bedding was all snowy white with a puffy comforter and a bunch of pillows, all in different shades of blue for a nautical effect.

There was also a watercolor painting of the harbor on the wall, and Hannah remembered her aunt telling her it was done by a local artist and she'd bought it at a shop downtown. Hannah looked forward to poking around downtown, and walking along Main

Street, which reminded her a bit of a Hallmark movie as there were so many cute shops. She remembered her aunt had mentioned the bookshop had changed hands and she was curious to pop in there, too, and see if they had any copies of her book. She headed back to the kitchen.

"Here you go." Her aunt handed her a glass of wine and they settled in the sunroom, which looked over the ocean. It was her aunt's favorite room. She ate most of her meals there and relaxed in the evening watching TV or reading a book. When the weather was warmer, she cracked a window to let in the fresh air and the soothing sound of the waves crashing on the beach.

Hannah took a sip of the wine and closed her eyes for a moment, savoring the smooth, creamy taste.

"It's very good. Kind of oaky and buttery," she said.

"I thought so, too," her aunt agreed.

They chatted for a while about nothing in particular and then her aunt asked how she was feeling. "Have you had any more panic attacks?"

"No. I think I'm feeling a little better about it all. It's just sometimes it catches me by surprise, when I just don't expect it. That's when it's really hard."

Her aunt nodded. "I'm still struggling with it, too. She was my only sister and we were so close. We talked almost every day, even if it was only for a few minutes. I miss that the most."

Hannah realized it was likely just as hard for her aunt as it was for Hannah and Sara. Different, but similar. Hannah and Sara were close, but they didn't talk every day or even every week. Lately it seemed like they spoke once a month, if that, and it was always a rushed few minutes as one of them was always busy and couldn't talk long. Hannah was looking forward to spending more time with her sister over the summer. They were only five years apart but their lives were so different. Hannah couldn't imagine having four children at her age—like her sister had done. And four boys—it just seemed so exhausting.

"Feel free to use my office when I'm not here. There's also a small den, or you could even just sit here in the sunroom and write. Whatever works for you," her aunt said.

"Thanks. I'll probably roam around and see what feels good. I thought I might head downtown, too, and see if there's a coffee shop to hang out in and write for a bit. I did that a lot in Brooklyn."

"You can use Richie's car. He left it here. And there's a cute new coffee shop next to the bookstore." Her aunt looked at her curiously. "Can you really get writing done in a place like that? It's not too distracting?"

"You'd think it would be, but there's something about the hustle and bustle of people coming and going and the sounds of the cappuccino machines. It's like white noise that my brain recognizes and knows that it's time to get to work. Or at least it used to be . . ." Lately, no matter where she went, the words refused to come. She hoped it would be different in Chatham.

"Well, don't be alarmed if it doesn't happen for you right away. It may take a while for you to settle in and for your brain to be ready. I've been reading up a lot about this lately. How grief affects the brain. The bottom line is that it just takes time. Getting out and walking might help, too."

Hannah smiled. "I was thinking that as well. It's a great area to walk—along Shore Road and back. Do you want to go with me?" She knew her aunt liked to walk and at fifty-eight, she was slim and fit and looked five years younger.

"If I'm up, I'll go before Joy and Ben come for coffee. It's a great way to start the day. If I'm not up, go on without me and we'll go another day."

☙

Hannah went to bed early and slept deeply. The fresh Cape air and the day of traveling caught up with her and she drifted off as soon as her head hit the pillow. Which meant she woke earlier than usual, too. It was not quite six when she eased out of bed and padded softly to the kitchen. Her aunt was still sleeping, and she didn't want to wake her.

She found the coffee in a cupboard and made herself a cup, then brought it to the sunroom with her laptop. Usually her best writing time was first thing in the morning. When she was still half-asleep it was easier to tap into her creative zone. Usually. She'd hoped that the combination of being out of the city and her aunt's spectacular ocean view would inspire her. But when she opened her laptop and pulled up her manuscript, the empty page seemed to taunt her.

She tried her usual trick of reading through the last few scenes she'd written, but that didn't work because a little voice in her head whispered that it was unusable. Hannah tried to remind herself that it was just the normal writer insecurity and if she kept going, it would be fine at the end. That's what her writer friends said anyway. She hoped they were right, but she worried that it really was rubbish and that she wouldn't be able to fix it or keep going.

Hannah sighed and sipped her coffee. She stared at the empty page and then out the window, then back at the empty page. Sometimes after doing this for a few times, an idea would come to her and she'd type one sentence and then another and it wouldn't be long before she'd lose herself in the story.

But by the time she finished her coffee, she realized that it just wasn't going to happen this morning. She closed her laptop and decided to go for a walk. Her aunt was still sleeping. She grabbed a house key, put on her sneakers, sweatshirt, and jeans, and headed off for a walk. Sometimes when she walked, the ideas would come. But it was never something she could count on.

Walking was always a good stress reliever. Hannah did a lot of walking in Brooklyn. She used to walk to her office and once she started working from home, she made a point to get out of the house and walk at least once a day. Maybe if she headed to the coffee shop later in the afternoon, the writing might come more easily.

She was halfway down Shore Road, heading toward the Chatham Bars Inn, when her phone rang. It was her sister. Sara was also an early bird and often called once she'd gotten the kids off to school.

"Are you all settled in?" Sara asked.

"Pretty much. I'm out walking now. Aunt Maddie is still sleeping. Did you know she and Uncle Richie are separated? He's been living in the Manhattan apartment."

"What?" Sara sounded as shocked as Hannah had felt. "No, I didn't know that. Did she say why? I've been so busy, I haven't actually talked to her in almost a month. I feel bad now that I didn't call."

"She just said they have some issues to work out. I wouldn't feel bad. The kids keep you busy. We're going to dinner at the Impudent Oyster. She said to invite you out tonight with us, if you can make it."

"Oh, I would love that." Sara hesitated a moment before adding, "Maybe Tom will watch the kids. Though he just did that last weekend."

Hannah stopped walking for a minute. "Let me guess. He watched them because you invited him out, but he needed to work?"

Sara sighed. "He had a big client project. It was disappointing though. It would have been fun if he'd come out, too. Courtney and Kevin are our best friends, and we never get out to see them anymore."

"Is there a chance you could get a sitter?" Hannah asked.

"Impossible on this short notice."

"Well, it would be nice if you could come."

"I'll ask him. It's a Saturday, after all, so I'm sure he won't mind.

I haven't seen Aunt Maddie in ages." Sara sounded like she wanted to join them.

"It will be fun. We'll swing by and pick you up."

"How are you doing? Did you get some writing done this morning?" Sara knew Hannah was a morning writer and her normal routine was to go for a walk after she got her daily words done.

"It feels good to be here. I slept like a baby last night. But the words wouldn't come this morning. I'm going to go downtown this afternoon and bring my laptop. Maybe I'll be able to get something done at the coffee shop."

"Did Aunt Maddie tell you there's one right next to the bookshop? New owners took it over last year and are running the coffee shop, too. It's always busy."

"She did. I'm looking forward to checking it out. And the bookstore, too."

"You should introduce yourself. Maybe you can do a signing there?" Sara suggested.

"That's a great idea. I was just planning to browse and maybe buy a book or two, but it could be fun to do a signing at some point."

"I've got to run, the school is calling on the other line. I'll call you later about tonight."

Hannah continued walking for another forty-five minutes and made it back to the house a little after nine. Aunt Maddie was up by then and in the sunroom, drinking coffee and reading the morning paper. Hannah said a quick hello, then showered, changed, and dried her long hair. She'd just walked into the sunroom with a second cup of coffee when there was a knock at the front door.

Her aunt jumped up. "That must be Joy and Ben."

It was. Her aunt held the door open and welcomed her next-door neighbors. They were both in their mid-seventies. Joy had short straight gray hair and round wire-framed glasses and big blue-gray eyes. She was petite, about five-three, and slim. Her husband was almost a foot taller and had white-gray hair and a matching beard. He had rosy cheeks and warm brown eyes. Both of them exuded warmth and Joy seemed to be aptly named. Her eyes lit up when Hannah's aunt introduced them.

"It's so nice to finally meet you. Your aunt talks about you and your sister all the time."

Aunt Maddie poured coffee for Joy and made a cup of English breakfast tea for Ben, who was British and preferred tea. They all went in the sunroom and Hannah's aunt also brought a coffee cake and plates and they all helped themselves.

"This is delicious, did you make it?" Joy asked.

Aunt Maddie laughed. "No. I'm not much of a baker, or a cook, for that matter. I got that at the market, they have a great bakery." It was a cinnamon-walnut coffee cake and Hannah inhaled her piece. She hadn't eaten anything yet and had worked up an appetite from the walk.

As they chatted, Hannah learned that Joy was a semiretired minister who also taught creative writing. She was also a published poet and mystery author for a small press. Ben was retired and enjoyed woodworking.

"He has a full shop of machines in the basement. Ben makes the most beautiful bowls. He sells them at local craft fairs," Joy said proudly.

They chatted for a half hour or so before Hannah's writing came up.

"I'm hoping the change of scenery might help Hannah find her story," her aunt said.

Joy looked sympathetic. "It's hard when the words don't cooperate. You know, sometimes it's helpful to be around other writers. I lead a small group of local writers every Monday. Why don't you join us? We all read a few pages of whatever we are working on and it's a friendly group. They'd be tickled to have you there."

The idea appealed to Hannah. Her writing friends were all online and she missed the real-life company of other writers. "I'd love that."

"Good. Pop by around three. We're usually done by five."

The visit flew by. Hannah enjoyed listening to Joy and Ben talk about their recent adventure. They'd just visited Venice.

"It's a beautiful city and the food everywhere in Italy is so good. Venice is unique. Imagine, every day, the water rises and floods just a little. And no one is bothered about it. They just go about their day."

"That sounds wonderful. Italy is high on my list of places I'd like to see," Hannah said.

"You should go. Go everywhere. It's a big, beautiful world," Joy said. She and Ben stood and said their goodbyes.

"I'll see you on Monday then. Oh, if you see a young man about your age on our property, that's our grandson, Spencer. He insists on cutting our lawn and doing odd jobs when we need them. Actually, maybe you know him? I think he's about your age. He's a lawyer now, works right on Main Street. We're very proud of him."

"I do remember him. I'm not surprised he's a lawyer. I think he was valedictorian of our class."

"He was! Well, we'll see you both soon."

Hannah and her aunt walked them to the door and Hannah tried to picture Spencer. It had been years since he'd seen him or even thought of him. When she was in high school she'd had such a crush on him and he'd never looked at her twice. He'd always had a bit of an attitude, like he was too important to bother with someone like Hannah. Spencer had been a serious student, on the debate team, and one of the years he was class president. Other than English and art, Hannah's grades had been somewhat mediocre.

Hannah had enjoyed high school and had loved being a cheerleader and a member of the creative writing club. That club had started her dreaming about being a writer someday and her teachers had been encouraging. But she'd known that most of the students didn't take romance writing seriously. Hannah was used to that by now. For some reason, even though it was the top-selling genre, romance was also the one genre that people, including other writers, often looked down on.

Spencer had been one of those people. Her crush on him had been short-lived once she actually got to know him a little and realized they were much too different to ever be compatible. She hadn't thought about him since high school and had to admit, now that Joy had mentioned him, she was curious to see if he'd changed at all since then.

Chapter 4

After lunch at home with her aunt, Hannah decided to head downtown. She eased her uncle's charcoal-gray BMW sedan out of the garage and waited longer than she needed to pull onto Shore Road. She hadn't driven a car in several years and even though it came right back to her, she still felt a little nervous, especially as it wasn't her own car.

Downtown Chatham was less than a ten-minute drive away, and she found a parking spot right on Main Street, which was lucky. Someone was pulling out just as Hannah drove up. She parked and put her laptop in her oversized tote bag and got out of the car. It was a sunny Saturday afternoon and there were lots of people out and about.

Hannah strolled along, popping in and out of shops that looked intriguing. There was a great boutique that had some gorgeous shoes and sweaters. She was tempted by a really cute pair of dressy shoes, but didn't really need anything, and she was trying to be careful with her spending. She'd read about other authors who blew through their six-figure advances in a year and then their next book didn't sell and they were dropped by their publisher.

If she had to, Hannah knew she could always go back to doing administrative work, even if it was just a temporary assignment.

There was always a demand for it. But she hoped she wouldn't have to. Her sister had thought she was jumping the gun by quitting a perfectly good job that had great benefits. Sara had always been the more conservative, practical sister. Whereas Hannah had always dreamed of being a full-time writer, and as soon as she received the first installment of her advance, she'd put in her two weeks' notice. And had never regretted it.

She spotted the bookshop and admired the books in the display window before stepping inside. The arrangement was attractive with a dozen or so different titles stacked on a bright blue beach towel. The books were mostly bestsellers across a variety of genres, with a few authors she wasn't familiar with as well.

Hannah had so many memories of this shop when she was growing up in Chatham. The same owner had run the shop for as long as she could remember. When she stepped inside it still had a wonderful timeless feeling of peace about it. People were browsing the many sections, and two little kids were sitting on the floor in the children's book area. They were flipping through picture books while their parents chatted nearby.

The shop had a slightly different look, with a fresh, fun feel to it and lots of smaller tables scattered here and there highlighting different genres. And there was a large rectangular table right by the front door that featured local authors. Hannah was a little disappointed that her book wasn't on it. Or anywhere else that she could see.

But she still enjoyed browsing and noticed that all of the smaller tables had little sticky notes with staff recommendations and thoughts on various books. It was fun to read the notes and consider their suggestions. Hannah picked up two new novels by debut authors that looked intriguing and made her way to the counter to pay.

The woman at the counter had a name tag that said ALISON.

She looked familiar to Hannah. She was about her mother's age and she smiled as Hannah handed her the two books she'd chosen.

"Did you find everything you were looking for?" Alison's voice was warm and friendly.

Hannah nodded. "I did. The store looks great. I really like the little note cards you have with a lot of the books. It helped me decide."

Alison's eyes lit up. "Oh! That's wonderful to know. That was my daughter Julia's suggestion."

"I also wanted to introduce myself. I'm a local author. I grew up here in Chatham and am staying here for the summer, working on my second book." Hannah felt like she was rambling a bit. She wasn't used to randomly introducing herself to bookstore owners.

Alison seemed interested. "We love local authors. What is the name of your book?"

"*Time Flies.* I write as Hannah McIntosh, but my real last name is Brewster."

Alison's eyes widened and Hannah saw sympathy there. "Hannah, I am so sorry about your mother. We were friends and worked together at the magazine for years. I'm Alison Page."

That's why she looked familiar. Hannah vaguely knew her daughter Julia, too, though she'd been a year ahead of her in school and they hadn't hung out with the same crowd.

"Of course. I've been living in Brooklyn for close to ten years and don't get home as often as I'd like. How is Julia?"

Alison beamed. "She's great. She makes jewelry and has a shop a few doors down. You know, we're actually totally sold out of your books. I have more on order, but once you hit the *New York Times* list, people came in looking for it." She looked thoughtful for a moment. "Would you ever be interested in doing a signing?"

Hannah didn't hesitate. "I'd love to."

"Good. We can do a Saturday afternoon, maybe in a few weeks.

The books should be here in a few days and I can order more for the signing as well." Alison smiled as she rang Hannah's books up.

"I'm here all summer, so any weekend works for me." The summer stretched before her and Hannah had no plans. A signing would be fun.

"Okay. Let me get your email address and I'll check the calendar and let you know. It will be fun!"

While Alison ran her credit card, Hannah fished around in her purse for one of the cute business cards she'd had made and seldom used. They came in handy when she visited bookstores. Then Alison handed her a cute green paper bag with her two books.

"Here you go! I'll talk to you soon about setting up that signing."

Hannah wandered into the connecting coffee shop and immediately liked the vibe. It had a welcoming feel, with lots of small tables. She set her shopping bag and laptop on a corner table and went to order coffee. There were a few others in line and several people sitting by the big windows that looked out over Main Street.

Hannah decided on a caramel latte and a chocolate-chip cookie. She settled at her table, opened her laptop, and took a sip of her coffee and a bite of her cookie. Both were excellent. She read her story from the beginning and was relieved to see that it was better than she remembered. She made small tweaks here and there as she read and by the time she finished, she had a few new ideas for scenes.

Before she knew it, two hours had passed and she'd written two new scenes, and for the first time in a long time, she felt good about her story again. Her phone rang just as she was closing her laptop and getting ready to head home. It was Sara.

"Are you coming to dinner with us?" Hannah asked.

"Yes! Tom agreed to watch the kids. Where are you? I hear voices in the background."

"At the coffee shop by the bookstore. I've been here for a few hours. I'm on my way home now."

"A few hours? Does that mean the writing went well?"

Hannah smiled. "Yes. I got some good words in today."

"That's great news! We can celebrate over dinner." Hannah tossed her laptop and phone in her tote bag and stood to leave. It had been a good day. She felt happy and optimistic that she might actually fix her book and she looked forward to catching up with her sister and aunt over dinner.

Chapter 5

W hat happened here?" a vaguely familiar voice asked. Although it was apparent what had happened. Hannah had clipped Joy and Ben's mailbox. Which meant she had to be just about the worst driver ever. And when she turned and saw it was Spencer, she wanted to die. He looked all grown up and even more handsome than she remembered with his dark wavy hair and intense hazel eyes. Eyes that were scowling at her. And she didn't blame him.

She bit her lip and took a breath before speaking. "I feel awful. I was just trying to get close enough to get the mail before heading into my aunt's house and I misjudged the distance. I'm not used to driving this car. I'll pay for it, of course."

Spencer assessed the damage. The post itself wasn't damaged, just pulled out of the ground, which was soft from recent rains.

He nodded. "It's not a big deal. I can fix it. I'm Spencer, by the way. Spencer Smith."

"And you're Joy and Ben's grandson. She was talking about you this morning. I'm Hannah Brewster. I'm staying with my aunt for the summer."

He studied her quietly for a moment as if trying to place her.

"I was a year ahead of you in high school," he said. "Where do you live now that you don't have to drive?"

"I've been living in Brooklyn for almost ten years. Today is the first time I've driven in several years," she admitted.

"Well, you're lucky this is an easy fix. Maybe be a little more careful till you get used to driving again." His tone had a sharp edge to it that took her by surprise and she stepped back.

"Of course. I'll get out of your way. Thank you for helping." She turned to walk back to her car. He was the same as ever; she didn't know why she thought he might have changed.

"Hannah."

She glanced back and Spencer was smiling and his eyes were apologetic.

"What?"

"It's nice to see you. I'm sure I'll see you around." He picked the mailbox up and pounded it back into the ground. "See, good as new."

Hannah was relieved that she hadn't killed the mailbox. "Thank you."

Hannah climbed into her car and drove up her aunt's driveway. She thought back to high school and wondered what Spencer thought of her now. She was pretty sure that he'd thought she was flaky in high school. She'd always been creative, hung with the artsy crowd, and she'd had a tendency to run late. Whereas Spencer was always early and he used to roll his eyes when she would rush into class late. She liked to think that she'd matured since then, but running over his grandparents' mailbox wasn't a great look.

✾

"I can't believe you ran over Joy and Ben's mailbox!" Sara looked thoroughly amused as she reached for her glass of chardonnay and took a sip.

Hannah was sitting at a table at the Impudent Oyster with her aunt and sister. She'd just shared her embarrassing run-in with Spencer Smith and the poor mailbox.

"I wanted to die," she admitted. "I used to have such a crush on Spencer and after not seeing him in years, that's what happens. I'm so glad the car wasn't damaged."

Her aunt waved the concern away. "I'm not worried about the car. You weren't going fast enough to damage it. And Spencer put the mailbox back in place. He's pretty handy around the house and he's over there often. Joy and Ben pretty much raised him."

Hannah hadn't known that. Her aunt had only moved into this house a few years ago. "What happened to his parents?"

"Drunk driver. They were on their way home from a night out and were killed instantly by someone going the wrong way on Route 28. I think he was only two or three when it happened."

"How awful," Sara said. "Does he have any siblings?"

Aunt Maddie shook her head. "No, it's just Spencer. He was so little that he probably hardly remembers his parents. Joy and Ben showered him with attention. I think he did very well in school."

"He was valedictorian," Hannah confirmed. "And he may be hot, but he's still insufferable. He told me to be more careful. How rude!"

Sara laughed. "Well, can you really blame him?"

Hannah smiled. "I suppose not. But still, he annoys me."

"He's probably just being protective of his grandparents. I wouldn't take it personally. I'm not worried about your driving," Aunt Maddie said.

"I will be more careful though," Hannah assured her.

"I know you will. So, what are you two having?"

It was hard to choose. The menu had so many things that sounded good. They decided to share two appetizers, fried calamari and the oysters Rockefeller, which they always ordered. They were local oysters baked with fresh lobster, sambuca, spinach, and cheese béchamel sauce, and they were to die for. For their meals, Sara ordered the steak au poivre and both Hannah and her aunt got the filet and lobster tail.

Everything was delicious. They all packed up half their dinners to take home and shared a piece of cheesecake topped with cherries and whipped cream for dessert.

"Have you lost weight, Sara?" Hannah's aunt asked. Sara had the most food left over from her dinner and she only had one bite of the cheesecake that Hannah and her aunt devoured. Sara had always been the thinner of the two of them. She was more active and had never had to worry about her weight. Hannah hadn't noticed it before but now that her aunt mentioned it, Sara did look a little thinner and she had dark circles under her eyes, more than usual.

Sara nodded. "I haven't gotten on the scale but my clothes are looser. I haven't been trying to lose weight, I just haven't been as hungry lately."

"Are you feeling okay?" Hannah heard the concern in her aunt's voice.

"I feel fine. I've just been more tired than usual lately. I love my boys dearly, but I need to find a part-time job soon. I've been looking for a while, but there's nothing out there. And Tom's been working such long hours lately. It's just getting to me."

"Something will turn up soon," Aunt Maddie said. "It will be good for you to get back out there and have more balance in your life. Tom will have to help more though. You can't do everything you do now and work, too."

"Do you miss your day job at all?" Sara looked at Hannah and the question surprised her, at first.

"Not even for a minute. I never loved the work. I did like the people, and sometimes I do miss going into an office and having coworkers. Writing is a solitary job. Thanks to the internet and my phone, I am in touch with writer friends while I work. We have Facebook groups and there's a group of us that meet up on Clubhouse most afternoons and chat in between writing sessions. That's what I missed the most and now I sort of have it again."

"I love working from home," Aunt Maddie said. "Maybe it's partly my age, but the daily commute gets old fast. It's the best of both worlds for me now, as I still go into the city occasionally and meet up with editors for lunch, and that gets me out of the house."

"Will you be meeting with editors next week?" Hannah asked. She'd always thought her aunt's job sounded glamorous. When Aunt Maddie used to live and work in the city, she was always visiting publishers and going to lunches or dinners to build relationships with editors. Some of those editors regularly sent her emails telling her what they were eager to see in submissions, so when she'd come across a manuscript set with a knitting theme, she might know of an editor looking for exactly that.

"I have a bunch of meetings set up and most of them are lunches or after-dinner drinks. One of my favorite editors told me she's looking for a female Jack Reacher book. I'm curious to chat with her more about that."

"That would be difficult to find, I would think," Sara said.

"It does seem impossible. But I want to find out how flexible she might be. I just read a story last week that has a similar vibe, but the book is set in a small town and the woman is a sheriff. I'd like to tell her about it and see what she thinks."

"Do you think other publishers will be interested, too?" Hannah asked. She was already intrigued by the little she'd heard. Though she wrote romance, she also loved reading mysteries and thrillers.

Her aunt nodded. "I think they may be. I plan to talk about this book to most of the editors that I meet with and tease it a bit. The author is revising it slightly. My hope is when it's ready to be submitted, we'll have editors eager to read it." She smiled. "I like to build that anticipation ahead of time, so then they read more quickly."

"That sounds right up my alley. I love edge-of-my-seat suspense," Sara said.

"I'll send it to you if you like, when she sends it back with her revisions. I should have it in a few days. And I'd be curious to get your impressions."

"Oh, I would love that!" Sara looked excited to read it.

Hannah felt her chest tighten as she thought about how far her current book was from having edge-of-the-seat suspense. One didn't expect that in a romantic comedy, but still, there needed to be a reason for the pages to turn. She took a deep breath and tried to will the sense of panic away. If she needed them, she had the bottle of Ativan in her purse. But she'd already had a glass of wine and didn't want to mix them. She decided to change the subject.

"What are you up to tomorrow, Sara? I'm going for a long walk in the morning and thought I'd head to the coffee shop in the afternoon again to try and get a little more writing done."

"Sundays are crazy around here. I'll be running around with the boys for various sports practices and Tom's parents are coming for dinner tomorrow night. Your day sounds much more relaxing."

Hannah sighed. It would be more relaxing if she wasn't so stressed about her lack of production. But she'd had a good writing session today and hopefully a good, long morning walk would help her shift into a more relaxed and productive state.

"That sounds like a good plan, Hannah. I may need a ride to the airport later in the afternoon, if you don't mind. I have a five o'clock flight to New York from Hyannis."

"Of course!" It would be strange having the house all to herself with her aunt in the city all week, but maybe it would help Hannah to focus.

Chapter 6

Hannah gave Aunt Maddie a hug goodbye at the airport the next day.

"Have fun in New York."

She hoped that her aunt and uncle might use the time together to work on whatever wasn't right with their marriage. Aunt Maddie still hadn't shared any details about what wasn't working. And Hannah hadn't asked.

"I will. Call me if you need me and don't forget about Joy and Ben next door if it's something I can't help with."

Hannah smiled. "Will do. I'm seeing Joy on Monday for her writing group meeting."

"Oh, that's right. Well, have fun, honey, and I'll see you in a week."

"I'll be here next Sunday."

Hannah waved goodbye to her aunt and drove off. Since she was in Hyannis, she decided to stop by the Barnes & Noble at the Cape Cod Mall and see how her book was doing there.

The mall was mobbed as usual and it was a challenge to find a parking spot. But finally, she found one and headed into the store. She found her book on the second floor in the romance section and there were only a few copies on the shelf. She didn't know if it was because they had only ordered a few copies or if they'd had more and already sold them. She decided to introduce herself to the store manager and see if they might also consider putting some of her books on the local authors table, which was by the door where people entered.

She stopped by the information desk and asked for the manager, and when he walked over, she introduced herself.

"I grew up on the Cape, in Chatham, and I'm here for the summer so I thought I'd stop in and say hello."

"Thank you for stopping in. Your book has sold well for us. Especially for a new author. If you're interested in doing a signing sometime this summer, we can order extra copies and also add you to the local author table."

"I would love that!" She handed him her card. "All my contact info is here."

"Perfect. I'll shoot you an email and we can pick a date that works. Saturday afternoons seem to be our best times for readings."

"Great, I look forward to it."

Hannah browsed around a bit after that and got herself a cup of hot cinnamon-spice tea from the cafe for her drive back to Chatham. She also picked up a new release from one of her favorite authors.

The tea smelled amazing. It was one of her favorite flavors. She sipped it slowly as she drove down Route 28 heading back to Chatham. It was a more scenic route and as she passed through all the towns on the way to Chatham—Yarmouth, Dennis, Harwich—she couldn't help notice how they'd changed over the years. Different restaurants and shops had come and gone. This time of year, things were still quiet; many of the tourist-related businesses like mini-golf hadn't yet opened for the season. In a few more weeks everything would be open. Memorial Day weekend would welcome the beginning of the summer season. Hannah looked forward to it. She enjoyed the peace and quiet in the off-season, too, before the traffic tripled.

As she drove along she realized it had been over a week since her last panic attack, and that had been a small one that she'd felt coming and had been able to divert. She felt more relaxed now, especially after finally having two good writing days in a row. That's why she wanted to test driving home this way. When she took the highway to Chatham, she was able to go to her aunt's place without passing by her mother's house. By taking Route 28, which was a main road that ran through all the towns, she would pass right by her mother's house a few minutes after entering Chatham.

She took a deep breath as she saw the familiar landmarks, and then up ahead, her mother's home on the right. It was a typical Cape Cod–style house, with weathered gray shingles and white shutters and a white picket fence. Her mother's car, a baby-blue Toyota Corolla, sat in the driveway. The sight of her car made Hannah's eyes instantly well up. It looked as though her mother was home. The house looked the same as ever, except that the grass was starting to grow a little too long and would need to be cut soon. She'd have to talk to Sara about that and see if there was someone she knew who could cut it for them.

Hannah took a deep breath and drove on. She felt a bit calmer once the house was out of sight and she was relieved that it hadn't triggered a panic attack. She felt sad, which was normal, but she didn't feel the awful tightening and pressure that came with a panic attack.

She stopped at the Kream 'N Kone in downtown Chatham and decided to splurge on a fried clam plate, which came with French fries, onion rings, and coleslaw. She got it to-go and ate it in the sunroom while watching the waves on the water.

She'd just finished eating when she got a message on Facebook from Joy. *Don't forget about writing group Monday afternoon. We*

meet at three and go until five. And why don't you plan to stay for
supper after that? I'm making a big pot of split pea soup and some
fresh bread.

Hannah immediately wrote back. *I'd love to. Thank you. What*
can I bring?

Nothing for supper, just yourself. For the group bring a few pages
of whatever you are working on. We'll take turns reading our work.

Perfect. See you tomorrow. Hannah didn't want to show up
empty-handed, though. So, she thought she might head to the
coffee shop again tomorrow afternoon and when she left, maybe
she'd buy some of their brownies to bring for dessert.

Hannah had another productive session at the coffee shop the next
day and left with two thousand new words and a dozen brownies
to bring to her neighbors for dessert. When she got home, she
printed a few pages of her first chapter and headed next door at a
few minutes before three.

There were already several people there when Hannah arrived.
She handed Joy the box of brownies.

"In case we have room for dessert."

Joy laughed. "There's always room for dessert. Thank you, Hannah. Make yourself comfortable. We're meeting in the family room."
Joy introduced her to the others. Vern was in his seventies and explained that he was a retired healthcare consultant who had always
written a little poetry on the side and was now working on a novel.
Mary was in her sixties and was also retired. She used to be an ele-
mentary school teacher. Anna was the youngest of the bunch, and
looked to be about Hannah's age. She was a stay-at-home mother
of two small children.

"My husband works from home on Mondays. He was the one
that insisted I come. I love my children, but I needed to get out
of the house. I've only been coming for a few weeks, but I look
forward to Mondays now."

Joy joined them at three on the dot.

"We might as well get started. There is one more who often joins us, but she usually runs late." It was clear that Joy did not appreciate the tardiness.

"Since Hannah is new here, I thought she could introduce herself and then we'll get started with the writing prompt." She nodded at Hannah to go ahead.

"Hi, I'm Hannah. I write romance—romantic comedies, actually. I'm working on my second book and I've had a lot of writer's block this time. I'm spending the summer here, where I grew up, to see if a change of scenery might help."

As soon as she finished speaking, the door opened and a woman came rushing into the room full of apologies.

"I'm so sorry, Joy. I didn't realize my gas was so low. I had to stop and fill up and then I think I hit every red light on the way over."

"Have a seat, Louise. You haven't missed anything yet. We're about to start the writing prompt. Meet Hannah, she's staying next door for the summer and is a published author. Hannah, meet Louise. She's a fantastic mystery writer and she will finish her first mystery this year. Right, Louise?"

Louise ran a hand through her shoulder-length tumble of wavy gray hair. She grinned at Joy. "Yes, I will finish it this year."

"Good. Okay, today's prompt. The phrase is 'Victorian house.' Write five hundred words about a Victorian house. Go!"

Hannah picked up her pen and opened her notebook and thought about the chosen words.

"Don't think too hard now. Just start writing whatever comes to mind and see where it takes you. This is just an exercise to warm up our writing muscles and have some fun," Joy said. She glanced at Hannah and winked. Hannah smiled. She knew the words were mostly directed at her—a reminder to just have fun with the exercise and not take it too seriously.

And just like that an idea came to her and Hannah started scribbling. They all wrote for about ten minutes before Joy called to take another minute if they needed it to wrap up and then they'd all read their work.

Everyone read what they'd written and Hannah found it interesting how different everyone's mini-story was. Some had a bit of romance while others had a murder happen at the Victorian house. Hannah's went in the romance direction and she found that it was more fun than she'd expected.

For the rest of the session they took turns reading whatever they'd brought to share, and taking feedback and questions from the group. It was interesting and helpful for Hannah to listen to everyone else's feedback.

When it came time to read her own work, she felt nervous but took a deep breath and dove in, reading the first four pages of her book. She knew it needed work. The opening scene wasn't really working for her and she couldn't quite figure out what it needed, what was missing.

But the feedback she received from the group helped. Anna had the most insightful comment that seemed to hit on what Hannah was sensing.

"I really liked it. But I wonder if you might give us a little more of her background in the beginning—of why what she wants matters so much. Then I think it will matter more to me, too."

"Thank you so much. That's really helpful." Hannah made notes and planned to spend the next day thinking more about Anna's suggestion.

When everyone had had a turn and had received feedback, it was almost five.

Joy stood, signaling that the meeting was over. "All right, everyone. Thanks for another good session. Same time next week?"

Everyone agreed and said their goodbyes before heading for the door. Once everyone left, Joy turned to Hannah.

"So, what did you think? Was it helpful? We'd love to have you join us again if you're up for it."

Hannah nodded. "I'd like to. I wasn't sure what to think. I've never been to a group like this, but it was fun, and helpful, too."

"Good. Come on out to the kitchen. You need to taste this soup and let me know if you think it needs anything."

Hannah followed Joy into the kitchen and over to the stove where she had a pot of soup simmering. She looked around the room—it was a big, warm kitchen, with hunter-green walls, cream counters, and matching cream subway tiles. Colorful artwork hung on the walls and lush green plants filled every corner. It looked like Joy had a green thumb. Hannah's plants never looked anything like that.

Joy dipped a spoon into the soup and handed it to Hannah. "What do you think? It's vegetarian, so no ham, but I have another secret ingredient."

Hannah took a taste. The soup was rich with caramelized onions, carrots, and celery, and there was something else that made it delicious. She didn't even miss the ham.

"It's wonderful. What is your secret ingredient?"

Joy grinned. "Sherry! Lots of it." She walked to the spiral staircase that led down to the basement, where Ben was in his woodshop, and hollered down, "Ben, supper is ready. Come on up!"

As she walked back into the kitchen, Hannah heard the door behind her open. Spencer stepped into the room and stopped short when he saw her.

"I didn't realize you had company over." He didn't look thrilled to see her and Hannah shared his feelings. Joy hadn't mentioned that Spencer would be joining them.

"Oh, hi, honey. Hannah joined the writing group today and I asked her to stay for supper. Do you want to slice the bread for us? I made a few loaves earlier today." Joy handed him a big crusty loaf of homemade bread and Spencer got busy slicing.

"Can I help you do anything?" Hannah asked. She suddenly felt awkward with Spencer there. The relaxed and welcoming vibe vanished when he walked into the room.

"Why don't you help yourself to whatever you'd like to drink? I have bottled water or iced tea in the refrigerator."

Joy filled four bowls with soup and Hannah helped her to carry them to the table. Ben joined them a moment later and Spencer brought over the cutting board with the sliced bread. Joy went back for the butter and they all sat down around the table.

"I'm so glad you could join us, Spencer." Joy glanced at Hannah. "I called him earlier and invited him for dinner. Spencer loves my pea soup."

He grinned and Hannah couldn't help but notice that it made him look so much friendlier and more handsome. "I do. When she told me she'd made bread, too, it was an easy decision. Gram's bread is the best."

Hannah spread some butter on a slice and took a bite. "It's so good. I've never made homemade bread. Is it hard to do?"

Joy laughed. "It really couldn't be easier. Next time I make some, I'll have you come over and watch me. It's just a few ingredients and time."

"I would love that." Hannah liked cooking but living in Brooklyn in a small apartment with a tiny kitchen, she mostly got takeout or made simple things like pasta.

"Spencer, how was that event that you told me you didn't want to go to—some networking thing at the Chatham Bars Inn. Did you end up having a good time?" Joy asked.

"I did actually. I went with Natalie from my office. She sort of dragged me there kicking and screaming." He grinned. "But it turned out to be pretty good. We had a few drinks, a nice selection of cocktail snacks, and I met a few interesting people. One of them referred a new client to me and I am meeting with him this week."

"So, it was worth going. That's good," Ben commented.

"It was. And it's an interesting case. It's a young Brazilian man who works for the person I met. He's trying to sponsor him for a green card. Ernesto is a good worker and wants to stay here in the States."

"Does he send money home to Brazil?" Joy asked.

Spencer nodded. "He does. He's the oldest of eight children and he sends money home every week to help his mother. If he can get a green card, that will give him even more options as he can grow with the company."

"Is there a reason why they might deny him?" Joy asked.

"Visas have been more difficult to get lately. They will have to make a case that a local person couldn't do the job they want to have Ernesto do. They don't make it easy to get the visas."

"Hannah's story is about an attorney," Joy said.

Spencer glanced her way. "Really? What's it about?"

Hannah took a deep breath. "It's a romantic comedy about a female attorney who is trying to make partner. She has a crush on her coworker who is also up for partner. He's grumpy, though, and wants nothing to do with her until they're assigned a big case together and they have to work side by side and he realizes he's attracted to her, too, but he resists it."

"Oh, that sounds fun!" Joy said.

Spencer raised an eyebrow. "That's not very realistic. Coworkers at a law firm shouldn't date."

This time his grandmother was the one who looked skeptical. "I think it's more realistic than you realize. People meet at work all the time."

Ben changed the subject to update them on a new woodworking project he'd started. After they'd all had second helpings of soup, Joy put Hannah's brownies on the table. While they enjoyed the brownies, Joy looked deep in thought and then a smile spread across her face.

"I have the best idea. Hannah's writing a story about an attorney and Spencer is an attorney. Spencer, why don't you have Hannah shadow you for a week so she can really learn what an attorney does?"

The shocked expression on Spencer's face perfectly mirrored Hannah's own feelings.

"I'm not sure that's a good idea. I don't want to be a bother," Hannah protested.

"I don't think that would be very . . . interesting for her," Spencer added.

"Nonsense. Hannah won't get in the way and you can make sure she gets it right, Spencer. You can have her sit in with clients and go to court with you. You mentioned you have a court date later this week, I think?"

"We do. It's an interesting case, actually. I suppose that might be good for her to see," Spencer admitted.

"Good! Then it's settled. Hannah can meet you at your office tomorrow. What time should she be there?"

Spencer hesitated. "Maybe nine? I'm in earlier but my first client meeting is at nine so if you want to come a few minutes before that?"

"Okay." Hannah recognized it was a great opportunity to really see inside a law firm and how it worked, but the idea of spending all day shadowing Spencer was a little intimidating.

And apparently he wasn't too keen on having her spend the entire day, either. "Why don't we do mornings for the rest of this week? That should give you enough time to get a feel for it and in the afternoon you can do your own thing, get some writing done?"

Hannah relaxed a little. That sounded better to her, too. "That's perfect. I like to write at the coffee shop in the afternoon so I can just head over there when we finish up."

"I guess I'll see you early tomorrow morning then," Spencer said.

Joy and Ben exchanged glances and looked pleased with themselves.

"See you in the morning." Hannah made a mental note to make sure she left early enough to get there at a quarter to nine. She would be horrified to be late on her first day at Spencer's office.

Chapter 7

Tony's eyes lit up when he saw Maddie and he held the door open wide.

"Miss Madeline. It's been too long. We miss you here."

"I've missed you, too, Tony. It's nice to be home."

Maddie smiled at her favorite doorman. He'd been manning the door of her building on the Upper West Side for as long as she could remember. She loved everything about their Manhattan apartment. The location on Riverside Drive was excellent, close to everything. She'd just walked home from the literary agency.

She'd spent the day in the office and it had been crazy busy with two publisher meetings, one of them a lunch. She was looking forward to a quiet night at home and she was curious if Richie was going to be there. He'd been out when she arrived the night before and she'd gone to bed before he arrived home. His bedroom door was shut when she left for the office this morning, so she hadn't seen him yet.

And when she walked in, the apartment was empty. It was still light out and sunshine streamed in through the oversized windows that overlooked the Hudson River. The apartment was large, the prewar layout a sprawling ten rooms. Maddie loved the architectural details, the wood-paneled library, fireplaces, classic moldings, and gleaming hardwood floors. Richie used the den as his office while Maddie claimed the library as her space.

Richie took the guest bedroom that was farthest away from the primary bedroom where Maddie slept. They would be able to avoid each other pretty easily. Maddie felt both sad and relieved about this. She wasn't up to a big talk with Richie just yet. Everything felt too unsettled with them. They'd had a mostly wonderful marriage over almost thirty years. But they'd hit a rough patch in recent months. Since before her sister passed, actually. Though Richie had been good about that. He'd loved her like a sister, too. But things had already changed between them and her passing just seemed to push them further apart.

And it didn't help that Maddie didn't know what to do about it. She wasn't sure what she wanted and Richie wasn't saying much, either. When he was unhappy he tended to withdraw and go silent and their house had been very quiet for many months. Maddie found the quiet of the apartment both soothing and unsettling at the same time.

Maddie found an open bottle of Decoy cabernet in the kitchen and poured herself a glass. She brought it into her bathroom, along with her waterproof tablet, and a few minutes later, sank into a blissfully warm bubble bath. She stayed in the soothing water until her muscles relaxed and she felt the stress of the day seep away.

She only had a few sips of the wine. After she toweled dry and changed into a soft sweatshirt and matching pants, she brought her wine to the library, her favorite room, and debated what to order for dinner. There was still no sign of Richie, so she guessed he had other plans for the evening. Which was fine with her. She didn't have the energy to go out somewhere and try to make conversation when things were so awkward between them.

She ordered an eggplant, spinach, and feta pizza from her favorite restaurant and thirty-five minutes later it was delivered. It smelled amazing and her stomach grumbled as she opened the cardboard box and got a plate out of the cupboard. She heard the door open behind her. Richie was home. He looked tired, but so handsome, too. She'd always loved the way he looked in his charcoal-gray suits with his dark wavy hair that was always slightly long. His eyes were as dark as his hair and had been the first thing she'd noticed about him, so many years ago.

He gave her a small smile. "That smells good."

"Do you want some? Your timing is perfect, it just arrived."

He shook his head. "No. Thank you. I'm just stopping here for a minute to drop off my stuff. I'm playing cards at Andrew's. He's having a few of the guys over."

"That sounds fun."

"Are you around tomorrow night? Maybe we could get dinner and catch up?"

Maddie shook her head. "I can't tomorrow. I have dinner plans with Kathryn. Maybe the night after that?"

Richie nodded. "We'll figure something out. I should run."

Maddie loaded her plate with three big slices of pizza and headed into the living room to watch TV and relax. A few minutes later, Richie waved goodbye and once again, the apartment was empty. Maddie took a sip of her wine and stared out the window at the sun setting over the water. By the time she finished the pizza, she was already yawning and knew it would be an early night.

She didn't mind being alone as much as she'd thought she would. It was still new to her, and when she saw Richie again, she just felt confused. It was easier to get used to being alone when he wasn't around. Being here in the apartment with him wasn't going to be easy. She sighed and wished she knew what she wanted to do.

Chapter 8

Hannah arrived at the law firm right on time. Her hair was tousled and going in every direction, as it was unusually windy. She could feel a gust of air rush by her when she opened the door. She'd debated what to wear and settled on a fluffy, bright pink sweater with dark gray pants, and she had a scarf tied around her neck. It had flowers in vibrant blues and purples. She felt like she stood out and not necessarily in a good way, as both Spencer and Natalie were dressed conservatively. But before she could say a word, the door opened again and a woman about her aunt's age, who Hannah guessed was the firm's owner, strode in. She was in a pink-and-gray tweed suit and stopped short when she saw Hannah.

"That sweater is gorgeous. I love the color."

"Thank you."

Spencer introduced Hannah to Natalie and Donna. "Donna, this is Hannah, the one I emailed you about. She's going to shadow me this week until about noon or so."

"You're the romance writer?" Donna asked.

Hannah nodded somewhat shyly.

Donna grinned. "I read your book a few weeks ago and loved it. Natalie, have you read it yet?"

"No, not yet."

"I'll bring my copy in for you. Hannah, make yourself at home. If you have any questions that Spencer can't answer for you, feel free to ask."

"Thank you." She glanced at Natalie. "I have some extra copies with me. I can bring one in for you tomorrow if you like?"

Natalie smiled and her whole face lit up. "That would be great!"

Hannah couldn't believe that Spencer's boss had already read her book. She wasn't used to hearing that from people and it always took her by surprise and thrilled her at the same time.

"Hannah, if you want to follow me, you can use this desk," Spencer said. "My client should be here any moment and we'll go into the conference room then."

Hannah followed him to the empty desk that sat right behind his. She had brought her laptop with her and pulled it out of her tote bag and set it on the desk. Natalie sat nearby and was on the phone talking with a client. Hannah noticed that Natalie's and Spencer's attire almost matched. They were both in crisp black pant suits and white button-down shirts. Natalie had a sleek blond bob that was stick straight and barely touched her shoulders. She was very put together and polished. Her lipstick and nail polish were both a soft pink.

Spencer looked equally sharp in his suit. He wore a green tie with preppy pink whales on it. A common look on the Cape. His hair was cut short and slicked over his ears, but it was wavy and stray curls popped up here and there. She was actually thinking it looked cute on him, until he spoke.

"Hannah, did you hear me? Let's head into the conference room. My client just texted me that he'll be here in a minute."

"Sorry." Hannah stood, grabbed her laptop, and followed Spencer. The conference room was spacious with chocolate-brown leather chairs and an oval dark pine table that was polished to a shine.

"Why don't you sit along the side," Spencer suggested. He

opened the blinds, which sent a stream of sunlight into the room, warming it and giving it a more welcoming feel.

A moment later, Natalie tapped on the door. "Here's Mr. Fontes to see you."

"Thanks, Natalie. Ernesto, come on in. Meet my colleague, Hannah. She's just going to be observing today. If that's okay with you?"

Ernesto, who looked to be in his late twenties or maybe early thirties, glanced Hannah's way and looked confused. "Sure. That's okay."

"Please, have a seat."

They all sat. Hannah opened her laptop and just listened as Spencer asked a series of questions and took notes as Ernesto answered them.

Hannah was impressed by the way Spencer spoke to Ernesto, who was clearly nervous when he first entered the room. Spencer quickly put him at ease. He asked about his family and what he liked to do on his days off.

"I love the beach and fishing. If I catch anything, I invite friends over and cook the fish on the grill."

"I love to fish, too, though I'm not very good at it," Spencer admitted.

By the time the conversation finished, Ernesto had opened up and Hannah found him very likable. He was exactly thirty and he'd been in the country for five years on an H-1B visa. And now his employer was willing to sponsor him for a green card.

"The first step is we'll apply for your EAD—your Employment Authorization Document. If that is granted, then we'll wait for the green card to be processed."

Spencer had Ernesto sign some paperwork and when he finished, they walked him to the door and Spencer said he'd be in touch as soon as he had an update, but that it might be a while.

For the rest of the morning, Hannah listened to both Spencer and Natalie as they spoke with their clients. After each call, Spencer explained what was going on with the client and what would happen next in the process. Their office was a general law firm, meaning they handled a variety of different things, from DUIs to criminal to family law and immigration.

"The case on Friday is a DUI, Gerry Easton. That should be an interesting one for you to observe," Spencer said.

"Was he drinking?" Hannah asked.

Spencer nodded. "He had two drinks at dinner with friends. He's a big guy, so that probably wouldn't have registered, but you never know. He didn't want to risk it as he needs to drive for his job, so he refused to take the Breathalyzer."

"Why was he stopped? Was he driving erratically?"

"Broken taillight. He'd meant to get it fixed and hadn't gotten around to it yet." Spencer frowned. "That was asking for trouble. You should always fix car lights immediately. When the officer approached him, he smelled bourbon on Gerry's breath."

"So, how do you defend that?" Hannah was curious.

"It's not enough to just smell alcohol. Gerry was driving fine and the officer will have to admit to that. He also has no priors and a clean driving record overall. That will help. There's also the chance the officer might not show. That's common when they don't really have a case. That would be ideal as then it's immediately dismissed. It's not likely though."

He looked contemplative for a moment and Hannah wondered what he was thinking. "Are you sure he's telling you the truth? What if he actually had more than a few drinks? What if he's guilty?"

"I don't think he's lying. I wasn't keen to take the case at first. You know about my parents, right?"

Hannah nodded.

"It would have been harder if he'd actually been drunk or if something bad had happened. I'm not sure if I would have been the right lawyer in that case. But when I talked to him, I felt better about it and wanted to help him. It made me also realize that things aren't always black and white."

"No, they're not," Hannah agreed. She was glad that Spencer had opened up to her a little. It was nice to see his less prickly side.

The morning actually went by quickly and at noon, Hannah started packing up her tote bag. Natalie glanced over at them. "I'm going to go grab a sandwich. Do you guys want to join me?"

Spencer shook his head. "I'm good. I brought lunch in with me. Hannah, I'll see you tomorrow?"

"I'll be here." She looked at Natalie. "I didn't even think about lunch, so I'll join you."

Natalie led the way down Main Street to the Public Cafe.

"I am addicted to their turkey pesto panini. I get it at least once a week."

That sounded good to Hannah, too. They ordered their sandwiches and it didn't take long. While they ate, Natalie asked Hannah about living in Brooklyn.

"Do you love it there? I went to Manhattan once with friends and had a blast, but by the end of the weekend, I was glad to get back to the Cape. I think I'm just a small-town girl. But I love visiting the city. It seems so glamorous."

Hannah smiled. "I love it. There's a certain energy there, like anything is possible, and there's always something going on. For someone like me, interested in books and publishing, there are always fun events to go to."

"So many good restaurants, too," Natalie added.

"Yes, although everything in the city is crazy expensive. We tend to have house parties more than nights out at restaurants because cocktails especially are so overpriced. We still go out, just not all the time."

Hannah took another bite of her sandwich. The pesto on the toasted bread was so good. She could see why Natalie came here so often.

"So, are you dating anyone?" Natalie asked.

Hannah shook her head. "No. I actually ended a two-year relationship a few weeks ago. He wanted to get more serious and I didn't, so it seemed the right thing to do. I probably should have ended it sooner," she admitted.

"Oh, that's too bad. Do you miss him?"

"No. I don't actually." Hannah hadn't thought about Jeremy once since the last time she and Lucy discussed him, at the party. The realization surprised her.

"Well, there you go then. You made the right decision."

Hannah laughed. "What about you? Are you dating anyone?"

"I am. I've been with my boyfriend, Adam, for three years now. We're not engaged yet, but we've talked about it. Things are going well. He's out of town for a few months now, which I'm not crazy about. We text and FaceTime but it's not the same. He's a security software consultant and is actually on a long project in Dubai of all places. It's too far to come home until the project is over and the money is so good that he couldn't pass it up."

"I've never been to Dubai but I have a college friend who is there with her husband and they are both teaching at a university. They have free housing and are able to save a lot of money by doing it."

"I bet it would be interesting to visit. But I don't know about living that far from home. I'm one of those Cape natives that rarely crosses the bridge." Natalie laughed. "Although I do go to Boston once or twice a year to see a show or have dinner in the North End."

"I love to do that, too. Boston reminds me of New York, just a smaller version of it. I like that I can walk all over Boston. I walk a lot in New York, too, but it's more spread out and sometimes I have to take an Uber or use the trains to get places."

"So, Spencer is your neighbor's grandson?" Natalie said.

"He is. We went to school together, but he was a year ahead of me. I didn't really know him then, though."

"We're the same age then. I'm a year behind him, too. Though I didn't grow up in Chatham. My family lives in West Yarmouth, so I went to D-Y." That was Dennis-Yarmouth, the regional high school. "A few years after graduating from law school, I got the job with Donna and moved to Chatham."

"Just like Spencer."

"Right. Spencer is a great guy. He was dumped recently. Did you know that?"

Hannah shook her head. She knew very little about Spencer.

"We all thought he was about to propose. His girlfriend, Michelle, was one of those people who always looks perfect, never a hair out of place, and always dressed to impress. They looked like the perfect couple." Natalie paused to take a bite of her sandwich.

"Michelle surprised us all by falling in love with a fisherman. Not that there's anything wrong with that. It's just that George is the total opposite of Spencer. He took it hard, at first. But I don't think she was ever right for him. He needs someone that will loosen him up a little."

Hannah smiled. "He does seem a little uptight at times."

Natalie laughed. "That's an understatement. He's a real softie, though, once you get to know him. He'll do anything for his family or good friends."

Hannah glanced at her phone and noticed the time. It was almost one. Natalie finished her sandwich and stood. "I should get back to the office. I have a client coming in soon."

Hannah walked back with her and stopped when she reached the coffee shop. "This is where I'm going to stay for a bit and try to get some writing done. I'll see you in the morning."

Chapter 9

Hannah fell into a routine of sorts for the rest of the week, while her aunt was away. She woke early, did her morning walk along Shore Road, then showered and went into Spencer's office for the morning. After the first day, she found that she'd connected with Natalie and looked forward to chatting with her each day when Spencer wasn't showing her something.

It was helpful to sit at the desk behind him and listen to him and Natalie as they spoke to their clients on the phone. She sat in on a few other meetings with Spencer as well and it was interesting to watch him with clients. She'd expected him to be somewhat formal and abrupt, like many lawyers she'd come across, but he was actually a good listener and seemed to care about his clients' problems and reassured them that he would do everything he could to help. For those who faced a potential court trial, he would gently warn them that if they went to court there were no guarantees and things might not go their way. Hannah wasn't surprised when Natalie informed her that Spencer's track record was very good.

The topic had come up on day two, when they were off getting sandwiches at lunch. "Spencer almost never loses when he goes to court," Natalie said. "If he thinks his case isn't strong enough to win, he will always advise his client that they may be better off settling."

"He is very reassuring with his clients," Hannah said.

"They love him. I've learned a lot by sitting next to him."

Spencer wasn't one for idle chitchat. He stayed focused the entire day and always ate lunch at his desk. Natalie, however, liked to chat in between client calls and Hannah enjoyed talking with her. Although Natalie had a different style, she seemed equally capable with her clients and Hannah learned a lot by listening to her as well as Spencer.

Each afternoon, after lunch, she headed to the coffee shop and spent a few hours at her favorite corner table. The book was still coming along slowly, but a bit more smoothly now. A few new plot ideas had come to her after sitting in the office and she was eager to work them into her story.

Hannah usually left for the day around three, when the coffee shop slowed and she was often the only person still sitting at a table. She headed home that Wednesday afternoon and carefully pulled up to the mailbox to collect her aunt's mail before turning onto the driveway. She was extra careful not to hit the mailbox again. She parked and waved hello to Joy, who was walking toward her.

"How is your week going?" Joy asked as they both reached the mailboxes and Hannah grabbed her aunt's stack of mail.

"Good, I'm keeping busy. I was at Spencer's office this morning and at the coffee shop this afternoon."

"I hope Spencer is being helpful?"

"Yes, thank you for suggesting it." Hannah had been horrified at first, but she was grateful now that Joy had come up with the idea for her to shadow Spencer. Her impression of what a lawyer did had been very different from how it actually was, and she would be able to add a layer of authenticity to the story now that would make it better.

"Of course." Joy cocked her head. "Your aunt is still in New York?"

Hannah nodded. "Yes, she's coming back on Sunday. The house is quiet without her."

"Well, if you don't have plans for supper, why don't you join us? I tried a new recipe, an eggplant pasta baked dish, and we have tons of it. Ben has to eat and run to chorus practice, but we can sit and chat a bit."

Hannah didn't hesitate to accept. The evening stretched ahead of her and she hadn't even given dinner a thought.

"I'd love that. Can I bring anything?"

Joy shook her head. "Not a thing, just yourself. Come by around five thirty."

✾

"This is so good!" Hannah had just taken a bite of the roasted eggplant that was thinly sliced and tossed with rigatoni, tomato sauce, and lots of mozzarella and Parmesan cheese. It was like an eggplant Parmesan but lighter as there was no breading. Joy had toasted up slices of her leftover homemade bread as well.

They ate around the kitchen table. Ben had inhaled his food in record time and said a quick goodbye as he dashed out the door to get to his chorus practice on time.

Joy and Hannah were only halfway done with their meals and Joy encouraged Hannah to help herself to seconds as she piled another scoop onto her own plate. Hannah finished hers and added a little more.

"So, things are going well with Spencer?" Joy said. She had a little gleam in her eye and Hannah sensed she wasn't just asking how the shadowing was going.

Hannah smiled. "It's definitely helping. Thanks for suggesting it."

"I was never all that fond of the last one he was dating. He'd told me he was close to proposing. I don't think he would have been truly happy with her. I told him that when she broke things off."

"Why didn't you think she was right for him?" Hannah asked.

"I only met her once. Pretty girl, perfectly polished and very driven. Kind of cold, I thought. I didn't see her as the mother of Spencer's children."

"Does Spencer want children?" He was so focused on work that Hannah wasn't sure she could picture it.

"Of course he does. He's great with kids. Spencer was so confused when Michelle said she was leaving him for that fisherman. But it made perfect sense to me."

"It did? Why?" It seemed confusing to Hannah, too. It sounded like Michelle and Spencer had so much in common.

"George was the complete opposite of Spencer—and of Michelle. Opposites really do attract, you know. Sometimes it's just an attraction that burns out when there's not enough shared interests. But often, in a good marriage, they balance each other out. At the end of the day, I think she was too similar to Spencer and they would have gotten tired of each other."

Hannah thought about it and realized that was true of many couples she knew. They seemed like opposites and those differences kept things interesting and had a positive effect on each other. She thought of Tom and Sara and how Tom was always early and very conservative with money, great at saving, whereas Sara tended to run late and was much more of a spender than a saver. She'd encouraged Tom to relax a little and splurge now and then, and now that she did all the shopping and managed their checking account, she was more careful about spending.

"Are you and Ben opposites?"

Joy laughed. "Most definitely. I'm the outgoing one. We'd never leave the house if it was up to Ben. I encouraged him to join the local choral group and he loves it. He's happy just hunkering down in his shop, or reading a book. I need to be busy. I always have a project or two going and if we are just staying in and watching TV, I'll usually be knitting at the same time. I find it relaxing and it also works my hand muscles in the opposite way that typing does. So, it helps prevent sore hands and wrists."

"I didn't know that. Maybe I should learn how to knit," Hannah joked.

But Joy took her seriously. "I'm happy to teach you if you really want to learn. It's not hard."

"Oh! Maybe I'll take you up on that if I ever get this book finished."

Hannah helped Joy clear the table when they finished and they took cups of tea and a few chocolate-chip cookies into the living room. Hannah settled on a comfy sofa that faced the window and the ocean beyond it. Joy and Ben's home was smaller than her aunt's but the view was every bit as good.

"How did you meet Ben?" Hannah asked. She knew it was a second marriage as Joy had mentioned once that she'd been married before. She wondered if Joy had met Ben in the UK.

"It was fate." Joy smiled. "I had recently divorced and a friend talked me into going skiing for a long weekend in Vermont. Ben was staying at the same hotel and we were all in the pub for after-skiing happy hour. Ben was visiting a college friend and they weren't supposed to be there at all. They'd planned to leave the day before we arrived, but they had car problems and it couldn't be fixed right away. The shop had to order a part so they stayed through the weekend. We hit it off, skied together the next day, and kept in touch after that. I didn't think much of it because I knew he was going back to England."

"Oh, he was just on vacation?"

"He was only here for two weeks. I didn't think I'd ever see him again. But we wrote to each other and he invited me to come visit. I still wasn't thinking it would be more than friendship. My family is here, after all, and I couldn't possibly move to England. But once

I went there, it was clear that it was more than that. And here we are! I never would have met him if my friend hadn't forced me to go with her on that trip."

"That does seem like fate. You two seem perfect for each other."

Joy picked up her knitting and without even looking, started clacking her needles together as she spoke. "He really is my best friend. Sometimes he drives me crazy and we need a little space from each other. He'll go to his shop and I'll work on my writing and then all is good again. What about you, are there any interesting men in your life?"

"Not at the moment. I actually ended a relationship not long before I came here. I'm not sure how much my aunt told you, but I was having panic attacks, from stress. I realized that Jeremy wasn't the person I wanted to grow old with. And my mother's passing hit me really hard. I also have a deadline hanging over me and the words weren't coming. So, right now, I'm very single and not focusing on dating at all. I need to finish this book first."

Joy nodded. "Stress is a difficult thing to deal with. Anything you can do to decrease it is a good thing. Take a walk on the beach, sit outside in the sun, and just let your story come to you. Love will find you the same way when you are ready for it."

Hannah smiled. "I've always heard that, how love finds you when you're not looking. But I'm not sure I believe it."

"I've found it to be true. You can't force it, though. That never works. It's good that you're not focusing on it. Give your energy to your book and once that is flowing well, everything else will fall into place for you, eventually." Joy sounded so sure of it that Hannah relaxed a little. Her writing was going a little better and she was hopeful that the book would turn out okay.

Chapter 10

Sara walked into the coffee shop at a quarter to two. She spotted Hannah immediately. She was sitting at a small table in the back of the shop, with a paper cup of coffee by her side and a half-eaten sugar cookie next to it. Hannah was typing on her laptop and looked oblivious to the rest of the world. Sara got herself a coffee before walking over to say hello to her sister. Hannah didn't even notice her.

"I take it the writing is going well?" Sara asked.

Hannah looked up in surprise. "What are you doing here?"

"I have an interview at three at the bookshop. They advertised for part-time help."

"Oh, that might be perfect! And I bet you'd get a good discount on the books, too."

Sara laughed. "I didn't even think of that. But you're probably right. And I think it would be fun. I don't know how much competition I'll have, though. I don't want to get my hopes up."

"Well, good luck. Pop in after and let me know how it went. You can leave your coffee here if you want."

"That's probably a good idea. I should have bought it after the interview. I guess I'm a little nervous. It's been years since I've interviewed for anything."

"You've got this. With your library experience, they'll be lucky to have you."

Hannah's encouraging words calmed Sara a little. She took a deep breath.

"Okay, I'm off. Will be back in a bit."

She headed into the bookshop and looked around. Her interview was with Alison, one of the owners. At two in the afternoon, the store wasn't too busy. There were a few people browsing in the aisles and one paying at the register. The woman ringing up the sale looked to be in her fifties and Sara guessed that might be Alison. She waited until the customer left with their bag of books before she walked up to the counter.

"Hello, I have a meeting with Alison. I'm Sara."

The woman glanced at the clock above the door. It was a few minutes before two. She looked pleased.

"Wonderful, and you're right on time. Let me just grab Brooklyn to watch the register and we can sit down in the back." She disappeared into the back office and returned a moment later with a younger woman who went behind the counter and smiled at Sara. "Good luck," she said as Sara followed Alison to the back office.

There was a big desk and two chairs facing it inside the office. Alison gestured for Sara to have a seat.

Once she was seated, Sara opened a folder and handed Alison a crisp copy of her résumé.

"I printed some extras out, just in case."

Alison took the résumé. "Thank you. I meant to print a copy earlier and then things got busy." She looked over the résumé for a moment.

"I love that you worked as a librarian. I think you mentioned in your email that you took time off to raise your children?"

Sara nodded. "Yes, I have four boys and the youngest is in school full-time now, so I am eager to work again. I miss it."

"Are you looking for part-time, mother's hours?"

"Yes, ideally anytime between nine and two or two thirty. As long as I can be home by three."

"That should work. Brooklyn is taking some college classes so she's looking to shift her hours to evenings and weekends. We need the most help during the week. Have you ever worked retail?"

"No. But I think library work is similar. I used to help people find books and make recommendations."

Alison smiled. "I think that's close enough. Do you have any questions for me?"

Sara thought for a moment. "How long have you owned the shop?"

"Not very long. Just over a year now. This store was a long-held dream of mine. I'd worked for years as an editor until the magazine had layoffs. Timing is everything—the owner of the bookshop mentioned she was looking to retire and a good friend knew this was my dream and she helped to make it happen."

"Oh, that's wonderful. And is it what you'd hoped it would be?"

Alison nodded. "Yes. There was a learning curve, but when you love what you're doing, it doesn't feel like work."

"That's how I feel about books and why I liked working in the library. I really think this will be a good fit for me. I am addicted to reading." Sara grinned.

"Would you be able to start on Monday?" Alison asked.

Did that mean she got the job? Sara wasn't sure if Alison was just generally asking about her availability.

"Yes, that would be perfect, actually."

"Excellent." Alison told her the hourly rate, which was about what Sara had expected. "If that works for you, you're hired."

"Yes, that works for me."

Alison stood. "Great. If you want to follow me, I'll introduce you to Brooklyn."

Sara followed her to the counter and Alison made the introductions. "Brooklyn will be here Monday and she can train you on the register and then when she leaves at noon, you can take it from there."

"Perfect! I will see you both on Monday."

Sara walked back into the coffee shop in a daze. This time Hannah saw her coming. "How did it go?" she asked when Sara reached her.

"I start Monday! I can't believe it." Sara reached for her coffee and took a sip. It didn't quite seem real that finally, she had a job lined up and it was at a bookstore.

"I'm so happy for you. I'm here just about every afternoon now, so I'll pop over and say hello. And maybe this weekend, we'll celebrate, if you can get out."

"If not, then you can come over and we'll relax in the backyard and have a cookout. And there will be celebrating." Sara couldn't wait to tell Tom and everyone else.

Sara was in such a good mood as she left the bookshop that she stopped by the local butcher shop on the way home, to splurge on steaks for dinner. She decided to serve them with baked potatoes and roasted asparagus. She poured herself and Tom a glass of cabernet when he got home and when they were all gathered around the dinner table, she shared her big news.

"I finally got a job. I start Monday at the bookshop on Main Street!"

Two of her boys weren't paying attention but her oldest gave her a thumbs-up. "That's great, Mom!"

Her youngest looked confused. "Will you still be here when I get home?"

"Yes, honey. Nothing will change for you. I'm going to be working part-time."

"What will you be doing there?" Tom asked.

"Whatever needs doing, I suppose. Stocking the shelves when books come in, ringing up customer orders. Helping people find books."

He frowned. "I didn't realize you were looking at retail jobs. Do you think that will be enough for you? I thought you'd probably go back to a library." And just like that, her happy moment ended.

"I tried. I've mentioned before that I've been looking for ages and they never have an opening. And if they did, I don't know that it would work with what I need for hours. This really seems perfect. I'm excited about it." Or at least she was, until Tom's lack of enthusiasm burst her bubble.

Tom took a sip of his wine and smiled slightly. "Well, if you're happy with it, that's all that matters. And the hours will be good. Cheers."

He tapped his glass against hers but her celebratory mood was gone.

Chapter 11

Maddie was the first one in the office the next morning. As much as she enjoyed working from home when she was in Chatham, she also found being in a busy office energizing. Theirs was an open environment, a big room with work stations scattered throughout. They could all hear each other on the phone and it helped with collaboration and communication.

Kathryn and Maddie and a few other senior agents had their own offices, but they all kept the doors open and could hear what was going on. Maddie made herself a black coffee from the Nespresso machine. She loved the thick foam that the machine somehow made even though there was no dairy. She'd just taken her first sip when she heard voices and footsteps. Within fifteen minutes, most of the office had arrived.

Maddie's day was busy. Her author, Shelley, had the last of her Zoom calls with publishers, one in the morning and one in the afternoon. The offers had already started rolling in and Maddie knew it was a bit overwhelming for Shelley. Like many authors, Shelley was an introvert, so to be the center of attention and on Zoom calls with as many as five other people all focused on her was a little intimidating. But everyone loved the book and as they communicated that, Shelley relaxed a bit and let them tell her how excited they were and how they hoped to help.

Maddie let both publishers know that Shelley had offers already so they knew they had to move fast. One of them got an offer to her later that afternoon and the other said they'd have something in the morning. All of the offers were good but one of them was quite a bit better than the others. Maddie called Shelley after her second Zoom call to give her the newest offer.

"This is great news," Maddie said. "And we'll have one more offer in the morning."

"Then what happens? Do I pick one of them?" Shelley asked.

"Not just yet. Once we receive the last offer in the morning, I'll reach out to all of them and let them know we've had multiple offers and they should submit their best and final offer. And then you decide."

"Do you think they'll all come up?"

"Probably not. But they will all have the opportunity. And it's not just about which advance is the highest. You should consider which house you liked the best and how comfortable you feel with each one. They are all good publishers."

The rest of the afternoon flew by and as soon as they were able to wrap up for the day, Maddie and Kathryn made their way to I Sodi, the restaurant in the West Village that Kathryn had been dying to try.

It was crowded when they arrived and the restaurant was small, but Kathryn had made a reservation and they were seated quickly. They ordered a bottle of a Super Tuscan wine that their server recommended, along with a special fried artichoke appetizer to share and they both decided to have the twenty-layer lasagna.

The wine and the artichokes were both amazing. Maddie hadn't paid close attention when the server recommended the wine, but after he walked away she saw the price on the menu. It was almost two hundred dollars for the bottle. She expected it to be good and when she took her first sip she wasn't disappointed. It was smooth and rich and she savored it.

They chatted about business as they ate. Maddie updated Kathryn on the offers Shelley had received so far.

Kathryn nodded. "They should go up some, most of them. A few of them probably won't budge much, but they could surprise us. She's a debut author and there's no sales figures to hold them back."

That was one of the things that had surprised Maddie when she first started agenting. Most offers from publishers were carefully crafted after closely analyzing an author's prior sales figures and forecasting what was likely for the next book.

But with a debut author, there was no track record and sometimes the offers could be unusually large if there was an auction and several publishers wanted the book badly enough. They could overpay. And the high advance amount would become part of the book's marketing, designed to get attention and create buzz.

When their lasagna arrived, they both marveled at the many thin layers of delicate pasta filled with meat sauce and creamy cheese. When they tired of talking about work, the conversation turned personal. Kathryn was one of the few people who knew that Maddie was having issues with her marriage.

"How has it been, seeing Richie?"

"It's strange. I'd almost gotten used to being alone on the Cape. He's been gone for over a month. But being here with him in the same apartment is a lot harder than I thought it would be. I don't really know what to think." She felt sad imagining her life without Richie.

"How does he feel? Have you had a chance to talk to him about it?"

Maddie took a sip of her wine. "I've hardly seen him for more than a few minutes. He was out with friends last night. We're going to do something tomorrow night, maybe grab dinner."

"That's good. Go to one of your favorite places, and see how it feels to be there together. See if there are any romantic sparks."

Maddie laughed. "It's been a long time for that. We've been sleeping in separate bedrooms now for almost a year. It's more like having a distant roommate."

Kathryn smiled. "Does he snore?"

"Yes, especially if he's had a few drinks. That's how we started sleeping in separate bedrooms and after a while it was just easier to do it all the time."

Kathryn lifted her wineglass, took a long, slow sip, and set it down again. "Marriage is work. There are plenty of times when I can't stand David. The older we get the more opinionated we both are, and when he goes off on one of his rants, usually about something political, I make a quick exit. He can be annoyingly stubborn and it used to upset me. Now, I know not to push those buttons. I can usually redirect him, but if not, I just ignore him until it passes."

Maddie nodded. She agreed with Kathryn, but it wasn't quite the same thing. "I learned to do that, too. That's everyday stuff though. It's different with Richie. Ever since that woman joined his team, it's like he's checked out, and has grown more distant. And I suppose I have, too. It's not just him."

"You don't think he's been unfaithful? I don't think I could forgive that," Kathryn said.

"He swears he hasn't been and I don't think he has. But it's more of an emotional thing. They speak the same language—finance—and they can talk for hours about hideously boring mathematical concepts that they both find fascinating. I guess I feel a little left out because I just can't relate. It sounds silly, but his job is so consuming that it seems like there's not a lot of time left for us."

"She's married, too?" Kathryn asked.

"She is. We've had her and her husband down to the Cape. She's married to a lovely man. He's a teacher. He and I laughed together about how the two of them are in a secret relationship, speaking a language that only they can understand. It was just a joke. It clearly doesn't bother him. He said they're eager to have another child."

"But it bothers you," Kathryn said.

"Yes and no. I'm really not worried that there's anything going on there. It's more that I just don't feel like I'm a priority anymore—that our marriage is a priority."

"And you've told him that?"

"To be honest, we haven't talked much about this at all. It's like we both know we're not happy and so far it's been easier to just deal with it by spending time apart."

"Well, you have to decide if you want to save your marriage. And if you do, you need to talk to your husband. Be honest with him. Ask him how he's feeling and see where you go from here."

Maddie sighed. It sounded so sensible. Of course they needed to talk. She was a little nervous, though, because not only wasn't she sure of what she wanted, she was even less sure of what Richie wanted. But she knew they needed to figure it out.

Chapter 12

started the business close to thirty years ago and we've built it primarily on word-of-mouth referrals," Donna said proudly.

"Did you have the same focus when you started?" Hannah asked as the bartender at the Chatham Squire set down a second round of drinks for them. Natalie had texted her while she was at the coffee shop writing to see if she wanted to meet everyone at five thirty for drinks. They were seated at a corner of the bar, which made it easy to talk. Spencer and Donna sat along one side, then Hannah and Natalie. The bar had been empty when they first arrived but it was packed now, as it was prime time for dinner.

Donna laughed. "When I started the firm I was all of twenty-six and newly married. I'd worked in Boston at a law firm for a few years but Bill and I both had family on the Cape and when he decided to take over his father's business here in Chatham, I took the leap and hung out my shingle. It was just me at first, and I did whatever came my way. Anything from family law to real estate to criminal. I liked the variety. Still do. We are a little more focused now, though."

"When you do a good job for someone, and they tell their friends, they tend to refer the same kind of business, so after a while, that's how you develop a specialty," Natalie said.

"There's never a dull moment," Donna said. "We've had all kinds of interesting cases come our way. Some of them are pretty incredible stories."

"I like the variety," Spencer said. "I'd get bored if I was doing the same thing all the time. I have friends who do that. They work for big law firms in Boston and just do tax law all day or patent stuff. They say they like it, but it sounds monotonous to me."

"I don't think I'd like that, either," Natalie agreed.

"What did you do before writing books?" Spencer asked Hannah.

"I was an assistant in the marketing department of a technology company. I didn't love the work, but it was a fun group of people. That's the one thing I miss—having coworkers," Hannah said. "Although a few of my friends work there and I still see them often, so it's not too bad."

"I have friends that are totally remote. I don't think I'd like that. I like having an office to go to and coworkers," Natalie said.

"We do work from home sometimes," Donna said. "If the weather is bad, for instance. These two know that if there's even a hint of snow, there's a good chance I won't want to drive in. We can easily work from home if we need to."

"Except for court appearances," Spencer added.

"I'm looking forward to going to court with you tomorrow," Hannah said. It would be her last day shadowing Spencer and she was sorry to see it end. The week had gone by quickly and she liked being around people again, especially as it was just in the morning.

"Tomorrow is your last day?" Natalie seemed sorry to see her go, too.

"It is. This has been a fun week. Thanks for having me," Hannah said.

"Did you learn everything you need to know?" Natalie asked. "If you want, I'd be happy to have you shadow me next week. If that's okay with Donna?"

Donna took a sip of chardonnay. "Of course. It's fine by me. You can sit in with me on one of the days if you like, too. I have a few interesting clients coming in next week."

Hannah glanced at Spencer before answering. She didn't want him to be stuck with her for another week if he didn't want her there. But he looked amused.

"You might as well," he said. "I think you said your attorney is a woman, so it might be helpful to get their perspective."

"I'd love to come in for another week then, as long as it's not too much trouble."

Natalie smiled and lifted her glass. "Good, it's settled then."

After Donna finished her drink, she excused herself to head home to have dinner with her husband. Spencer, Natalie, and Hannah decided to order some nachos to share.

"I miss this," Natalie said. "My best friend, Taylor, got a job in Boston and she and her husband moved there a little over a month ago, so I haven't been getting out as often."

"It's fun for me, too," Hannah said. "Other than my sister I don't really know many people here anymore, and my sister has her hands full with four young boys. She hardly ever gets out."

Spencer didn't say a whole lot. He just sat there listening and eating nachos as Hannah and Natalie chatted away.

"I haven't been out since I dragged Spencer to a networking thing at the Chatham Bars Inn last week," Natalie said. "He really didn't want to go, but I think he had a good time?"

Spencer laughed. "She's right. I really did not want to go. I usually end up having a decent enough time once I get to those things, though."

Natalie turned to Hannah. "Maybe I'll bring you along the next time one of those comes up. It's something to do."

"I would totally go. Especially if it's at the Chatham Bars Inn. I haven't been there in years."

Natalie looked thoughtful. "And you're here all summer, right?" Hannah nodded.

"We will definitely have to get together then. Summer is so much fun in Chatham."

"Uh-oh," Spencer said. "This sounds like trouble."

Natalie laughed. "Spencer, you know you're always welcome to come out with us, too."

Spencer just grinned and opened his wallet. He took out an American Express card, set it on the bar, and waved to get the bartender's attention. "I should probably get going. I need to be up early tomorrow for that court case. If you guys want to stay and have another drink, feel free. Just have the bartender put it on the tab. Donna is paying so you might as well."

"I don't think I want another whole drink," Hannah said. "But we could split one maybe?" She and Natalie were both drinking the same chardonnay.

Natalie nodded. "That's perfect. Let's split a glass."

The bartender topped off their glasses and Spencer paid the bill and said his goodbyes. After he left, Hannah asked Natalie about her boyfriend.

"When does he come back from Dubai?"

"Not soon enough. In about a month he'll be back. He has some cute friends. We'll definitely have to make a plan to do something when he's back."

They stayed at the bar for another half hour or so, sipping chardonnay and laughing. Hannah was glad that she was getting to know Natalie. She seemed like a lot of fun and she had so many funny stories about clients and just in general. Hannah looked forward to shadowing her next week. She was already getting a lot of good material that she might be able to use in her book.

When they both yawned at the same time they decided it was time to head home.

"I don't have a court case in the morning," Natalie said, "but

I do need to get a good night's sleep as I have a busier day than usual for a Friday."

"I want to make sure I'm on time for Spencer tomorrow, too. I'm not sure when he plans to head out to the courthouse, so I want to make sure I'm there early."

"Well, this was fun," Natalie said as they walked out to their cars. "I'm glad you came out with us."

"Thanks, I am, too. See you in the morning."

The next morning, Hannah rode with Spencer to the district courthouse in Orleans, the town immediately to the east of Chatham. Spencer was quiet on the ride over and Hannah didn't want to bother him with idle chitchat so she gazed out the window as they drove.

When they reached the courthouse, Gerry was waiting for them just inside the door. Spencer introduced them and Gerry shook her hand. He was wearing a navy suit, his hair was short and neat, and he looked freshly shaved. He had a friendly smile and Hannah found herself rooting for him immediately. Spencer had also told her how important it was that the defendants show respect to the court.

"It goes a long way. When people show up looking like bums it just makes it harder on themselves. I always advise my clients to look their best."

They waited their turn and at a little after eleven, Gerry's name was called.

The police officer was there, seated by the prosecutor. Hannah paid close attention as Gerry was called to the stand and questioned by both the prosecutor and Spencer. Gerry stated that he'd been pulled over on his way home because of the broken taillight.

The prosecutor walked through the events of the evening, asking Gerry a series of questions, and then the police officer took the stand and the prosecutor asked him to walk them through the conversation he'd had with Gerry.

Hannah watched with fascination as Spencer expertly walked Gerry through the details of the night. In his closing summary he reminded the court that Gerry had a clean driving record. "In fact, Gerry Easton drives for a living. He has no priors of any kind. He is a family man with two children. He had a broken taillight, which he repaired the next day. He didn't do anything wrong here. There is no evidence that he was driving under the influence. The officer stated that is not why he pulled him over and that his driving was, in fact, fine."

Spencer spoke with passion and conviction and Hannah was impressed. She glanced at Gerry and he sat tall in his chair as Spencer spoke. He looked equally impressed and hopeful as Spencer sat back down.

The judge, a man who looked to be in his late sixties, took a moment to gather his thoughts and then spoke.

"After listening to both sides on this and looking at the defendant's record, the court is comfortable dismissing these charges. Case dismissed."

Gerry high-fived Spencer and looked so relieved. As they walked out of the courthouse, Gerry thanked him profusely.

"This is so huge. I can't thank you enough. I don't know what I would have done if I'd lost my license. There would have been a good chance I'd have lost my job, too."

"I was happy to help."

Gerry went on his way and Spencer and Hannah headed back to the office. It was almost noon and Hannah planned to see if Natalie wanted to grab a sandwich.

Spencer was in an unusually good mood and was chatting about another similar case that was coming up. He felt good about his chances for that one, too.

It made Hannah wonder, though, and before she could stop herself she blurted out, "That's good. But what if they do it again and this time they hurt someone or even kill them?"

Hannah quickly realized that she'd killed Spencer's good mood. She saw a muscle clench in his jaw before he spoke. "If that were to happen, they'd pay the consequences. Loss of license and likely jail time."

"That doesn't help the person they killed though," Hannah said softly.

Spencer sighed. "No. It doesn't. The system isn't perfect. All we can do is operate within the laws as they exist, present the facts, and let the judge decide. That's our job."

"I suppose. I think it would be difficult sometimes to defend certain clients if I knew they were guilty."

"It's rarely that black and white. There is a lot of gray, in everything. Even murder. It may seem black and white that if you kill someone you should go to jail, right?"

Hannah nodded. "Yes, of course."

"Right. But what if the victim was actually a burglar that entered your home with a gun and you shot him in self-defense? Or what if it was your husband and he was abusive and you defended yourself?"

"Well, that would be different."

"Exactly. Every case is different and the judge looks at the whole picture. For what it's worth, we don't do a lot of criminal cases and I personally couldn't defend someone accused of murder unless I believed they were innocent. I wouldn't be the right choice for that person because I wouldn't be able to defend with conviction. So far, we haven't had any cases like that come in and we aren't likely to as it isn't our strength."

Spencer reached the office and they walked back inside. He immediately went to his desk and Donna and Natalie waited for an update.

He grinned. "We won!"

"Excellent!" Donna said.

"Congrats!" Natalie turned to Hannah. "Do you want to run and grab lunch?"

They walked to their usual place and ordered two sandwiches and took them to a table by the window.

"So, what did you think? Was it helpful to go to court with Spencer?"

"It really was. Though I think I may have insulted him on the ride home." Hannah relayed the conversation and Natalie was quiet for a moment.

"Spencer actually does the most pro bono work of all of us. He's helped quite a few elderly clients that were taken advantage of. And he does the most immigration work, helping people get their visas and green cards. He's a good guy, Hannah."

Hannah felt even worse now for grilling Spencer. "I know he is."

"I wouldn't worry about it. You were just asking questions to better understand how it all works, right?"

"Yes, exactly."

"So, we'll see you Monday morning then? I have a new client coming in and you can sit in with me. It's a divorce."

"Yes, that would be great."

"Any fun plans for the weekend? I'm heading up to Boston to visit with my best friend at her new place."

"I'm going to my sister's tonight, I think. We need to celebrate her new job. She starts Monday at the bookshop."

"Oh, fun! See you on Monday, then."

Chapter 13

Sara sighed with contentment as she stepped into the bubble bath. The house was blissfully silent. She had a few precious hours to herself as Tom took the boys fishing, and they weren't due back until later that afternoon. She intended to stay in the warm water until it grew cold and her skin was all wrinkly. She had candles lit, her favorite Norah Jones music playing in the background, and a book she'd been dying to read waiting for her on her waterproof e-reader. She'd just swiped it on when her cell phone rang. She'd thought about leaving the cell in the kitchen so she wouldn't be bothered, but ended up bringing it into the bathroom, just in case something happened with the kids. She glanced at the caller ID and saw it was her sister.

"Good morning!" she answered cheerily.

Hannah laughed. "Same to you. You're in an awfully good mood."

"Tom is out with the boys, and I just sank into a hot bubble bath with a good book. Life is pretty good right now."

Hannah knew how rarely Sara got to enjoy a good bubble bath. "Yay! I won't keep you then. Just wanted to see what you were up to. That was fun last night."

Hannah had come over for dinner and she and Sara had stayed

up late after Tom and the boys went to bed. They'd cooked burgers and hot dogs and drank wine and later had big bowls of ice cream as they watched *When Harry Met Sally* on Netflix. It had been so fun to just hang out with her sister.

"Are you and Tom still on for dinner tonight?" Hannah asked.

"We are. This may be one of the best Saturdays I can remember. Best weekends, actually. And then I start the new job on Monday. I'm excited, but a little nervous, too," she admitted.

"Don't be nervous. You'll do great. I'm sure they will love you and I really think you'll enjoy the work. I'll let you go, so you can enjoy your bath before the water gets cold."

"Thanks, Hannah. Talk to you soon."

Sara added a swipe of dusty rose blush and two coats of black mascara, then stepped back and assessed her appearance in her bathroom mirror. She turned left and right to check the fit of the black dress she'd found at the back of her closet. The dress she'd bought several years ago and hadn't worn once. It still had the tags on it. She added her favorite gold hoop earrings and ran a brush through her shoulder-length light brown hair. The dress was flattering and she hadn't worn makeup in so long that she'd forgotten how it could make her feel. She looked refreshed, with her dark under-eye circles erased and a bit of color added to her otherwise pale skin. She was excited to finally have a night out with her husband—a date night—as the babysitter was due to arrive any moment.

The doorbell rang and she hollered downstairs, "Tom, can you let Emma in?"

Sara grabbed her small black clutch and made her way downstairs. The kids were watching television in the family room. She'd fed them earlier.

Tom was dressed and waiting by the kitchen door. It hadn't taken him more than a few minutes to get ready. He'd just changed his shirt and was wearing a navy-blue button-down and a newish pair of jeans. He'd shaved, too, and the five o'clock shadow was gone. He always looked good in navy.

Emma was a neighbor's daughter, a sophomore in high school, and she'd sat for them a few times before. She was a good student and responsible. Still, Sara made sure that Emma had both of their cell numbers and told her to be sure to call if she needed anything.

"If you're hungry, help yourself to whatever you want. There's snacks in the cabinet above the refrigerator and Popsicles in the freezer."

"Thank you."

"Tom, are you ready to go?" Sara was a little disappointed that he didn't seem to notice she was wearing a new dress. Or that she looked nice.

He glanced her way and smiled. "I'm ready. Do you want to drive or should I?"

"You can drive," she said shortly as she grabbed her coat from the closet.

Her mood improved as they drove to the restaurant. It was a new place, in Orleans, and she'd read a review recently that raved about the food. She'd been dying to try it, and since they so seldom went out these days, it was her first choice. Tom was easy that way; he didn't really care where they went. Food was food to him. She had a feeling he wasn't going to be happy about the prices, but it wasn't like they couldn't afford it—especially since they so rarely went out.

Sara was glad that she'd made a reservation as when they arrived the front bar area was crowded with people waiting for tables. When Sara gave them her name, though, they nodded and said their table was ready. They were led to a cozy table for two next to a cheerful gas fireplace.

They sat and the hostess handed each of them a menu and said their server would be over shortly. Sara glanced around the restaurant. It was on the water, but it was too dark now to see the view. During the daylight she guessed it would be stunning. The ceilings were high with dark wooden beams that gave the room a rustic, cozy look. The luxurious tablecloths were smooth to the touch and the silver was polished to a shine. Soft yellow candles glowed in the center of each table and the overall ambiance was one of comfort and elegance.

She opened the menu and the feeling continued. There was a wide selection from seafood to steaks and several vegetarian dishes. Quite a few had a comfort-food feel to them, such as lobster potpie, short ribs over blue cheese mashed potatoes, and seafood risotto. When their server came, she told them about a few specials and took their drink order.

"I'm going to have wine—should we get a bottle? Or did you want something else?" Sara asked.

"I'll just have a draft beer." Sara wasn't surprised. Beer was Tom's usual drink of choice but once in a while when they'd gone out, he'd had wine with her. She ordered a glass of cabernet and welcomed the time to decide as she was torn between several options.

"What are you going to have?" For some reason when she had a hard time deciding it helped to know what others were going to have.

"Sirloin strip steak. It's the only thing that appealed to me on the menu. Hopefully it will be good."

Tom wasn't an adventurous eater. He rarely got anything other than steak.

When the server returned with their drinks, they put their orders in and Sara decided to go with the lobster potpie. "I'll have a Caesar salad to start, too. Tom, you'll share that with me? Or would you like something else?"

"I'll have a few bites of your salad."

Sara took a sip of her wine and looked around the room. There was a low hum of conversation. It wasn't too loud like some places.

The floor was covered in a thick carpet, which she guessed helped to muffle the sounds. People seemed to be enjoying themselves. She saw trays go by carrying meals that looked delicious.

"So, how was your day?" she asked Tom. They'd hardly had a chance to talk since he'd gotten home.

"Fine. Nothing unusual. What about you?"

She smiled. "It was nice, relaxing to have the house to myself. I stayed in a bubble bath reading a book until the water grew cold. I am really looking forward to starting work on Monday."

Tom frowned. "How will that go, exactly? Will you still be able to help the boys with their after-school stuff?"

Sara leaned forward. It was disappointing that Tom didn't share her excitement, even a little. His question was about the boys, but she knew he was really more concerned with how it would affect him and if he'd need to do more. "Yes. I made sure of it. I go in after they head to school and I'll be home when they finish. I really need this, Tom."

He looked skeptical. "Working a minimum-wage job at a retailer? Do you really think that will make you happy? Or make a difference with our finances?"

Sara took a sip of her wine and felt her good mood evaporate. Tom just didn't understand why this was so important to her.

"It's not about the money. Your job pays well and you love it, so we're very lucky there. But I used to have a career that I loved, too. I put it off to raise our children, and I'm grateful that I was able to do that. But now I need more."

Tom took a sip of his beer and stayed silent.

"Honestly, I don't know if I will like the job. I won't know until I try it. But I like the idea of it. I'll be surrounded by books and talking to people about books and helping them to find books and recommending books that I love. Just thinking about it makes me happy. I'm ready for more than doing laundry and being a car service to our kids."

"You're more than that," Tom protested.

She smiled. "Yes, I'm a lot more than that. And I think it will be good for all of us if I'm doing something that makes me happy, too. Not that taking care of our kids doesn't make me happy. This will just add to that."

Their server arrived and set down two Caesar salads. Sara was about to protest that they'd only ordered one when their server smiled. "Since you said you were going to share, the kitchen split it for you."

"Oh, thank you." After she walked away, Sara took a bite and it was delicious. It was an obviously homemade dressing, heavy on garlic with the richness of anchovy. "I love that they did that," she said.

"Did what?" Tom said absentmindedly. His gaze was on his cell phone and a text message he'd just received.

"Split the salad for us. So few places do that and it's a really nice touch. What do you think of the salad?" Tom had already eaten half, shoveling it in as he typed on his phone.

"It's fine."

"Who are you texting?" Sara felt her irritation rise. It was a pet peeve of hers when people focused on their phones instead of the people sitting across the dinner table. Especially when that person was her husband.

"Just Andi at work. She had a client with a question."

Since Tom was the VP of product development, overseeing engineering and product management, he often fielded off-hour questions that came as the sales team worked on closing a big deal. His company was headquartered on the West Coast and that three hours' difference meant he often worked after hours since it was still normal business hours for them. Tom's phone pinged again and he smiled as he read the message.

Sara felt herself fuming. There were a few more back-and-forth texts until finally she spoke up.

"Are you done yet? Does Andi have everything she needs?"

Tom looked up, confused. "What do you mean?"

"This is supposed to be a date night for us. We almost never go out. I'm just asking if you are done texting for work. Can you put your phone away and try to enjoy having dinner with your wife?"

"Sure. I'm sorry." Tom sent one final text and then slipped the phone into his pocket. It immediately chimed again with a new message.

"I'll turn the ringer off." Tom fished the phone out and glanced at the text, hit one button, which Sara guessed was a thumbs-up or similar. He turned the ringer off and put it back in his pocket. "You still have yours on in case Emma calls?"

She nodded. "Of course." She finished her salad and took another sip of her wine, which was almost gone. Tom hadn't said another word. He sat silently sipping his beer.

They used to have so much to talk about. Now sitting in a nice restaurant, she felt herself struggling to make conversation.

"Do you like my dress? This is the first time I've worn it."

He glanced at her outfit and nodded. "It's nice. Did you just buy it?"

"No, I just hadn't worn it yet." She smiled. "We need to do this more often, get out, just the two of us."

"It's hard with the kids. Maybe Emma will be available more often. I'd like to get out more, too," Tom said.

Their meals arrived a few minutes later and they focused on their food. The lobster potpie was even better than she'd expected. It had big chunks of lobster and a creamy sauce with a flaky puff-pastry topping. Tom seemed happy with his steak.

They talked about the kids over dinner. How they were doing with their various sports. And the weather.

"Supposed to be nice all weekend," Tom said. "I thought I'd get a round of golf in with the guys."

"I invited Hannah over for dinner tomorrow again. I thought

we could grill up some burgers and maybe even eat outside on the back deck."

"How is she doing?" Tom asked and that made Sara feel more warmly toward him. He could be thoughtful at times.

"She's doing better, I think. She's been going to the coffee shop downtown most afternoons and it seems to help her get some writing done. I ran into her before the interview."

By the time they finished and their server had cleared their plates, Tom was yawning and Sara fought the urge to join him. She was full and content and ready to head home. Neither one of them wanted dessert and after they paid the bill, Tom drove home.

When they arrived home, Emma and the two older boys were watching a movie. The younger two were in bed. The house was quiet. Sara paid Emma and thanked her.

"What does your availability look like for the next month or so if we wanted to use you again?"

"I'm pretty flexible, just let me know and we can work something out."

Tom yawned again as Emma closed the door behind her. "I'm beat. I'm going to head to bed." He leaned over and kissed Sara lightly before heading upstairs.

Sara sighed. Her earlier hopes for a romantic ending to the evening had vanished hours ago as Tom quizzed her about her job and seemed more interested in his cell phone than talking to her. But it hadn't been entirely awful. They were just out of practice. Maybe if they were able to have date nights more often, things could improve all around for them. She hoped so.

✧

"Where's Tom?" Hannah asked. She'd just arrived at Sara's house and they were sitting on the back deck drinking chardonnay and keeping an eye on the grill that Sara had just covered with marinated steak tips.

"He's golfing with his buddies. I don't expect him back until later." Sara took a sip of her wine and made a face. "I sort of hate him at the moment."

"What's wrong? Did you guys have a fight?"

Sara sighed. "Of course I don't really hate him. But he can be so frustrating sometimes. We went to dinner last night. We finally had a night out and he was more interested in texting a woman he works with. He didn't even notice that I was wearing a new dress. And it looked good!"

"I'm sorry. Guys can be pretty unobservant. I'm sure you looked great."

"You're right. It was just annoying."

Sara seemed in a bit of a mood, which was out of character for her. And she was quiet, sipping her wine and gazing off into space. Distracted.

They sat in silence for a moment, while Hannah sipped her wine, too, and wondered what was bothering her sister. Finally she asked, "You're not worried about the woman he was texting? I can't imagine you have anything to worry about there. Do you?" Tom didn't seem the type to cheat. Hannah supposed you never really knew, though.

Sara shook her head and smiled sadly. "No. It's just the time difference. What annoyed me the most was he just doesn't understand why I'm looking forward to starting this job at the bookshop. It's not about the money."

Hannah sympathized. Her life was so different from her sister's. She couldn't imagine being home all day and running around with four children. Just the thought of it made her tired. She'd always thought she'd have children someday, just not anytime soon. And not four of them. But her sister had always seemed happy, for the most part.

"I get it. You want to be doing something you enjoy. We all want that. Tom has it."

"You're right. He does. Maybe he'll understand once I start. It would be awful if he was right."

Hannah laughed. "I can't imagine you won't like the job. It seems perfect for you."

"How is everything going for you? Was it helpful going into the law office? I know you were a little nervous about doing that."

"I just felt bad that Joy didn't give Spencer much of a choice. It has been really helpful though. I've made a ton of notes."

"That's good. Friday was your last day?"

"No, I'm actually doing another week. This time I'm going to be shadowing Natalie, Spencer's coworker. We've become friends."

"Interesting. Spencer doesn't mind?"

"I worried about that, too. But he seemed fine with it."

Sara got up and flipped the steak tips. When they were done, she put them on a big platter and brought them into the kitchen. She set out two big containers of store-bought potato salad and coleslaw and hollered for the boys to come fix themselves plates. Once the kids were all set, Sara and Hannah helped themselves and took their food out to the deck. It was a beautiful night and it was nice to eat outside. Sara invited the boys to join them but they had no interest and ate in the living room watching TV.

"What time are you picking up Aunt Maddie tonight?" Sara asked.

"Her flight comes in at ten. I wonder how her week went—if she and Uncle Richie are working things out. Do you have any idea why they separated?"

Sara shook her head. "No. I didn't even know they were having any issues. She hasn't said a thing to me. I hope it's fixable, whatever it is."

"I hope so, too. I always thought they seemed so solid."

"How are you feeling? Have you had any more panic attacks since you came here?" Sara asked.

Hannah took a sip of her wine and looked around the yard. A

soft breeze made the leaves on the trees sway and the sky looked almost pink as the dark orange sun began to set. The air smelled clean and fresh and she felt more relaxed each day.

"I'm feeling better. I haven't had any panic attacks since I left Brooklyn. The stress is starting to ease up a bit now that the writing is getting better. It's still like pulling teeth sometimes. I've had more than one afternoon where the words are still a struggle, but it's better than it was and I feel like I'm moving forward."

"That's good. I thought it might help to be here for the summer. It's been so long since you've been here for more than a week or so. Have you been by Mom's house at all?"

Hannah's mood shifted at the mention of their mother and a wave of sadness washed over her, taking her by surprise with its intensity. She sighed. It felt like this heavy sadness would always be with her when she thought of her mother. She supposed it would be easier if they weren't so close. She just still missed talking to her.

"I drove by once—a week ago on my way back from dropping Aunt Maddie at the airport. It was strange to see her house, just sitting there, like it was waiting for her to come home."

"I know. I'm still not used to it. I stop by every few weeks, and check on the house and to see if there's any mail we missed canceling. It might be good for you to go there, maybe? I could let you know the next time I swing by and you could come with me, if you want."

A sense of dread swept over Hannah. "I don't think I'm ready for that yet. Maybe later this summer. I know I need to go there eventually."

"It might help you to get closure. I get it though. It's still hard for me, too. Eventually, we will have to decide what to do about the house. If we want to sell."

Hannah knew they couldn't put it off indefinitely. But she just wasn't ready to deal with anything yet when it came to her mother's house.

"We have time still. We agreed that we wouldn't do anything for at least a year."

Sara nodded. "I know. I only mentioned that we need to think about it. A year will be here before we know it."

Hannah sighed. "You're right. Do you think you will want to sell it? I don't really know what our options are."

"Well, we could sell it or keep it. We could rent it out. You could live there if you wanted to buy me out. Or we could just share it and both use it. Like you said, we don't have to figure that out yet. There's still time."

"I don't know that I could ever live there. It might be too sad being in Mom's house, the house we grew up in, without her."

Sara nodded. "I can see that. But maybe it would be comforting, too. It might feel like she's still there in some way. I don't really know how I feel about it either, to be honest."

Hannah got up and returned with the wine bottle, topping off both of their glasses before settling back into her seat. As sad as it was talking about their mother, she was glad that she had Sara to talk to and that she understood completely. Though she and Sara talked often when Hannah was in Brooklyn, it wasn't the same as spending real time together. She would miss this when the summer ended and she went back to the city.

Chapter 14

Maddie and Richie decided to go to one of their favorite local restaurants, which was a short walk from the apartment.
Maddie met him at the restaurant as it was on her walk home. They
agreed to meet just before six. It was a small place and neither of
them wanted to stand around waiting.

Richie was already seated at a table when Maddie walked in.
Mario, the host, smiled from ear to ear when he saw her.

"It's so good to see you again. Your husband just arrived. Follow
me." This was one of the things they loved about this restaurant.
Even at the beginning, before they became regulars, Mario greeted
them the same way, as if they were his favorite customers. She
knew he did it with everyone, but she still appreciated it. Mario led
her to the table and pulled out her chair.

"Thank you, Mario. I hope Evelyn is well?" Mario spoke of his
wife often and Maddie knew they lived nearby.

He smiled again. "Very well, thank you for asking. We just became grandparents again last month—grandchild number six!"

"That's wonderful, congratulations."

Richie sat silently, watching the exchange. He didn't speak
until Mario mentioned the new grandchild and then he offered

his congratulations, too. After he walked away, there was a long, awkward silence. Exactly the kind that Maddie had feared. Richie was the one who broke it.

"So, here we are. How was your day?"

Before she could answer, their server approached the table and asked if they'd like to order drinks.

"Want to split our usual bottle?" Richie asked.

Maddie nodded. They'd found a red they liked, an Italian blend that was inexpensive and delicious. They ordered it almost every time.

The waiter brought the wine right out, and poured a taste for Richie to try. He approved it and they put in the rest of their order. Eggplant Parmesan for Maddie and veal marsala for Richie. Their usual selections. While they waited for their food, they sipped the wine and made small talk. Maddie talked about her author's auction.

"All but one came back with a better offer."

"Are they close?"

"One is a little ahead of the others and it's also her favorite after the Zoom calls. She said she clicked with that editor the most. She's going to sleep on it and call me in the morning with her decision."

Richie lifted his glass. "Congratulations."

"Thank you. How was your day?"

"Busy. And interesting. There's a new company we may invest in. They have a technology that we think could be a game-changer, totally disruptive." He told her all about it, a new social network that was only available on their unique smartphone.

"They are positioning it as invite-only initially. Which creates insane demand."

"That sounds intriguing. But a little risky, too. Will people give up their current phones just to join a new social network?"

"If enough of them do, that's all that matters. We think it has the potential to be the next iPhone."

Maddie smiled. "Well, that is exciting then."

They kept the conversation light until halfway through dinner when there was another awkward silence and once again Richie spoke first.

"Maddie, what are we doing? What do you want to do about us?" He held her gaze and she saw both her husband whom she'd adored for years and a stranger. They hadn't slept together in almost a year. She'd never felt so distant from him.

"I don't know." She turned the question back on him. "What do you want to do?"

He sighed. "I love you, Maddie. I think I'll always love you. But I don't love how things are with us. I feel like I've lost you."

"I'm still here. But I agree. Everything feels different. I think we've grown apart, some. Our priorities have changed."

He nodded. "We've both been so focused on work. I thought at this point my workload would slow, but it's only gotten more intense. And I've lost myself in it."

"Is it too much for you?" This was the first time Richie had admitted to being overloaded with work.

He smiled though. "No. I love it. It challenges me and it's always something new. But being here this past month has had its pros and cons. It's been great to be in the office with everyone. But I've been working even longer hours because the apartment feels so empty without you. I've missed you." He picked up his wineglass and took a sip, keeping his eyes on hers. "Have you missed me, too?"

She answered quickly. "Of course. It was strange trying to get used to an empty house. But it's getting easier. I haven't totally minded having the place to myself. It's been a nice break in a way after this year, and losing Melanie."

Richie's eyes clouded and he stared off into the distance. He stabbed his veal with his knife and tore a ragged piece off and swallowed it. He said nothing and continued to attack the remains of his meal, until it was gone.

"So, are you saying that you want this separation to be permanent?" he asked.

"I'm not saying that. I honestly don't know what I want. I think it's too soon for us to make a decision that final. I feel like I need more time."

"Time apart, you mean? Separated." His voice was flat, emotionless, but she saw a muscle twitch in his jaw. Part of her wished that he'd fight more for them, insist that they try harder. But that wasn't his way.

"I think so. I have Hannah staying with me for the summer. Maybe we take that time, too, and reevaluate in a few months? I don't need to be back here again until mid-August. Does that work for you?"

"Sure. I suppose it has to, right?" He smiled sadly and finely etched laugh lines danced around his eyes and the corners of his mouth. She loved those lines. Her heart hurt and she wondered if she was making a horrible mistake by insisting on keeping their separation going. But it didn't feel right to do anything else. Not yet.

"Want to split a piece of tiramisu?" she suggested.

"I'm not hungry. Get it, though. I'll have a Grand Marnier."

After they finished eating, Richie did have a few bites of the dessert—she knew he probably would. They walked back to the apartment and retreated to their bedrooms. Maddie felt a heavy sadness mixed with confusion. She hoped she'd made the right decision by asking for more time.

Chapter 15

After a more chaotic morning than usual when Cody almost missed the bus because he couldn't find his favorite green sweatshirt, which he had to wear that day, Sara breathed a sigh of relief when her last child was out the door. She had just enough time to jump in the shower, dry her hair, change, and get to the bookstore by nine thirty.

Alison wasn't there, but Brooklyn unlocked the front door to let her in. They had a half hour before the shop opened.

"Welcome! We got a new shipment of books in yesterday. I figured we could start with that, unboxing and putting everything on the shelves. Then I'll show you how our computer system works. It's not hard but it can be a little intimidating at first. I made a cheat sheet to help, and it's right next to the register.

"Great! Sounds good to me."

Brooklyn led the way to the back of the office where several cardboard boxes were stacked. She opened each box and first checked the contents against a printout of the order Alison had placed. Once everything was in order, they carried the boxes out to the shelves and put everything away.

"It's all alphabetized by genre. If you've read any of the books, let me know and we can have you fill out an index card with your thoughts—if it's one you'd recommend, of course."

Sara laughed. "Can you imagine if I put something like 'worst book ever' or 'DNF'?"

"Did Not Finish is the worst. I know more people do that these days, but it just feels wrong to me," Brooklyn said. "I hate giving up on a book. I feel like if I bought it that I owe it to the author to finish. Usually it gets better. Though I admit, I do DNF occasionally if I'm just not feeling it."

As they chatted, they shared notes on books they'd loved and it turned out they had similar taste. They both loved a suspense author who was wildly popular and wrote dark, twisty psychological thrillers.

"I actually almost didn't finish that book," Sara admitted. "I thought the beginning was slow. But so many people raved about it and said it was unputdownable, so I picked it up again one night and couldn't stop reading. The mid-book twist changed everything."

"Totally. And it's one of the few times where the movie was as good as the book."

"The ending got people talking, too. So many hated it, but I actually loved it," Sara said. "They were basically horrible people that got exactly what they deserved—each other."

Brooklyn smiled. "I thought the ending was perfect, too."

They discussed books they were currently reading as well.

"My aunt is a literary agent and I just recently read a book she is submitting soon. It was so good, it will be interesting to see where it lands."

Brooklyn looked intrigued. "What is it about?"

"It's about a female sheriff in a small town. It is loaded with twists that I did not see coming."

"Very cool. Alison mentioned that your sister is an author, too. I read her book when it first came in and loved it."

"She is. I'm super proud of her."

"Romantic comedies are big sellers for us. Especially when they are set on the Cape or by a beach somewhere." A few minutes later, she pulled a dozen copies of Hannah's book out of a box. "We sold out last week. There were a few people that placed orders, so we'll need to call to let them know the book came in."

After they put all the books away, and called the customers who had ordered Hannah's book, Brooklyn spent the next hour showing Sara how to use the computer system. It tracked all the books in the store and was also how they placed orders for new books. It wasn't difficult, but Sara was grateful for the lesson and the cheat sheet that Brooklyn made for her.

It was a quiet morning, which Brooklyn said was typical for a Monday. "People tend to start coming in more just before lunchtime and it stays busy all afternoon."

Sara didn't mind the slow start. It gave her time to get her bearings and learn her way around the shop.

"Oh, I'm not sure if Alison mentioned it, but employees get a forty percent discount. That's one of the nice benefits about working here."

"That's great." Sara grinned. "I will probably be reinvesting a good chunk of my paycheck here. I may have a book-buying addiction."

Brooklyn laughed. "We all do. I think it may be a requirement for the job!"

"Should I offer to help everyone that comes in?" Sara asked.

"I usually wait to see if they look like they want my help. Some people clearly know what they are after and go right to it. I don't want to be a bother if that's the case. But I'll always ask them when they bring their book up if they found everything they were looking for. Usually they have, but now and then, they want help finding something else."

An elderly woman came up to the counter a moment later

holding the newest Danielle Steel hardcover. Brooklyn smiled at her.

"Hi, Mrs. Winston. Did you find everything you were looking for?"

"Yes, dear. I have all of Danielle Steel's releases marked on my calendar and I make sure to come get each one."

Brooklyn watched as Sara took the book, scanned the barcode into the register, and took the woman's credit card and ran it through the processor. She printed out a credit card slip and after she signed it, Brooklyn put the book and receipt in a paper shopping bag and handed it to her.

"Here you go. Hope you enjoy!"

The woman smiled. "Thank you, dear. I know I will."

As soon as she left the store, Sara turned to Brooklyn. "I'm impressed that you remembered her name."

"Mrs. Winston is one of our regulars. She'll be back in a few weeks for Nora Roberts's new release. Or her sister will be in. They both read a lot and like to share books."

"I used to do that with my sister, when we were younger," Sara said. With the five-year difference, they mostly had different friends growing up, but after graduating, before Hannah moved to Brooklyn, they grew closer. Even after Hannah moved, for the first few years they talked more. But once Sara had her third boy, she didn't seem to have time like she used to. And Hannah was busy with her new life in the city. They still talked but not as often. Now that Hannah was in Chatham for the summer, Sara hoped they'd be able to catch up more often.

"Do you want to see if that woman needs any help?" Brooklyn asked.

Sara glanced at a woman who had just walked in and was looking around the store, trying to decide where to go. She walked over to her.

"Good morning. Are you after anything in particular today?"

The woman looked to be a little younger than Sara. She was carrying a tote bag that had a child's sweater hanging out of it. Sara guessed that she had popped into the store for a quick break.

"I'd love to find something light and easy to read. Women's fiction that I can escape into, maybe a series of some kind with a woman my age?"

Sara smiled. "Have you read Robyn Carr's Virgin River series or Debbie Macomber's Cedar Cove?"

"I watched *Virgin River* on Netflix. That's exactly the kind of thing I like. I haven't read the Debbie Macomber series."

"I think you'll like that. It's also a series, on Hallmark, I think. But the books are really wonderful." Sara led her to the section that had Debbie's books and after a quick look at the back-cover blurbs, the woman grabbed the first three books in the series. Sara rang them up for her and after she left, Brooklyn looked pleased. "Nice job. If she likes those three books, there's plenty more in the series."

The rest of the morning went quickly as the store was steady with customers and Sara split her time helping them find something to read and ringing up sales at the register. At a little before twelve, Brooklyn asked if she felt comfortable handling things alone for a half hour.

"I'm just going to eat lunch in the office. If you get slammed, don't hesitate to come get me. When I come off break, you can take a half hour as well."

It stayed busy, but Sara managed and was glad she didn't need to interrupt Brooklyn's lunch. She'd been so busy rushing around earlier that she hadn't thought to pack a lunch. And a half hour wasn't a lot of time, so she just went to the coffee shop and ordered an onion bagel with cream cheese and a cup of vegetable soup. She'd just settled at a table when her sister came in, with her laptop. Sara waved at her and Hannah headed over to her table.

"Are you already done for the day?" Hannah asked.

"No, I'm just on a quick lunch break. As soon as I finish here, I'm heading back until two thirty. How did your morning go?"

"Good. I'm going to grab a bagel, too. Be right back." Hannah set her stuff down, then went to order her lunch, and returned a few minutes later with the same thing Sara had ordered, right down to the onion bagel and chive cream cheese. Hannah laughed when she realized it.

"Great minds think alike. My morning was good. A little more fun than shadowing Spencer. Natalie likes to chat. How did it go for you?"

"The computer system is a little tricky to get used to, but I think I've got the hang of it now. It was slow at first but it's been pretty steady for the past hour or so. It's really fun, actually. Oh, and we got a shipment of your books in. You could stop by and sign them if you want, and we'll put a gold sticker on it that says 'autographed.'"

Hannah nodded. "I'll be sure to do that before I leave for the day."

"How's Aunt Maddie? Did she give you an update last night on how things went with Uncle Richie?"

Hannah frowned. "Sort of, but not really. All she said was that they decided to stay separated for the rest of the summer and see how they're feeling after that. I worried that I might be in the way and told her I could go home early or go elsewhere, but she insisted that she wanted the time and that she was glad for the company."

Sara's heart sank. "I really hope they can work things out. I always thought they were the most solid couple."

"I know. I guess it just goes to show you never really know what is going on with people."

They chatted for a few more minutes, while Sara finished up her bagel. The morning had flown by and she'd enjoyed working in the bookstore even more than she'd expected. It was fun to chat about books with Brooklyn and it was really satisfying to share her thoughts about books that she loved with customers and to help them find their next perfect read. She looked forward to getting back to work for a few more hours before she had to head home and put her mom cap on again.

Chapter 16

Hannah enjoyed the rest of the week shadowing Natalie. Spencer mostly ignored them and focused on his own work. He was very busy, though, so Hannah couldn't fault him for that. Friday morning she sat in with Donna as she met with a woman who was getting a divorce. It was a messy one as she'd been married for close to thirty years. And the wife was the one who wanted the divorce.

"Are you sure that you and Alan can't work things out? Divorce is an expensive and permanent solution to what could be a temporary problem. You could try counseling," Donna suggested. She turned to Hannah and added, "Christine and I go way back, at least twenty years, right?"

"At least that," Christine agreed. "And we're done. We're long past the counseling stage. We tried that a few years ago. It helped for a month or two and then we fell back into our old patterns. We just grew apart." She grinned. "And I met Ron."

"Ron? You didn't mention anything about another man on our call." Donna sounded surprised.

"I thought that would be better told in person. We're in love. He's a little younger than me." She almost giggled when she said it.

Donna raised her eyebrows. "How old is he?"

"Thirty-eight. He's my Pilates instructor. We just have so much in common. It couldn't be denied."

Hannah smiled. If she wrote this as a storyline her editor would tell her it was too far-fetched. Christine was almost twenty years older than her boyfriend. It wasn't unusual when it was the man who was older, but it was rare to see it the other way around. Hannah immediately wondered if Christine was rich and then felt guilty for the thought.

But Donna didn't hesitate to bring it up. "Does he have any idea how wealthy you are?"

"I don't think so. We've never discussed it. He does know where I live and that I intend to keep living there once the divorce is final."

"So, he's seen your waterfront mansion on its double-sized lot, with its dock and private beach? That has to be worth at least four million, I would think?" Hannah was a little shocked at Donna's bluntness, but figured as her friend she probably had a good idea of the value, and as Christine's lawyer, she needed to know.

"Five, actually. I just had it appraised last week. Alan wants to keep the lake house in New Hampshire. That's fine with me."

"How is Alan doing with all of this?" Donna asked.

"I think he's relieved, to tell you the truth. He wants to get on with his life, too."

"Is he seeing someone?"

"Not that I know of. He's just been spending a lot of time with his former college roommate, Brian, who moved back to Chatham. The two of them have been inseparable. Brian just got divorced a year ago, so they've been catching up. Alan will be fine."

"Well, at least you're not wanting to kill each other like some of my clients. Divorces are stressful enough without constant fighting."

"Oh, Alan and I get along just fine. We just don't want to be married anymore."

Donna asked a series of questions after that, jotting down

information about all of Christine's assets and how they wanted to split things up. When they finished, Donna told Hannah she'd be right back and went to walk Christine to the door.

"Nice to meet you, Hannah," Christine said pleasantly. She then turned her attention back to Donna. "I'll be seeing you at the gala Saturday night, right?"

Donna stopped short. "Oh, shoot. I forgot all about that. I bought those tickets so long ago. Bill and I won't be able to make it. We're actually going off-Cape to a wedding."

"Oh, too bad. It's going to be more over-the-top than usual this year. Be sure to give your tickets to someone who can enjoy it."

"Of course." Donna walked her out and then returned a few minutes later.

"So, that wasn't your typical divorce, but I suppose it's good for you see the unusual ones, too. There's generally more bitterness and regret. Sometimes even violence. Frankly, I wouldn't mind having more like this one. I don't remember the last time I saw Christine so happy."

"I hope it works out for her," Hannah said.

"Hmm, the odds are against it, but you never know. She's happy now and that's a good thing. All right, let's head back to our desks." They left the conference room and as soon as Donna saw that Spencer and Natalie were off the phone she walked over to their desks.

"Do the two of you have plans Saturday night?"

"No plans," Spencer said.

"I am heading off-Cape to see a friend," Natalie said. "Why, what's going on?"

Donna looked at Hannah. "What about you? Are you free Saturday night?"

"I am."

"Good. The two of you can take my tickets for the Chatham Gala. It's at the Chatham Bars Inn and it starts at six with champagne and appetizers on the lawn. It's a charity thing, for a good cause, the local animal shelter, I think. Christine runs it every year and she said it's going to be the best ever this year."

"Is it a dinner?" Spencer asked.

"It's a five-course wine dinner and a silent auction. The tickets are already paid for. Bill and I always go but we're double-booked this year. One of his nieces is getting married. So, will the two of you go?"

"Together?" Hannah said. She couldn't imagine that Spencer would want to go to an event like that with just her.

Donna gave her a funny look. "Yes, of course together. The tickets are already paid for. Just go and have fun. It would be a shame to waste them."

"Okay, thank you," Spencer and Hannah both said at the same time.

Natalie looked back and forth between the two of them and her eyes glimmered with mischief. "Great, it's a date then. You guys are going to have a blast."

Spencer looked unsure about that. But he smiled. "It sounds fun. Hannah, I can swing by and pick you up at twenty to six, if that works."

The Chatham Bars Inn was less than a mile down the road from her aunt's house. "Sure, that's perfect."

Natalie invited Spencer and Donna to join them for after-work drinks, but Spencer already had plans with friends and Donna had dinner cooking in her Crock-Pot.

"We want an early night tonight as we're heading out first thing in the morning. Bill's niece lives in upstate New York," she explained.

Since it was just the two of them, and Hannah had told Natalie earlier that she had nothing to wear for the gala, they decided to do a little shopping first before having that after-work drink. They walked down Main Street to one of Natalie's favorite boutiques, If the Shoe Fits.

"It's not just shoes, though their shoes are fabulous. They have some interesting pieces there and you might find a good dress. If not, definitely shoes," Natalie assured her.

Hannah found both. They walked into the store and as soon as she entered, a dress displayed on the wall beckoned to her. It was cocktail length in a rich shade of shimmery gold. It was sleeveless, and had a high neckline that came to her collarbone. It tied in the back and the dress fell in a straight line. It was simple and very flattering. And Natalie found the perfect pair of dressy sandals to match. They had a kitten heel and the cut was both elegant and fun at the same time, as there was a fluff of cream-colored threads that swished when she walked.

"You look gorgeous!" Natalie said as Hannah walked back and forth in the shoes. The material of the dress was so soft. She was starting to feel excited about this event. Even though it wasn't a real date, it would be fun to dress up and enjoy a delicious dinner. Hannah had looked up the event information online and the wines were all from a top California winery and there was a different wine to match every course.

"Okay, this is perfect. Now I don't have to spend tomorrow shopping for something to wear. I'm ready for a glass of wine at the Squire."

Natalie laughed. "I am so ready, let's go."

Chapter 17

When Hannah returned from her morning walk the next day, she was surprised to see Spencer and Joy in the driveway next to Spencer's car. Joy smiled when she saw her and waved for Hannah to come say hello.

Hannah couldn't help noticing that Joy had that look on her face as Hannah drew near and Hannah wondered what she was up to. She didn't have to wait long.

"Hannah, I've double-booked myself, it seems. I totally forgot that I told Spencer I'd go with him to the animal shelter to help him pick out a dog or two. One of my oldest friends is in town and I'm off to meet her for brunch. If you're not busy, why don't you go along with him and offer a second opinion?"

Hannah was about to say she'd love to, but Spencer spoke first. "I'm sure she is busy, Gram. I can go by myself, it's fine."

"I actually don't have anything I have to do right now. I'd be happy to go."

Joy looked delighted to hear it. "Splendid! Spencer, I can't get out until you move your car, so off you go!"

Hannah climbed into the passenger side of Spencer's car and he pulled out of the driveway and headed toward the animal shelter.

"Is this something you've been thinking about for a while?" she asked.

"Yeah. I lost my last dog, Bixby, six months ago and I adopted him from the same shelter. I thought I would have him longer, but he got sick and was only eight when he died. It kind of hit me hard and I wasn't ready until recently." He smiled. "I mentioned it to my grandmother and she got all excited."

"Will you get the same kind of dog? What was Bixby?"

"He was a golden retriever. I don't know. I'm open."

When they got to the shelter, they met with Ellie, a shelter volunteer, and Spencer gave her a history of his experience owning a dog. She explained that they do a reference check and contact his vet. Because he adopted his last dog from the same shelter, she said that process should go quickly. Once he gave her all the required information, Ellie brought them out back to meet the dogs.

"Since you mentioned that you might want to adopt two, I'd like to show you Lady and Tramp first."

He smiled at their names. "That's creative."

"Their names fit. They're both very sweet dogs, but Tramp is older, almost nine, and it's hard to find someone that wants to adopt two dogs, especially when one is a senior."

"What is their history?" Spencer asked as Ellie stopped in front of a larger cage that held two dogs. Tramp was a big golden retriever with wise, sad eyes. He was sprawled on the floor with his head resting on his paws. Lying next to him was a smaller, more delicate-looking dog. Ellie explained that Lady was a husky and collie mix. She had long, beautiful fur and she was snuggled up next to Tramp.

"Their owner passed recently. He was an older gentleman, in his mid-nineties, and he lived alone. His children lived out of state and couldn't take the dogs so they brought them to us. Their father's wish was that the dogs would stay together as they are a tightly bonded pair. We promised to do our best, but it has been almost six months now. So, we may have to consider adopting them out separately at some point."

"Can I meet them?" Spencer asked.

"Of course." Ellie opened their cages and Spencer crouched down onto his knees. He waited for the dogs to come to him. Lady came first. She tentatively took a few steps forward, sniffing the air as she walked. She stopped when she reached him and lifted her head as if asking for Spencer to pat her. He complied and scratched her gently behind her ears.

Tramp watched this closely before getting to his feet and ambling over. He sat next to Lady and regarded Spencer quite seriously for a long moment. Spencer continued petting Lady. Tramp took a step closer and butted his head against Spencer's hand.

Spencer laughed and met Tramp's gaze as he petted the older dog and Hannah noticed a look flash across his face.

"How much does Tramp weigh?" Spencer asked. Hannah stepped forward and patted him gently, too. He was such a big boy. Lady rushed over and demanded attention, too. Hannah laughed and petted her as well.

"We just weighed him the other day. He's a hundred and ten pounds and he's in good health. They both are, and are up to date on all of their shots."

Spencer stayed with the dogs for a few more minutes and sat right on the floor, continuing to pet both of them and talk to them softly. Both dogs seemed to take to him instantly.

"They really seem to like you," Ellie said. "Tramp has been a little more reserved with most people that have visited."

Spencer looked at Hannah. "What do you think?"

"They're both adorable."

Spencer got to his feet and Ellie led the dogs back into their cage and closed the door. She turned to continue their walk to view the other dogs.

"I'll take them," Spencer said.

Ellie turned back. "Don't you want to see the other dogs?"

He shook his head. "No, I've seen all I need to see. I want these two."

Ellie's eyes grew damp. "If you're sure, that's just wonderful news."

"I'm sure."

"All right, then. I'll get started on your background check. As soon as I speak to your reference, I'll be in touch to schedule a time for you to take them home."

On the ride home, Hannah was amused at the change in Spencer's personality. She'd never seen him so relaxed and happy. He was excited to get Lady and Tramp home soon.

"As soon as I drop you off, I'm heading into Hyannis to pick up everything I'll need for them: dog beds, food, toys."

"You don't want to wait to make sure they approve you?" Hannah teased him.

He laughed. "I am not worried about that." He turned into Aunt Maddie's driveway and dropped her at the front door. "I'll be back later to head to the Chatham Bars Inn. Thanks for coming along with me today."

"I'm glad I went. They're really sweet dogs, Spencer. See you later."

Chapter 18

Hannah heard the car come up the driveway and, a moment later, her aunt's voice.

"Hi, Spencer, come on in. Hannah will be right down."

Hannah assessed herself in her bedroom mirror. The new dress showed off her lightly tanned legs and arms. She'd curled her hair slightly so that it fell in loose waves to her shoulders. A final swipe of gloss over pink lipstick and she was ready to go.

She made her way downstairs and caught her breath for a moment when her eyes fell on Spencer. He looked so good in a black suit with a crisp white shirt and a deep purple silk tie. His dark hair glistened as the overhead light hit it.

She smiled. "You look sharp," she said casually. "Love the purple tie."

"Thank you. You look very nice, too." He sounded more formal than usual and maybe even a little nervous. Hannah noticed that her aunt watched them with amusement.

"You both look great," she said. "Have so much fun. Hannah, I'll expect a full report . . . of the food, when you get home."

Hannah grinned. "If no one is looking I'll try to snap a few pictures."

"Are you ready to go?" Spencer asked.

"I'm ready." She picked up a small cream-colored leather purse from the kitchen island and wrapped a soft pink cashmere shawl over her shoulders. It was a clear night, warm and still sunny as they walked to the car. Spencer opened her door and she slid into the passenger seat. Three minutes later, they pulled up to the Chatham Bars Inn and Spencer handed his keys to the valet. They walked inside and he handed their tickets to the woman collecting them at the front door.

❦

"Welcome. Head on out to the front lawn for champagne and passed appetizers."

Hannah and Spencer followed the people in front of them through the reception area to the lush, rolling front lawn that had stunning views of Chatham Harbor. All the buildings were white and the overall feeling was crisp and luxurious. A waiter came by with a silver platter that held flutes of champagne and they each accepted one.

"Have you ever played croquet?" Hannah asked. She sipped her champagne and gazed at a family playing croquet farther down on the lawn.

"Years ago. My grandparents had my cousins over and we played. It's fun. I like bocce better though. They have that here, too."

"I've played that." It was a fun game also played on the lawn or in sand, with balls that were tossed toward a target.

Hannah looked around at the crowd. She and Spencer were among the younger ones there. Many of the people were her aunt's age or older. She supposed that they were more likely to have the money to spend on an event like this. Hannah had glanced at the ticket and the price was not inexpensive.

"Do you know anyone here?" she asked.

"I haven't seen anyone yet. I'll probably run into someone I know, though. Chatham is a small town."

Hannah saw a familiar face first. A few minutes later, Donna's client, Christine, walked by next to a younger, very handsome man who she realized must be the Pilates instructor she'd mentioned. Christine was an attractive woman. She was slim and toned—all that Pilates no doubt helped—and she was wearing a gorgeous red designer dress and a diamond necklace and earrings. Her date was laughing at something Christine said and his eyes were warm as he looked at her. Maybe it would work out for them. They certainly seemed happy.

A server came by with a platter of crab cakes and they each took one. They were small and light with a creamy splash of spicy mayo on top. A few more appetizers came around, shrimp cocktail and mini beef Wellingtons that were savory bite-sized pieces of filet mignon, smothered in mushrooms and baked in puff pastry, topped with a horseradish cream sauce. Hannah was content to sip champagne and eat the delicious treats. She and Spencer chatted about the different cases going on in the office that week.

"Oh, I got an email as I was leaving with an update on Ernesto's green card application. It looks good for him. He'll know more in a few weeks."

"That's great news. I really hope it works out for him."

Spencer looked at her thoughtfully. "How did it go for you these past two weeks? Did you get what you needed?"

Hannah nodded. "I think so. You were right at your grandparents' house when you told me I was all wrong about the law. This was so helpful to get it right. But also, sitting in the office and just listening and watching how you all work was invaluable." She grinned. "It actually gave me quite a few story ideas."

"Oh, that's good." Spencer smiled warmly and Hannah noticed how much more attractive he seemed tonight and it wasn't just the suit. She liked this more relaxed side of him.

Someone announced that it was time for them to take their seats. The dinner was about to get underway. Hannah and Spencer went inside to the main ballroom and picked up their name cards on a side table. It told them they were seated at table eleven.

"It almost feels like we're at a wedding," Spencer joked as they made their way to the round table assigned to them. It held ten people and the other couples were all older, but everyone was friendly.

Once everyone was seated, tuxedo-clad waiters poured the first wine, a crisp sauvignon blanc, followed by shrimp toast—a slice of sourdough bread that had been baked with a creamy white bean hummus, then topped with sweet, plump shrimp in a buttery scampi sauce. The acidity of the cool white wine perfectly complemented the richness of the dish.

Chardonnay followed along with diced raw tuna and avocado marinated in ginger, miso, and sesame oil, served with wonton chips.

They moved on to red wine, a fruity pinot noir served with duck confit over pureed parsnips. Hannah loved duck confit, the crispy, savory meat that had been cooked for hours in duck fat. Spencer seemed to be enjoying it, too.

"I'm not usually a fan of overly fancy food, but I have to admit, this is all very good," Spencer said.

"I'm with you, young man," said the older gentleman next to Hannah, who'd overheard Spencer's comment. "This is all fine, but give me a beer and a steak or a hot dog and I'm just as happy."

"Andrew!" his horrified wife scolded him.

"What? I'm only speaking the truth." He grinned. "It's all good. It won't go to waste."

The next wine was a reserve cabernet, rich and bold, and it paired well with the braised beef short ribs served with roasted mushrooms over a very cheesy polenta.

They didn't serve full glasses of wine and the portions were small, tasting size, but still Hannah was very full at the end of the meal.

"Hope you saved room for dessert," Spencer said. "Whatever that is, it looks good."

Hannah followed his gaze to a waiter serving dessert to the table next to theirs. She wasn't sure what it was but it looked very chocolatey.

The final wine was a fruity zinfandel blend that paired well with the dessert, which was a chocolate tiramisu with layers of chocolate ladyfingers soaked in espresso and Tia Maria, a creamy mascarpone cheese filling, hot fudge, more ladyfingers, and fresh whipped cream. It was decadent and somehow the entire table managed to eat every bit of it.

"I think you may need to roll me home." Hannah laughed.

"It's early still," the man next to her said. "You can dance it off."

"There's dancing?" Hannah hadn't realized that.

"There's a very good band that will play for the next hour or so. And don't forget about the silent auction," his wife added.

"That's right," her friend added. "There are some great prizes. We should be able to raise a good amount of money for the animal shelter."

"We'll have to go check out the auction and see if there's anything we want to bid on," Spencer said.

The band began to play as Spencer and Hannah got up to view the silent auction items. It felt good to stretch her legs and walk around. They browsed the tables that were all along the sides of the room. There were quite a few items that seemed interesting, including two pairs of Red Sox tickets. Spencer put bids on both.

"Are you a baseball fan?" he asked.

Hannah grinned. "I go to the occasional Yankees game."

"What?!"

"Hey, I live in Brooklyn, remember. Of course, I'll always be a Red Sox fan first."

He smiled. "As you should be. I try to get to at least one or two games every summer."

"I haven't been to a Red Sox game in years." Hannah continued looking at the spa gift certificates, gift cards from various restaurants, paintings from local artists, two nights at the Chatham Bars Inn, a lunch and autographed book from a *New York Times* bestselling author who lived nearby, Patriots tickets for the fall, and there was also a raffle. Each ticket was twenty dollars and the grand prize was a weekend at a bed-and-breakfast on Nantucket. Hannah bid on a pedicure and manicure at one of the spas. But she wasn't optimistic as there were quite a few that bid ahead of her and she guessed someone might be back to top her bid. She and Spencer also both bought tickets to the raffle.

They were on their way to sit back down at the table when a woman came by with a ballot box for the raffle. The box was covered with pictures of cute cats and dogs from the shelter.

"Would you like to buy another raffle ticket? You can buy as many as you like and all the money goes to help the animals." Hannah took another look at their sweet faces and opened her purse again. She fished out all the money she had left—four twenties—and handed it to the woman, who looked thrilled to receive it. Spencer bought a few more tickets as well.

"Thank you, honey. Best of luck to both of you." She handed them their raffle tickets and moved along.

"So, you're a softy for animals? Or do you just really want to go to Nantucket?" Spencer asked.

Hannah laughed. "I'd love to go to Nantucket. I haven't been in years. But yeah, when I saw their faces, that did it for me."

"Do you have any pets?"

"Not now. I had an older cat, Misty. She lived to be twenty-one. I took her with me when I moved to Brooklyn. She passed a month before my mother did. I'd had her for so long that I couldn't possibly get another cat so soon. I'm sure I will eventually, though. Maybe after the summer, when I head back to the city."

They were both quiet for a moment and then Spencer asked, "You're heading back in September?" She couldn't read his expression but it felt like the energy shifted a little. Though she couldn't tell if that was real or if she was just imagining it.

"Something like that. I don't have a firm date, yet. It's kind of open-ended and it depends how well things go with finishing the book. I'm hoping to be done in early August and then have about a month to just relax and enjoy the Cape."

"Pets are good company. I'm looking forward to bringing Lady and Tramp home soon."

"When do you think you'll hear?"

"This week hopefully."

"What is your place like? Do you have a good backyard for them?"

He nodded. "I do, and it's fenced in. I'm also near the beach, so I can walk there with them and let them run along the shoreline."

Hannah could picture it, Lady running ahead and Tramp saun-tering along the water's edge, dipping his toes in the water now and then.

Hannah definitely planned to visit the shelter when she went home in the fall. "I might get an older cat. I know they're harder to adopt out."

Spencer's eyes softened. "That's a nice thing to do."

The man to Hannah's right stood up and glanced at Hannah and Spencer. Everyone else from their table was on the dance floor.

"You two young people should get out there. It's a good song for dancing."

Hannah smiled. It was one of her favorite songs, Eric Clapton's "Wonderful Tonight," but it was also a slow song and she doubted that Spencer wanted that. But he got to his feet and held out his hand. "Shall we?"

She took his hand and he led her to the dance floor and pulled her close. They swayed to the music and she leaned against him and noticed his fresh scent, a mix of cologne and something else—either soap or shampoo, she wasn't sure, but she liked the combination.

She breathed in deeply and closed her eyes, enjoying the moment. It was not an unpleasant surprise to find that she liked the feeling of Spencer's arms around her.

Spencer's chin tickled Hannah's hair as they swayed to the music. She felt light and petite in his arms and as they made their way around the dance floor, she smiled up at him and saw something reflected in his eyes that made her shiver. The energy between them shifted into something unexpected. She held his gaze as he swallowed and leaned in toward her, and she braced herself for the kiss that she suddenly wanted, very much. But then something like confusion flashed across his eyes and he pulled back a little and he loosened his grip across her back.

The moment was gone, just like that. It was fleeting and Hannah was sure it was just the romance of the night, the good wine and food, the music, maybe even the dress Hannah was wearing. It was madness, that's all it was. She knew that he didn't think of her that way—he never had and he'd given her no indication to think that had changed. Plus, she was only here temporarily. She'd made that very clear. Hannah was home for the summer but her home wasn't Chatham anymore.

When the music ended, they were both quiet as they made their way back to the table.

"Spencer. I can't believe I didn't see you earlier." A beautiful woman with long blond hair was suddenly standing before him in a little black dress and red heels. A man who was handsome but looked bored and as though he'd rather be anywhere else stood next to her.

Spencer didn't look thrilled to see her. "You look well, Michelle. I didn't realize you were here, either. It's a big crowd."

"Our seats are on the opposite side of the room. We were actually just about to get going." She glanced at George. "Do you know George? George, this is Spencer."

Spencer nodded at George. "Good to meet you." He looked at Hannah. "Michelle, this is my friend, Hannah. We went to school together. She's home visiting for the summer."

"Oh, you go way back, then." She sounded curious. "Where do you live now?"

"Brooklyn."

"Ah, so you'll be heading home then?"

Hannah nodded. "Yes, that's the plan."

Michelle smiled enthusiastically but it didn't feel genuine to Hannah. Michelle glanced at a clock on the wall. It was a few minutes before ten.

"Well, we're on our way out. Good to see you, Spencer, and great to meet you, Hannah." She took George's hand and they headed toward the door.

"So, that was your ex?" Hannah asked.

"Yes. That was Michelle. I almost proposed to her." He shook his head. "That's the guy she dumped me for. I wouldn't have thought a fisherman would be her type. Anyway, we should probably think about heading home, too."

Spencer still sounded a little bitter about the breakup. Hannah supposed she couldn't blame him; if he had been on the verge of proposing he'd obviously thought things were going well. He must have been blindsided.

"They haven't announced the winners of the silent auction or raffle yet," she said. "They should do that in a few minutes. I think this event officially ends at ten."

And as soon as Hannah said the words, the band stopped playing and the evening's host took the microphone to announce the list of auction winners. Hannah did not win the spa gift card, but Spencer won one of the pairs of Red Sox tickets he'd bid on. When the host was done reading the list of winners, he moved on to the grand prize, the raffle for the Nantucket bed-and-breakfast.

"And the winner of the weekend on Nantucket is ticket number 00897."

Spencer glanced at his tickets. "Not me."

Hannah looked at hers while the announcer said the number again.

"I can't believe it. I have the winning ticket!"

"No kidding? Well, head up there."

Hannah made her way through the crowd and handed the winning raffle ticket to the announcer. He matched the numbers and then handed her an envelope with her prize.

"Congratulations! Just call the bed-and-breakfast when you're ready to schedule your weekend." As Hannah walked away, he thanked the crowd for coming.

Spencer grinned when she returned with her envelope. "Congrats, that's an awesome prize."

"It is. I haven't been to Nantucket for years. Maybe I'll schedule it for the end of August as a celebration for finishing my book."

"That sounds good. I'd book it soon, summer is crazy on Nantucket," Spencer advised.

Spencer gave the valet his parking ticket and they brought his car around quickly. There was a little bit of a wait to get out of the parking lot but once they were on Shore Road, they were home in just a few minutes.

"I don't think I've ever asked where you live. Are you nearby?" Hannah asked before she opened the car door.

"Just a few miles away. Near the beach but it's also a quiet neighborhood with big yards. Should be good for the dogs."

She nodded. "I'm glad you don't have far to go. Thanks for driving. I had a really good time tonight."

"I did, too. Sleep well, Hannah." Spencer waited until Hannah was inside the house before he drove off. She was still in a bit of a daze from the evening, from the almost kiss with Spencer, and then winning the trip.

Aunt Maddie was still up, sipping a cup of herbal tea and reading a book in her sunroom. The TV was on the Pandora music
channel, the Norah Jones station, playing soft jazz. She looked up
as Hannah walked in.

"Hi, honey, how did it go? Did you have fun?"

Hannah flopped down into one of the oversized armchairs that
faced the sofa her aunt was curled up on. "It was a lot of fun. So
much food and the wines were amazing." She described all the
courses in detail.

"That sounds incredible. Did you get any pictures?" her aunt
asked.

"No. I wanted to, but there wasn't an opportunity. It didn't feel
right. If I'd seen anyone else snapping pictures I would have, but
we took Spencer's boss's tickets so I didn't want to do anything
that might embarrass her."

Her aunt nodded. "Well, I can almost picture it anyway from
your descriptions. Did you bid on any silent auction items?"

"Yes, but I didn't win. Spencer won Red Sox tickets." She
grinned. "I did, however, win the big raffle prize—a weekend on
Nantucket at a bed-and-breakfast."

Aunt Maddie was impressed. "Oh, that's a wonderful prize. All
the gifts are donated; someone there must have a connection with
that bed-and-breakfast. I've heard of that one, too. It's supposed to
be lovely."

Hannah yawned. The many wines and food had caught up to
her and she was ready for bed. "I think I'm going to call it a night."
She stood to head to her room.

"Oh, how did it go with Spencer? The two of you looked cute
together. He is single now, I think Joy said."

"It went fine. We're friends. He's not really my type, and besides, I'm only here for the summer." Hannah felt like she was
trying to convince herself to ignore the sparks she'd felt when she
was in Spencer's arms. Even if there was an attraction, she knew it

wouldn't be smart to act on it. She wasn't looking for a fling and Spencer clearly wasn't over his ex.

Her aunt raised one eyebrow but only said, "Well, a new friend is always nice, too. Good night, honey."

Hannah walked to her room, undressed, and climbed into bed. She snuggled into the soft pillow and closed her eyes. Her last thought before sleep took her was that she'd gotten the strong feeling that Spencer wanted to kiss her and in that fleeting moment, she'd wanted it, too. But she may have imagined it—it was likely just the effect of the wine and the romance of the event. It did make her look at him differently, though, at least for a moment.

Chapter 19

Sara had the nagging feeling that there was something she was forgetting as she ran around the house Monday morning after sending the last child out the door. She remembered to pack her own lunch, a simple turkey sandwich and a bag of chips. She needed to start keeping a list as she'd missed a few things last week. She'd forgotten to sign Cody's permission slip for an upcoming field trip.

That wasn't a big deal, he brought it in the next day, but it wasn't like her to forget things like that. Even worse, she'd almost forgotten to pick up Dylan after practice on Thursday. She remembered at the last minute, but she was the last parent there and Dylan looked so relieved when she finally pulled the car up.

She finished getting dressed, dried her hair, and headed out the door. She liked to get to the bookshop a few minutes before nine thirty. Overall she was pretty thrilled with how her first week had gone. It was a joy to be working again, interacting with adults and talking about books—and getting paid for it. Sara enjoyed chatting with the customers and sharing her recommendations, especially for her favorite books.

She mostly worked with Alison, as Brooklyn was in classes during the week. That meant Sara had weekends off, which was perfect as there was always something going on with the kids on the weekends.

"Do you want to see if your sister would like to do a book signing in two weeks?" Alison asked. "It's a Saturday, and I was thinking from one to three. That seems to be our best time for author signings."

"Sure, I can text her now and see if that works." Sara sent a quick text message to her sister. She would definitely make sure she stopped down on Saturday as well. She wanted to support her sister and was also curious to see how they handled author signings at the bookshop.

"We're going to have our first author signing of the summer season this coming Saturday. Niall Peterson will be here."

"Really? I love his books." Niall was a big deal. He released a new book every few years and they always spent months on the bestseller lists. He wrote literary sagas about dysfunctional American families and they never had happy endings, but they were incredibly well written and insightful. Sara always wanted to talk to someone after she finished one of his books. They were ideal for book clubs. Maybe she might want to stop in for this one, too, and see if Hannah wanted to come along, to have an idea of what to expect for her own signing.

"His parents bought a place here a few years ago and he said he's spending most of the summer in Chatham."

"Where does he live normally?"

"Manhattan, I think. His parents are very wealthy. They bought the Thurston estate."

"Oh! Wow. I didn't realize that had sold." The Thurston estate was a sprawling waterfront mansion set on almost three acres, which was massive for an oceanfront property. It was very private. You couldn't even see the house from the main road.

"We got to chatting and he told me he's staying in the attached guest house for a bit of privacy," Alison said.

"I've seen pictures of that property. I think the guest house is the size of a normal home. I'll have to tell Hannah. She loves his books, too. We'll make sure to stop in for the signing."

Her phone dinged with a new text message. It was Hannah and simply said, *Of course! I'd love to.*

Sara smiled. "I just heard from Hannah and she's confirmed."

"Great. I'll bring some snacks, cookies, brownies, that kind of thing. Everyone loves sweets."

"Is there anything I should let Hannah know to bring?"

Alison thought for a moment. "Just her favorite pens to sign with. We'll take care of everything else. I'll put an order in today for extra books. If we don't sell them all at the signing I'm sure we will over the next few months."

The day went by quickly as the shop was busier than usual for a Monday. It was a clear, sunny day and there were lots of people out walking and shopping along Main Street.

With their location, and the colorful awning and adjacent coffee shop, they saw a lot of foot traffic from people who were just curious and wandered in to explore. Many of them ended up discovering something they had to buy. The coffee shop next door also sent plenty of customers their way. It was easy for people to buy their coffee, then wander through the archway into the bookshop. Unlike many retail stores, they didn't have a rule about no beverages because Alison and Jess, the co-owner, wanted to encourage people to go back and forth between the businesses.

Sara had asked Alison last week if it was ever a problem, people spilling coffee on the books or touching the covers with sticky hands.

"Only once so far. A child with gooey hands got frosting on a book cover. But the mother insisted on buying the book, so it was all good. We figured even if there is the occasional mishap, it's still worth it overall if it drives more people into the store."

"That makes sense. It is nice to sip a coffee and browse books at the same time."

When her shift was over, Sara went home and threw a load of laundry in the washer and put some chicken, vegetables, and water into her slow cooker to make a big pot of soup for dinner. At four thirty, she ran out to pick up two kids from after-school practices, and when she got home, she put a salad together to have with the soup. She also sliced a big loaf of Italian bread in half and slathered soft butter and minced garlic across both surfaces, then put the loaf back together, wrapped it in aluminum foil, and put it in the oven to bake for twenty minutes. Tom should be home by then and the kids loved her garlic bread with soup.

Tom walked through the door at exactly five thirty, just as she was taking the toasted loaf out of the oven.

"Perfect timing," she said.

He gave her a quick kiss hello and went to change out of his work clothes. A few minutes later, he returned wearing his favorite jeans and an old T-shirt.

"Something smells good."

"Thanks, it's soup and the garlic bread you're smelling. Want to tell the kids to come eat? Everything is ready."

Sara ladled out bowls of soup and brought everything to the table. The kids didn't eat much salad, but they went back for seconds on the soup and bread. As they ate, Tom told her all about a new client they were trying to win over.

"If we land this one, it will be huge. They are a global company and we may have to hire one or two people just to service their account."

"That's great. When will you know?"

"Probably in a week or so. We have a big meeting tomorrow. The corporate heads are all flying here."

"They're coming to Chatham?" That was a surprise. Tom's company was headquartered on the West Coast and the satellite office in Chatham that served much of the East Coast was small. It was just Tom and two others plus an administrative assistant.

"The client will be on the Cape. They have friends in Brewster and are visiting for a few days. So when I mentioned we had an office here in Chatham they asked if the meeting could be here. That reminds me, did you pick up my dry cleaning? I didn't see the bag in the closet."

Tom's dry cleaning. That was the thing she was supposed to do—pick it up for his big meeting.

"Tom, I'm so sorry. I totally forgot. What time is your meeting?"

He frowned. "It's early, nine o'clock. I can't believe you forgot." He didn't sound angry, just surprised. And she didn't blame him. It wasn't like her to forget things.

"I think they open at eight. I can run over in the morning for you."

Tom sighed. "Thank you. I can do it though. I'll just go straight into the office from there. I wanted to go in early anyway."

He took a bite of bread and chewed for a moment. "How was your day? Are you still liking the job? It's not too much for you, is it?"

Sara knew he was really asking if she could handle juggling everything.

"It's an adjustment, balancing it all. But I love it. I really do."

"Good. So, did I tell you about this other deal we have cooking?" Sara sighed in frustration as she half-listened to Tom tell her all about his other deal. It would be nice if he was genuinely interested in hearing about how much she was enjoying her new job.

Chapter 20

The characters had stopped talking to her again. Hannah's Monday afternoon writing session at the coffee shop was decidedly unproductive. She went there earlier since she wasn't shadowing at the law firm anymore. She took a long walk soon after she woke, enjoyed her coffee and breakfast with her aunt, did some laundry, and around eleven made her way to the coffee shop. Because she was going to sit there for several hours, she made sure to have a bagel for lunch and a few hours later, a cookie and a second coffee.

Hannah fired up her laptop as soon as she arrived, sure it was going to be a good day, and instead it felt like pulling teeth to get any words onto the page. She was totally stuck about where to go next and she was feeling the worst possible thing a writer could feel as they wrote—boredom. Though she also knew it might not be real, that it was just doubt and worry messing with her as it often did at this point in the process.

But she also knew that when this feeling crept over her that usually something needed fixing. She needed to find the joy and excitement in her story again. She smiled to herself thinking it would be so much easier if she wrote mysteries and could add a dead body or something. Instead she had to find an interesting new predicament that would either bring her couple closer together or temporarily put an obstacle in their path until they could overcome it and have their happily ever after.

But all her ideas felt so boring. And as she often did when she was stuck, she surfed the internet, catching up on all the celebrity gossip and what her friends were posting on social media. It fascinated and annoyed her the way people would sometimes gush on social media about their partner. It always seemed odd to Hannah to post something so personal that seemed like it would make more sense to say privately, either in person or on a lovely handwritten card.

Instead, they posted it on social media, for the world to see. The writer in Hannah often wondered if they did it to convince themselves, and if things in the real world were different and perhaps darker than they wanted to admit. It was easier, safer to pretend online that everything was just peachy, couldn't be better.

Hannah left the coffee shop around two and headed home to print out the pages that she planned to bring to Joy's for the writing group. She walked over a few minutes before three and this time everyone was there already, including Louise, the one who'd been late before.

Joy smiled and welcomed her in. "Excellent, everyone is here and ready to go. Let's get started." They did their free-writing exercise and then everyone went around and checked in. When it was Hannah's turn she sighed.

"Everything was going better, until today. I've reached a point, about halfway through the story, and I'm not sure yet where I need to go next. I honestly have no idea what to do with these people and wonder how I can possibly fill another forty thousand words of story."

Joy looked sympathetic. "You're not alone, dear. That happens to me at least once with every book. I used to panic but now I've just accepted that it's part of my process. I don't outline, either, so that may be a factor. But we have to do what works best for us."

The others all nodded in agreement.

"Even though you don't outline, what if you jot down some notes?" Joy said. "I do that when I get stuck. I take a little time to think about some things I know that need to happen next. And then I think about what the very next scene could be and what fun thing or twist I can include to make the scene fun for me and hopefully for the reader."

Hannah smiled. "Thank you. I like that idea. I tried fully outlining once and hated it. But maybe just a few notes might help me to think through where I need to go next."

They finished up a little earlier than usual and as Joy said goodbye to everyone, she whispered for Hannah to stay. Once everyone was gone, she turned to Hannah.

"Do you have time for a cup of tea? I want to hear all about that fancy dinner you went to with my grandson."

Hannah laughed. "Sure." She and Aunt Maddie were just planning to order pizzas for dinner and it was only four thirty. She had time to visit for a bit.

Joy kept an electric teakettle plugged in and had hot water ready to go for their tea. Hannah chose a vanilla herbal flavor and they sat in the kitchen. Ben was in the house, but was working in his shop in the basement. Now and then Hannah could hear the faint whir of one of his sanding machines.

She told Joy all about the event, describing the crowd and all the food they'd had and the band. Joy didn't drink, so she didn't mention the wines. Joy loved music and she and Ben both liked to sing in Christmas choral productions.

"I know that band. Ray, the vocalist, is friends with Ben. They are very good."

Hannah agreed that the band was great. "How is your book coming along?" She knew Joy was about a quarter of the way into writing a new mystery.

Her eyes lit up. "I think I know who the killer is. It came to me yesterday. Along with a few other scene ideas. It's shaping up quite nicely."

Hannah had read one of Joy's books and enjoyed it. It was a more traditional mystery, focused on puzzle solving with interesting social issues covered in each book. The sleuth was also loosely based on herself as she was a minister living on Cape Cod and her husband was British, retired, and forever embarking on a new home-improvement project.

A moment later, Hannah heard footsteps coming up the spiral staircase that led to the basement. Ben walked over to a drawer in the kitchen, muttering under his breath. He opened several drawers, still muttering. Joy and Hannah exchanged looks before Joy jumped up to help him.

"What are you looking for?"

"Have you seen my Phillips screwdriver?"

Joy opened another drawer and held up a screwdriver. "Is this it?"

"That's the one. Thank you!" He took it and started back toward the stairs.

"What do you need the screwdriver for?"

"I need to open the air-conditioning vent in the ceiling. Just getting ready for summer."

Joy faced her husband and put her hands on her hips. Her tone was firm, but Hannah also picked up a bit of anxious worry. "Ben, you don't need to do that now. I don't want you on a ladder. Wait for Spencer to do that for you."

"Maybe I could help?" Hannah offered.

Joy shook her head. "This is not urgent. Ben can wait for Spencer. He knows how to do it."

Ben muttered something under his breath and headed back down to his shop.

Hannah and Joy turned their attention back to their tea and conversation. Joy continued talking about what she was working on.

"So, I think I have a really good idea for the next book in the series too. It just came to me while I was watching TV last night."

A sudden loud crash in the basement followed by an angry scream of frustration brought them to their feet.

Joy ran down to the basement, with Hannah right behind her. Ben was lying on the floor, next to a ladder, and held the screwdriver in his right hand.

"Ben, did you fall off that ladder?" Joy didn't sound upset, just scared, and she'd gone pale.

He nodded, then grimaced in pain. "I've done it a million times before. But I just lost my footing for some reason." He tried to get up, but couldn't put any weight on his leg to stand.

"Don't move. I'm calling 911." Joy had her phone in her shirt pocket, pulled it out, and made the call. Less than five minutes later there was a knock on the door and the paramedics quickly assessed Ben, put him on a stretcher, and carried him out the front door of the basement, which was easier to navigate than the spiral stairs.

Joy's hands shook a little as she looked around the room for her purse. She found it on the kitchen counter and headed for the door.

"Joy, can I drive you to the hospital? I can keep you company for a bit." Hannah didn't want her driving when she was this worried.

Joy hesitated then quickly accepted. "If you don't mind, I'd appreciate that. I called Spencer but had to leave him a voice message. He may be tied up with work for a while, but I let him know we're heading to the hospital."

❦

Spencer arrived at the Cape Cod Hospital about two hours after his grandparents.

A nurse in the ER directed him to where his grandfather was being seen. It was one of those areas that had eight or so beds with curtain partitions separating them. His grandfather was lying in a bed with a cast on one leg and an IV in his arm. His grandmother and Hannah were sitting in chairs on either side of the bed. He looked surprised to see Hannah there.

His grandmother stood and he walked over and gave her a hug.

"What did the doctor say?" he asked gently, as it was clear Joy was still upset.

"Your grandfather shouldn't have been on that ladder." She glanced at Ben with disapproval. "He couldn't wait for you to check his air-conditioning vent—even though I told him not to climb that ladder."

"I should have listened to your grandmother," Ben said sheepishly. "I missed a step and went down hard. I wasn't even all the way to the top. I suppose it could have been worse."

"He broke his leg and will have to wear a cast," Joy said. "The doctor wants him to take it easy and keep all weight off his leg for a while. But other than that, he's okay. His blood work came back fine. He's just a little low on potassium, which could have been a factor. He said he was a little light-headed. They gave him some pills."

"Well, I'm glad it wasn't worse. I am sorry you broke your leg, though, Gramps. I guess this means you won't be able to come to the Red Sox game with me on Wednesday?"

His grandfather glanced at his grandmother and she answered for him. "Absolutely not, I'm afraid. Your grandfather isn't going anywhere for a while."

"Okay. No problem. I'm sorry you'll have to miss it, but we'll go to another game later this season."

The nurse came in a moment later, took his grandfather's IV out, and handed him a stack of discharge paperwork. She smiled at his grandfather. "The doctor said to be sure to remind you to stay off all ladders."

His grandfather chuckled. "Message received. My wife said the same thing."

"He didn't listen to me though," Joy said.

"I promise. No more ladders." His grandfather picked up the pen and signed the paperwork and handed the signature page back to the nurse.

"You're good to go," she said cheerfully.

"Spencer, do you want to drive your grandfather home and I'll ride with Hannah? He could use your help getting into the house."

"I can manage fine," his grandfather said. "They're sending me home with crutches."

"Which you've never used before," Joy reminded him.

"Of course, I'll help get him settled when we get home," Spencer said.

When Spencer pulled into the driveway, Hannah and Joy had just arrived and were standing by the car waiting. Spencer helped his grandfather out of the car and stood close by as Ben slowly moved on the crutches.

"Hannah, thanks a million for going to the hospital and keeping us company," Joy said.

"Of course. I'm glad Ben is going to be okay."

Ben looked at her thoughtfully. "Yes, thank you, Hannah." His gaze shifted to Spencer. "You know, maybe Hannah might want to go to that game with you? Unless you have someone else in mind."

Spencer looked surprised by the suggestion. "No, I don't have anyone else in mind. I took the day off and it's too short notice for any of my friends to do the same. Would you want to go, Hannah? It could be fun. And I really do appreciate you helping my grandparents."

Hannah eagerly accepted the invitation. "I haven't been to a Red Sox game in years. I'd actually love to go."

"Great. It's an afternoon game. A one o'clock start. I was thinking we'd leave a little before eleven, just in case we hit traffic. I like to just grab lunch there if that works for you?"

She smiled. "Hot dogs at Fenway are the best. Sounds good to me."

His grandfather looked pleased. "It's settled then. You two have fun." They all headed in as Hannah waved goodbye and climbed back into her car. She didn't expect that she'd see Spencer so soon after the charity event and she was excited at the thought of spending the day in Boston with him.

Chapter 21

The next afternoon, Hannah was at the coffee shop struggling with a scene that just wasn't coming out right. It was almost three thirty and she'd been there for three hours. There was no one else in the shop and she thought she might as well pack up and head home. She put her laptop in her tote bag and as she stood to leave, the front door opened and Spencer strode toward her, looking more excited than she'd ever seen him.

"Are you busy right now? Want to go for a quick ride? The shelter called and said I can pick up Lady and Tramp today. Since you helped me pick them out, I thought you might want to come along. And I wouldn't mind an extra pair of hands to get them in and out of the car, if you are available." Spencer's enthusiasm was contagious.

"Sure, let's go."

At a few minutes before four, Spencer arrived at the animal shelter. Ellie smiled when she saw him. "They're ready for you. I'll bring them right out."

She walked out back and returned a moment later with both dogs. They saw Spencer, and Tramp immediately began wagging his tail while Lady ran over and licked his hand.

Ellie shook her head. "It's like they know. I told them you were coming." Ellie handed their leashes to Spencer. She also gave him a packet of information for him to share with his vet.

"I wish you many happy years together," she said.

Spencer smiled. "I know Tramp likely only has a few more years, but I intend for them to be good ones."

Hannah knew that Lady was only two and a half years old, so hopefully she would be around for much longer.

The two dogs followed him to his car and jumped right in his back seat. Spencer and Hannah climbed into the car and fifteen minutes later arrived at his house. Spencer and Hannah got out first and each went to one back door. Hannah grabbed Lady's leash and Spencer got Tramp. They led the dogs to Spencer's backyard, which was completely fenced in.

Hannah noticed that he also had a dog door on the deck that led inside. Spencer noticed her looking at it.

"I had that installed when I moved into the house six years ago, for Bixby. He was a little smaller than Tramp. But the door should be plenty big enough for both of them."

Spencer put some water and a bowl of food on the deck and Tramp ran over to it. He didn't eat but had a good drink of water. Lady did the same.

"They're not hungry yet," he said. It was a quarter past four.

"Did you say there is a beach nearby? We could take them for a walk," Hannah suggested.

"Sure. If you have time. I can drop you back at your car after."

They each took a dog and set off down the road. The beach, as Spencer had said, was just a short walk away, maybe a quarter of a mile or so. They walked along the beach, following the dogs to the water's edge, where both dogs ran in and out of the surf.

As they walked, Spencer told her about some of the new cases he was working on. He didn't share any names so he didn't divulge any confidential information and Hannah loved hearing the details of the cases. They were all so different and it gave her more story ideas to consider.

"I actually have to work tonight. Once we get back and I get them settled. I need to stay ahead since I'll be taking most of tomorrow off," Spencer said.

Hannah wasn't surprised. She knew that both he and Natalie often took work home if they needed to. Sometimes their caseloads demanded it as they never knew when new clients would call with work.

Hannah liked this side of Spencer. He seemed more relaxed outside of the office, with the dogs. She was inspired to try and get a little writing done when she got home, too, since she would be missing her usual afternoon writing session the next day.

She looked around as they walked, taking in the bright sun shining over the water, the families swimming and relaxing on the beach, and the sand that varied from sugar soft in areas to rocky in others—a typical New England coastline—beautiful and, in the off-season, remote.

"Did you ever wish you'd lived off-Cape for a while, after graduating law school?" Hannah wondered.

"I did live off-Cape, for years while I was in college and law school. I lived in Southie with roommates and went to school in downtown Boston. That was enough for me. Boston is fun, but I couldn't wait to get back here. I mean, look around you." He turned and gestured with one arm toward the ocean. "I have everything I need here. Lots of room for the dogs, the beach whenever I want it, a good job, and family nearby."

"Well, when you put it that way . . . you may have a point," Hannah agreed.

"What about you? Do you ever think of moving home to Chatham? Or do you love living in the city?" Spencer slowed his steps and faced her to see her response.

Hannah didn't hesitate. "I honestly never think about moving home. I love Chatham, but I really love living in Brooklyn. There's nothing like the energy of a big city. Have you been to New York City?"

He nodded. "A few times while I was in college. Fun place to visit, but too much concrete there. After a few days I couldn't wait to get home. Guess we're just wired differently," he said.

Hannah laughed. "Yes, I suppose so." She glanced out at the ocean. In the distance she could see a huge barge going by and several smaller sailboats. "It really is beautiful here though. I'm happy to be home for the summer. And I love playing tourist when people come to visit. It's fun seeing the Cape through their eyes."

Spencer smiled. "Yeah, you really appreciate it more when you share it with others."

They walked along silently for a few minutes, watching two other dogs race into the water, followed by their owners. Spencer and Hannah walked the dogs down to the water's edge one last time and let them go in a little until they'd had their fill and raced out shaking their fur and sending water everywhere.

Lady and Tramp both ran to Spencer as if they belonged with him and he petted them both. He looked madly in love with both dogs, and it was cute to see. After they'd had enough attention from Spencer, the two dogs walked over to Hannah for more petting and she happily complied.

"You'll have to bring them by to see your grandparents soon," Hannah said as they walked back into Spencer's yard.

Spencer grinned. "I will. My grandmother has been suggesting for a few weeks now that it was time for me to get a dog. As usual, she was right. She'll be thrilled to see that I got two."

Spencer locked the fence door, so the dogs were safe in the backyard, before driving Hannah back to her car.

"Thanks for coming along," he said as he parked next to her car. Hannah grabbed her purse and tote bag.

"That was fun. I was glad to see them again. I think they will love it there. And I bet you will enjoy the company," she said. She could picture Spencer working on his sofa with the dogs curled up beside him.

He smiled. "Yeah, I think they will be good company. I'll see you tomorrow."

Hannah pulled out of the driveway and headed back to her aunt's house. It had been fun going with Spencer to get the dogs. She found herself looking forward to the next day even more— watching the Red Sox and heading to Boston. It was something she hadn't done in so long.

✲

Hannah debated what to wear the next day. It was a sunny day, and warm—perfect weather to go to a baseball game. The only baseball T-shirt she had with her had the Yankees emblazoned all over it, which wouldn't be appropriate. She smiled thinking of Spencer's face if she dared to wear it. He would no doubt be wearing a Red Sox shirt. She decided on her favorite pair of faded jeans and a solid white T-shirt and a pink hair tie. She pulled her hair into a low ponytail, and added a matching pink baseball cap.

Her aunt was in her office working when Hannah heard Spencer's car outside. She waved goodbye and headed out to meet him. He was walking to the door and as expected, he was wearing a Red Sox shirt, matching baseball cap, and jeans. He looked just as good in casual wear as he did in a suit.

"Ready to go?"

They climbed into his car and drove off. Spencer went through a Dunkin' Donuts drive-through and they both got iced coffees for the ride.

"Do you like Pearl Jam?" he asked as they turned onto the Mid-Cape Highway.

"Sure. Especially their slower songs. I'm not as crazy about the harder rock," she said.

"Same. I have a playlist with their stuff and similar bands. Let me know if you get sick of it and we can change to something else."

Hannah relaxed and sipped her coffee while she gazed out the window and listened to the music.

"How's your grandfather doing?"

"Not too bad. I stopped in there before I picked you up. He's a little frustrated with the cast and not being able to move around easily. But my grandmother is taking good care of him."

They rode along for a while, just enjoying the music. Hannah sensed that Spencer wasn't one for a lot of small talk and she didn't want to bother him while he was driving. But the traffic was light and they sailed along, crossing the bridge over the Cape Cod Canal and merging onto Route 3, which led them up the South Shore toward Boston.

When they reached the Braintree split, Spencer veered right onto I-93, which would take them into the city.

"What made you decide to become a lawyer?" Hannah asked. "Did you always know you wanted to do it?"

"No. I really wasn't sure what I wanted to do. I majored in business just because that seemed like a good major with lots of options. Senior year I took two classes, philosophy and logic, that I really loved. A teacher mentioned that people who did well in those classes might have an aptitude for law."

"So, it was those classes that made you decide?"

"Partly. A neighbor of my grandparents' was an older woman. Her landlord threatened to kick her out even though she was paying the rent and had a lease. He wanted to sell the place. She was really upset and thought she had to move. She didn't have the money for an attorney but my grandparents found her someone that would help, pro bono, and he was great.

"The landlord was totally in the wrong and she had every right to be there until her lease was up. She was a nice lady and it just made an impact on me. I wanted to be able to help people like that, using the law."

"That's nice. Natalie said you do a lot of pro-bono work."

He stayed quiet for a moment before saying, "We all do. Donna supports it. It's a way to give back."

Spencer took the back roads to Fenway and found a parking spot on the far end of Boylston Street by the Longwood medical district.

"Do you mind walking a little way? It's nice out and we won't find anything closer unless we go into one of the paid lots and those can take a while to get out of when the game ends."

"I don't mind walking."

Spencer parked and they made their way down Boylston Street to Yawkey Way and into Fenway Park. The place was already crowded with people buying T-shirts, hot dogs, and beer.

"Are you hungry?" Spencer asked. It was a quarter to one, and the hot dogs smelled so good.

"I could definitely eat."

They both got hot dogs and fries and Sam Adams draft beers. Hannah wasn't much of a beer drinker, but it went well with the hot dogs and sunshine. They took everything to their seats, which were pretty good ones, about ten rows back with a nice view of the field. The sun felt great as it shone down on them.

The game got started on time, just as they were finishing up eating. The Red Sox were playing the Toronto Blue Jays and it was a close game with lots of scoring on both sides, so it was fun to watch.

They both switched to water as the afternoon went on, and at the bottom of the eighth inning, after singing along with the boisterous crowd to the classic song "Sweet Caroline," a tradition at all Fenway home games, Spencer went to use the restroom. He came back with two banana splits and grinned as he handed one to Hannah.

"This looked good, so I got you one, too."

She laughed. The dessert was ridiculously huge, with three different flavors, plus a banana, hot fudge, whipped cream, and nuts, but she was game to give it a go.

"Thank you." She managed to eat a good two-thirds of the sundae. Spencer polished off his and finished hers when she said she was done. The sugar plus the warmth of the sun made her a little sleepy as the game headed into the bottom of the ninth inning. She woke up, though, when a Blue Jays player hit a grand slam home run and tied the game. The Red Sox had had a comfortable four-point lead before that.

"It's never an easy win with the Sox," Spencer said. They paid close attention as it was time for the Red Sox to go to bat and try to pull off a win. They managed it with the last hit of the game and a solo home run.

Spencer and Hannah followed the happy crowd out of the stadium and walked back to the car.

There was a little traffic getting out of the city as it was rush hour, but it moved along and once they reached the Braintree split and turned onto Route 3, they picked up speed.

"How is your book coming along?" Spencer asked. "You're missing a writing day today. Unless you plan to write at night when you get home?"

She laughed. "I don't usually write at night. I'll try and get another writing session done at home before I head into the coffee shop tomorrow."

"Do you go there every day? Sort of like your office in a way."

Hannah nodded. "Most days. I like getting out of the house and having somewhere to go. And I like being around people, even if it's just customers coming and going. It's like white noise, and when I get stuck, I can people-watch for a while."

"I work better when it's quiet. That would totally distract me."

Hannah smiled, picturing Spencer trying to do his job in a busy, noisy coffee shop.

"Your grandmother said you worked in Boston for a few years right after you got out of law school. Do you miss being in the city at all?"

"No. I lived in Braintree and commuted into the city and I don't miss it—especially the rush-hour traffic. Working in downtown Boston was pretty cool, but we were too busy to really enjoy it. I'd go out with friends at night and that was fun, but when the opportunity at Donna's office came up, I jumped on it. I love the Cape. It's just tougher to find good jobs there, especially when you're just starting out."

"Yeah, there were no options when I graduated from college."

"What made you decide on New York over Boston?"

"I always knew I wanted to be a writer and I thought it might be fun to start with getting a job in publishing and those are all in New York."

"Oh, you worked for a publisher before you sold your first book?"

"No. I tried, but it's so competitive and I didn't have any relevant experience. Instead of working in a bookstore, I spent my summers waitressing. I signed on with a temp agency and they put me at a marketing agency doing administrative work and that turned into a full-time job. It was a nice company. It's where I met my best friend, Lucy, and Jeremy."

"Who's Jeremy?"

"My ex. We dated for almost two years. I broke it off right after my mother passed. He's a nice guy. He just wanted to get serious and I didn't feel the same way."

"Sounds like what happened with me and Michelle, the one

you met at the dinner the other night. Though I was the one that wanted to get more serious. But it just wasn't meant to be."

He didn't sound like he was still hung up on Michelle anymore. Hannah wondered if he'd actually started dating again. Though she guessed Natalie would have mentioned it if he had.

"I'm glad that I am able to spend the summer here. It's nice seeing my sister more and my aunt, too," Hannah said.

"Do you ever think about moving back to Chatham? Now that you're an author, you can live anywhere, right?"

"I really haven't thought about it. I love Brooklyn and have a life there, a cute apartment, and good friends. I may try to get back to the Cape more often, though. It's really not that far."

"It's not like living in Boston, though, where it's an easy drive to the Cape for a weekend. New York is a good six hours from here."

He was right. And that was why she hadn't gotten home as often as she would have liked. It wasn't a short drive.

"Do you ever get to New York?" she asked.

"Not so much these days. I had a college roommate that lived there so I went to visit a few times when I lived in Boston. But I haven't been back since I moved to the Cape. It's a great city, though. Lots to do."

"There's so much to do," Hannah agreed. She felt a pang of homesickness. She needed to give Lucy a call. They messaged each other all the time, but she'd only talked to her once since she'd been in Chatham. Hannah wondered what her friend was up to and what she was missing out on.

"I don't think I could ever live in New York," Spencer said. "It's a great city to visit, but there's too much cement there for me. I'd miss the trees, and the beaches. I didn't really appreciate the Cape as a kid. Not until I lived in Boston during law school and for a few years later. It gets busy in the summer with tourists, but nothing like city traffic. And it's a good place to raise a family, a lot safer than the city."

"That's true." Hannah had always felt safe in her Brooklyn neighborhood but was careful where she went at night. She never had to worry about that on the Cape. And truth be told, she hadn't given a lot of thought to starting a family. It wasn't a priority the way it was with some of her friends or her sister.

Though she supposed if she'd met her person in college like Sara had, she might feel differently. She just wasn't in a hurry for it. It was interesting to hear Spencer say he'd given it some thought and had been close to asking Michelle to marry him.

Spencer was starting to grow on her. She saw his earlier prickliness now more as protectiveness for his grandparents. Though he was still very much her opposite in how he approached things. Spencer was super focused, uptight even, and organized. Whereas Hannah was looser, more willing to go with the flow, and no one would ever call her organized. But she was starting to like him, as a friend. Even though for that split second at the gala she'd looked at him differently, she knew it was just a moment. And the moment had passed. He might be fun to hang out with more, though, along with Natalie and her sister. There was a whole summer ahead of her and once Hannah finished her book, she wanted to play tourist and just enjoy herself as much as possible.

Spencer pulled into her aunt's driveway and she thanked him for the day.

"Are you heading over to check on your grandfather?"

"Yes, and my grandmother wants me to stay for dinner, though I'm sure they've already eaten by now." It was almost six thirty.

"Well, tell them both I said hello."

"I will. I guess I'll probably see you this weekend, at Caitlin's party?"

Hannah had no idea what he was talking about. "What party?"

He laughed. "Talk to Natalie, she was going to call you about it. Caitlin at the coffee shop is having a cookout at her boyfriend's house. It should be a good time."

"I'll give her a call."

After Spencer drove off, Hannah checked her phone and there was a text message that she'd missed from Natalie asking her to call when she got home.

Chapter 22

Sara's week flew by. She was busier than ever between working at the bookshop and running around doing all the mom things she used to fit into a whole day into her afternoon window. She was learning to manage her time better by putting everything she had to remember on her phone calendar and setting up alerts so she wouldn't forget. But the week had been a good one. She was enjoying the new job, loved talking to customers, and was starting to recognize regulars who came in often.

Some came in several times a week to stock up on new books or magazines. Most of those customers were older and had more time to read and they liked to chat with her when they came in. She enjoyed it, too. It was fun getting to know them and their tastes in books. She'd introduced some of them to a few of her favorite authors already, based on what they seemed to like.

Alison had noticed and told her she was doing a great job, which was nice to hear. She met the other owner, too, Alison's best friend, Jess. Jess spent most of her time in her office down the street where she practiced law.

The store was more crowded than usual on Friday. It was still a week before Memorial Day weekend and people were already starting to head to the Cape now on weekends. Alison had signs all over the shop and on social media to promote the signing the next day. Sara looked forward to stopping in with Hannah, not only to get the latest book signed but also to see how busy it was. She wanted to be able to help Hannah have a good signing the following weekend and was excited that hers was on the long holiday weekend, which should bring plenty of foot traffic along Main Street.

Sara knew that Tom had his big meeting today with the huge potential client and she hoped that it was going well. It had been rescheduled from earlier in the week. They didn't have any plans for the evening or the weekend, so she decided to pick up a bottle of good red wine and make one of his favorite dishes for dinner, baked stuffed shells with Italian sausage. The kids loved it, too. And it was a simple dish to make.

She picked up the kids from their after-school sports and once everyone was home, she paid some bills, then started on dinner. She had everything timed to come out of the oven around five thirty, which was when Tom usually walked through the door. The kids were usually starving by then, too.

But at a quarter after five, Tom called to let her know he wasn't going to be home for dinner.

"Our afternoon meeting was followed by a round of golf. Now they want to go for dinner and drinks to celebrate working together. They signed a contract, so I sort of have to go. You don't mind, do you?"

Sara sighed. "Congratulations. I'll see you when you get home."

"You're the best!"

Sara hung up and called her sister.

"Do you have plans tonight?"

"No, Aunt Maddie and I were just talking about what to do for dinner."

"Do you guys want to come here? I have stuffed shells in the oven and Tom's not coming home for dinner, he's with clients, so I have tons of food. And I'd love the company." Sara heard Hannah ask their aunt and quickly said that they'd love to.

"We'll leave now and be there in fifteen minutes. Can we bring anything?"

"Perfect, just bring yourselves."

At five thirty, she heard a car pull into the driveway. She'd just taken the shells out of the oven and they were still bubbling in the casserole dish. She'd made extra garlic bread and skipped the salad. And she'd pulled some frozen brownies out of the freezer and popped them into the oven to thaw for dessert.

Hannah and Aunt Maddie walked through the door at the same time the kids came to the table for dinner. Hugs were given all around and everyone settled at the table. Hannah handed a bottle of Josh cabernet to Sara.

"Thanks! I just opened this bottle if you want to pour glasses for us while I bring the shells over." She gave Hannah the good bottle of wine she'd planned to have with Tom. She set the pasta and garlic bread on the table and let the kids help themselves. Hannah handed her a big glass of wine and she joined everyone at the table.

Aunt Maddie hadn't seen the kids in a while, and asked each of them what was new and exciting. The kids loved her and filled her in on everything going on—all the different sports they were in—and both she and Hannah did a great job of making each of her boys feel special. As always, her boys inhaled their food, had seconds, and then ran off. Meanwhile Sara, Hannah, and Aunt Maddie still chatted away with plenty of food on their plates.

"This wine is really good," Hannah said as she lifted the bottle and topped their glasses off.

"Thanks," Sara said. "I'd had it once before and really liked it. I picked it up thinking Tom and I might celebrate the end of a good week. He just closed a big deal and things are going great for me at the shop. I'm really enjoying it."

"I'm so glad you're liking the new job," Aunt Maddie said, then added, "You didn't know earlier that Tom was going out with clients?"

"No, it was a last-minute thing."

Hannah took a sip of wine and set her glass down. "Well, it's his loss, but our gain."

Sara laughed. "I'm glad that you guys are here to enjoy it. We should do this more often."

"Anytime. My schedule is pretty much wide open," Hannah said.

"Maybe Memorial Day weekend, I'll have a cookout at the house, then the kids can use the beach. It could be fun," Aunt Maddie said.

"They'd love that," Sara said.

When they finished eating, Hannah and Aunt Maddie helped her to clear the table and Sara put the brownies out. The boys ran out for them, grabbed a brownie, and headed back to watching TV.

Sara picked up a still-warm chocolate brownie and took a bite and then a sip of the good wine. They'd just finished the bottle.

"Brownies go very well with red wine," she said.

"They do. I think I need to open the Josh." Hannah jumped up and opened the bottle and brought it to the table.

"What are you doing tomorrow night?" she asked.

Sara laughed. "What do you think I'm doing? The usual. Nothing."

"Why don't you come with me to a party? Caitlin from the coffee shop is having it at her boyfriend's house and there's going to be a band. It sounds like fun."

"That does sound fun. But I can't just invite myself," Sara said.

"You'd be with me. Natalie told me about it and then Caitlin mentioned it again this afternoon when I went to the coffee shop. She told me to bring a friend if I wanted to."

"That is tempting. I don't know though." Sara felt a little guilty leaving Tom and the kids on a Saturday night to go to a party with her sister.

"Think about it. You can let me know tomorrow."

❦

Hannah and Aunt Maddie left a little before nine and Tom still wasn't home yet. Sara was surprised and a little annoyed. Especially that he hadn't texted to say he was staying out later than expected. She made herself a cup of herbal tea and curled up on the living room sofa to watch a movie with her two oldest boys. The two youngest had gone to bed. They watched the new *Top Gun* movie and Sara was surprised by how good it was. Because it was a sequel to a movie she'd seen a million years ago, she hadn't expected it to be so good.

The movie ended and the boys went to bed. Still no message from Tom. Sara climbed into bed herself and turned the TV in her bedroom on to watch the news. Just as the show ended, she heard the front door open. Tom was home.

She heard a crash as he bumped into something and then shuffled down the hall toward the bedroom. He stepped inside the room and squinted. Sara had turned the light off so the room was dark other than the glow from the television.

"You still up?" He slurred his words a bit and Sara sat up and turned the bedside light on.

"Did you drive drunk?" It wasn't like him to drink so much or to drive if he had.

He shook his head. "I took an Uber from the restaurant. I'll get my car in the morning."

"It's late. I started to worry when I didn't hear from you."

Tom sat on the side of the bed and pulled his shoes off.

"I'm sorry. I should have called or texted. I didn't realize how late it was. We were having a good time."

It irritated her that it hadn't even occurred to him to text her at least.

"I'm glad you had a good time. Where did you go?"

"We had dinner at Mahoney's and after-dinner drinks at the

Land Ho." Both of those places were in Orleans, the next town over from Chatham. She was glad he'd had the sense to call an Uber.

"The deal closed, though?" she asked.

"It did!" He attempted to high-five her and missed, then hiccupped. That decided it for her.

"You don't have plans tomorrow night with them, do you?"

"Of course not! I'll be home with you guys."

She smiled. "Good. You can watch the kids while I go out with Hannah. Good night, Tom."

❦

The signing started at one, so Sara and Hannah decided to meet downtown around two. Sara got to the bookshop first and was intrigued to see that there was a long line of at least fifty or so people that went out the door and down the sidewalk. Sara walked over and got in line. Hannah arrived a few minutes later and joined her. The line didn't move quickly, but it wasn't too bad. Sara thought it was a good sign that the author was spending a little time with each person and not rushing them along. It was a gorgeous day, too, so she didn't mind the wait.

"What time did Tom roll in last night?" Hannah asked.

"Just as the news ended. I think it was eleven thirty."

"Does he do that often?" Hannah sounded as surprised as Sara had been.

"No. That was late, for him. It did annoy me that he hadn't thought to at least text me that he was going to be out so late. They had an amazing dinner at Mahoney's, I guess, and then lots of after-dinner drinks at the Land Ho."

"That is a good combination. I love Mahoney's and the Land Ho is fun. They make the best White Russians. And have great chowder. We should go there sometime. I haven't been in ages."

"Yeah, it seemed like they had a very good time. Tom had to take an Uber home. I'm glad he did though. We ran up to the Land Ho this morning to pick up his car."

"So, I take it he didn't mind that you're going out tonight?"

Sara laughed. "I don't know if he minded. I just told him he was staying in and I was going out."

"Good! We'll have fun. I thought we'd head over around six or so, does that work?"

"That's good. I'll head home after this and get everyone set up for dinner. Though that may involve ordering pizza. I don't feel like cooking today. But I'll get them all settled and then we can head out."

The line slowly moved along and once they were inside the store, Sara got a look at the signing setup. Halfway between the entrance and the register, Niall Peterson sat at a table with a stack of books in front of him. Brooklyn sat beside him and sold the books before Niall signed them. He had another assistant with him, a young girl who looked to be in her early twenties. She had a camera and took pictures of customers with Niall after he signed their books.

Finally, it was their turn. Brooklyn smiled when she saw her and rang up two books for them.

"Has it been like this the whole time?" Sara asked.

Brooklyn nodded. "Yes. The line started immediately. People stopped in all morning asking about it. I think Alison is thrilled with the turnout."

The person in front of Sara finished having her picture taken and then it was Sara's turn. She handed her book to Niall.

"It's so nice to meet you. I love your books," she told him.

He smiled and picked up his pen. "Thank you. Who should I make it out to?"

"Oh, Sara. Thank you."

He signed the book and wrote, *Hope you enjoy.*

"Niall, this is my sister, Hannah. She's an author, too."

He looked at Hannah and nodded. "Nice to meet you. What do you write?"

"Romantic comedy. My first book came out this year."

"Congratulations."

Hannah handed him her copy of his book. "I love your books, too," she said.

He looked pleased to hear it. "Thanks so much."

Niall signed Hannah's book and wrote, *Nice to meet a fellow author.*

"Hannah is having a signing here next weekend," Sara said proudly.

"Well, I'll try to stop in. Thank you both for coming." He handed Hannah her signed book and the young assistant asked if they wanted a picture with Niall.

"Sure," Sara said. They got on either side of him and she snapped a picture with her camera and then with Hannah's.

Sara was going to say hello to Alison, but there were two people working the counter and it was so busy with people waiting in line that she didn't want to bother her.

"I'll send you a copy," Hannah said as they walked out. "And I'll post on social media, too."

"Oh, that's a good idea. I'll put it up on the shop's Facebook page, too. That will promote both of you. What did you think of him? He seemed nice. I read about him online this morning. *People* magazine had an interview. He's single. Hasn't dated anyone seriously in a while." Sara thought he was cute, and he was close to Hannah's age, and lived in the city.

"He was nicer than I thought he'd be. I wondered if he might be one of those literary snobs who look down on romance writers. But I didn't get that from him. And you're right, he is cute. Not that I'm looking."

"Well, he does live nearby." On paper, Niall Peterson seemed perfect for Hannah—he ticked all the boxes.

Hannah laughed. "New York City is huge. I'm not sure I'd say *nearby.*"

"Well, a lot closer than most people you're likely to meet in Chatham."

"That is true."

They stopped next door for a coffee and there was a line there, too, and all the tables were taken. They got their coffees to go and strolled down Main Street for a half hour or so, popping into some of the shops to check out sweaters and shoes, but neither of them bought anything.

They walked back to the lot behind the shop where they'd both parked earlier.

"I'll swing by a little before six to get you," Hannah said.

"Great." Sara was still smiling as she climbed into her car and buckled her seat belt. She looked forward to a night out with her sister.

Chapter 23

"W here are you off to? You look great. Love the shoes," Hannah said. Aunt Maddie was in a gorgeous ocean-blue sweater and flowing ivory linen pants. Her shoes were new ones that she'd shown off to Hannah the week before. They were pretty gel slides from the boutique she loved on Main Street.

"Thanks, honey. I'm meeting some friends for dinner in Hyannis. Have fun at your cookout."

Aunt Maddie left and Hannah checked the time—it was a quarter past five. Time to get a move on. She'd already showered and dried her hair, and now she just had to decide what to wear. She opened her closet and stared at her options, willing something to jump out at her. The cookout was in a backyard so she knew it was pretty casual. The temperature this time of year dropped down in the evenings. It was warm now, still in the high sixties, but she might need a jacket later. She tried on a few pairs of jeans and different tops and finally settled on dark jeans, a white tank top, and a rosy-pink V-neck sweater layered over it. She had treated herself to a pedicure earlier in the week so she chose a pair of comfortable open-toed sandals that would show off her polish.

Hannah didn't usually wear much makeup during the day but since it was a party, she added some bronzer, mascara, curled her eyelashes, and added blush and a swipe of her favorite glossy lipstick in a peachy-pink shade. She ran a curling iron through her hair to add a few loose waves and some shine.

At twenty to six she headed to her sister's house, and fifteen minutes later, pulled into her driveway. Before she could turn off the engine, Sara came out the front door and a few seconds later climbed into the passenger side.

Hannah laughed. "I would have come in to get you."

"No need. I heard the car and I was ready so I just came out. If you'd come in, we would have lost time saying hello to everyone. They just saw you, so it's all good."

"Good point. How's Tom?"

"He's fine. He's in his office eating leftover pasta and drinking a beer. I ordered pizza for the kids, so everyone is set."

"All right. Let's go, then."

"Are we picking up Natalie?"

"She's meeting us there. She lives right near Caitlin's boyfriend's house, so I think she was going to walk over."

"You said there's going to be a band there. Is it someone she knows?"

"It is. Her boyfriend's best friend, Tim, plays in a band. It's a side thing for them as they all have full-time jobs and just do it for fun. Caitlin said her boyfriend, Jason, used to play with them, too. He quit years ago when he took over his father's plumbing business and didn't have time for it anymore. She said they usually make him come up and sing at least one or two songs, though."

"That sounds fun," Sara said.

It didn't take long to get to the address Natalie had given her. Jason's house was a modest Cape with a huge backyard, perfect for an outside gathering. It was at the end of a cul-de-sac and there were already cars parked all along the side of the road. Hannah found a spot and parked. Sara had a bottle of chardonnay and Hannah had brought a tray of brownies that she'd made from a boxed mix that morning.

They knocked on the front door and a moment later, Caitlin opened it and welcomed them. "I'm so glad you guys came. Come on in." Hannah handed her the brownies. "Oh, these look so good. Thank you." She glanced at the bottle of wine Sara was holding. "There are wine openers in the kitchen if you want to open that or there might already be some wines open. Help yourself to whatever you want. Jason is cooking burgers and hot dogs and all the food is on the back deck. I'll set the brownies there."

Caitlin showed them where the kitchen and wine opener was, then headed to the back deck with the brownies. Sara opened the bottle of wine while Hannah found plastic cups for them to use. They took their glasses of wine and headed to the back deck and the yard where everyone was gathered.

Natalie was there, sipping a canned wine spritzer. She waved when she saw them and they walked over to her.

Hannah introduced Natalie to her sister. "I'm glad you could get out tonight. This should be fun," Natalie said.

"Thanks. I haven't been to a party like this in a very long time, other than stuff with the kids. I love them dearly, but it's nice to get out with just Hannah for a change to an all-adult party," Sara admitted.

"Do you know everyone here?" Hannah asked. She didn't recognize anyone other than Natalie and Caitlin.

"I don't know many people here yet, but there are more coming. It's early still. Have you met Jason, Caitlin's boyfriend?"

"No, she said he was cooking on the grill. Is that him?" Hannah glanced toward the deck where a dark-haired man was putting hot dog buns on the grill. Caitlin was nowhere in sight.

"Yes. I think Caitlin went to meet more people at the front door. I'll introduce you." She led them over to the grill and introduced them to Jason.

"Great to meet you both. Thanks for coming." They chatted for a minute and then Jason turned his attention back to his cooking and added cheese to the burgers.

"Let's move out of the way," Natalie said. They went to the corner of the deck, which was huge and wrapped around the side of the house. They could see everything from this spot and kept an eye on people coming and going as they sipped their drinks. After a little while, Jason hollered for people to come grab food. He'd piled a platter full of burgers and hot dogs. There were also bowls of potato and pasta salad, baked beans, and a creamy broccoli salad with bacon bits.

They took a little of everything and headed down to the backyard where there were several picnic tables and additional folding tables and chairs set up. Hannah could also see where the band was set up to play, in the middle of the backyard. Extension cords ran to the deck for power and all the equipment was there and ready to go. Hannah guessed they'd set it all up earlier so they could enjoy the party first, then just go and play when everyone was ready for some music.

By the time they finished eating, Hannah estimated that the crowd had grown to well over a hundred people. Out of the corner of her eye, she noticed Spencer walk onto the back deck and help himself to a burger. Natalie spotted him, too, and waved him over. He was with a friend, Chip, who Hannah vaguely recognized. He'd gone to school with them, too.

Spencer introduced Chip to everyone. "Do you remember Hannah from high school, and her sister, Sara?"

"Sure, I remember you. Nice to see you both." Chip had wavy red hair and a face full of freckles. He also had an easy smile and Hannah remembered that he'd been right up there with Spencer as one of the top students.

"Chip is a doctor at Cape Cod Hospital," Spencer said proudly.

"That's so interesting," Sara said. "What kind of doctor are you?"

"I'm in the ER."

"Is that as crazy as all the TV shows make it seem?" Hannah asked.

He laughed. "It's actually crazier. We see all kinds of things you'd never imagine in the ER. Never a dull moment."

Chip entertained them with a few patient stories and Hannah paid close attention. She never knew what might spark a story idea or end up in a book. Her sister often laughed when she read Hannah's stories and recognized things that had happened or little bits of conversation they'd both overheard. Without realizing it, Hannah had given the heroine of her recent book a navy BMW SUV just like the one her sister drove. Sara had teased her about that. Hannah promised never to use anything too personal without first running it by her. She didn't like to model her characters too closely after real people. They were all just bits and pieces of lots of people and ideas of people she imagined, and of course there was often a little of herself in some of her characters, too.

"I'm going to head in for a refill, can I get anything for anyone?" Natalie offered as she stood to head inside. Everyone was ready for more, so Hannah went with her to help her carry the drinks out.

Caitlin was in the kitchen talking to someone and she smiled when she saw them. When they drew closer, Hannah saw that it was Niall Peterson, the author. "Your ears must be ringing. We were just talking about you," Caitlin said. "I was telling Niall that we have another author here and that you come into the cafe almost every day to write."

"Nice to see you again," Hannah said.

"I stopped into the cafe this morning before the signing and Caitlin invited me. I do a lot of writing in coffee shops, too. There are a bunch of great places near where I live in the East Village."

"Do you go to the Lazy Llama?" Hannah asked. It was a coffee shop she'd ventured into one afternoon after a meeting with her editor.

"You know the Llama? It's one of my regular spots. I like the Coffee Project and Mud Spot, too. Do you live in the city?"

She nodded. "In Brooklyn. I'm here for the summer though. Grew up in Chatham."

"Best of both worlds. My parents bought a place here a few years ago and it's great. It's nice to get out of the city in the summer. I'm here till the fall, too. Though I might go back once or twice before then. It's nice that we get to do this from anywhere."

"It really is. I love Brooklyn. I've lived in the city for close to ten years, but I love coming home to the Cape, too."

Niall smiled and Hannah noticed a dimple in his left cheek. His hair was sandy blond and his eyes were greenish gray. When he smiled his whole face lit up and he was even more attractive. He was average height and on the lean side. She noticed Natalie glancing their way as she poured the drinks. Two women came over to Niall at that point and told them how much they loved his books. Hannah took that as her cue to go.

"It was nice talking with you," she said as Natalie handed her two cups of wine to carry.

"I'll catch up with you later," Niall said.

She followed Natalie outside. "Was there a spark there? You two seem to have a lot in common," Natalie said.

"Oh, I don't know. He's easy to talk to, though. We have the writing in common."

"That's a good start," Natalie said.

Hannah handed Sara a cup of wine and sat back down. Natalie sat next to Chip and had a medical question for him. That left Spencer sitting next to Hannah. He glanced at Chip and Natalie and looked amused. "It happens every time we go somewhere," he said.

"What does?"

"People have medical questions for Chip. He can't get away from it. He says he doesn't mind though."

"He doesn't look like he minds." Natalie and Chip were laughing about something.

Spencer smiled. "Not at all."

"Do you know many people here?" Hannah was curious since Spencer had returned to Chatham years ago.

He nodded. "Quite a few. I know Caitlin's boyfriend, Jason. We play on a winter hockey league together. And I know Tim through him, and his girlfriend, Julia. I recognized a few other faces, too. There's always a big crowd when word gets out that their band is playing."

"It looks like they are getting ready to play now." Hannah looked toward the area where the band had all their equipment set up. The guys were over there, checking to make sure everything was ready to go.

Sara and Natalie were talking and laughing about something. Hannah was glad that her sister seemed to be having a good time. She really needed to get out more. Though they talked often, Hannah had always just thought that Sara was busy with the kids and content with being a stay-at-home mom. She didn't realize until she came back to Chatham and saw her more often how things really were with her sister and her marriage. From what Hannah could see it looked unbalanced. Everything seemed to revolve around Tom and what he wanted and needed.

Sara had mentioned that he wasn't impressed with her job at the bookshop. He didn't seem to understand how important it was to her sister to be doing something of value outside the house. Something that would fill her well. She had loved working in the library. And it seemed like the job at the bookshop was working out really well. Hannah was happy for her. She just hoped that things might get a little better for her sister at home.

The band started to play and everyone stopped talking to listen. Hannah hadn't heard them play before and she was impressed by how good they were. They played a good mix of music, from popular current hits, both rock and some country, and older classic tunes. And they took requests.

"If they know the song, they'll try to play it," Spencer said. "What do you think of them?"

"I think they're great."

They played for about twenty minutes and then took a beverage break to refill their glasses and chat with friends. One of the guys stopped by the table to say hello to Spencer. He introduced everyone. "To those who don't know, this is Tim."

"You guys are great," Hannah said.

"Hannah likes Pearl Jam," Spencer said. "Can you guys do 'Black' or 'Just Breathe,' maybe?"

Hannah laughed. "I do like Pearl Jam, but not as much as Spencer does!"

Tim grinned. "I know. Yeah, we can probably do one of those tunes for you."

A pretty woman with wavy brown hair and turquoise tips walked over and wrapped her arms around Tim. He leaned in and gave her a kiss and then introduced her. "This is my girlfriend, Julia."

"You're Alison's daughter, right?" Sara asked.

Julia nodded. "I am."

"She mentioned you and your jewelry shop to me. I just started working at the bookshop a few weeks ago."

"Oh! Nice to meet you. You have four boys, I think my mom said?"

Sara laughed. "Yes. They keep me on my toes."

"I'll pop in and say hi. I usually make a coffee run midafternoon and spend most of that time chitchatting with Caitlin." She looked at Hannah as if she was trying to place her. "You look so familiar."

Hannah smiled. "I'm usually in the coffee shop when you come in every afternoon. I sit in the corner with my laptop trying to get some writing done."

"That's it!"

"I'm going to head inside and grab a beer and another burger before we go back on. Did you eat yet?" Tim asked Julia.

"No, I just got here about ten minutes ago. And I'm starving. I'll go with you." She turned back to Hannah and Sara. "It was nice meeting you both."

"Her hair is so pretty," Sara said. "My boys would tease me no end if I colored some of my hair blue."

"Hannah could do it. I usually see colors like that on artsy types," Spencer said. She could tell by the way he said it that he was teasing.

"Maybe I will one day. You never know. You're right. I have a few author friends that have pink, purple, or blue hair. It's a thing. And hers is gorgeous."

Spencer looked taken aback. "Would you really? I was just kidding. Your hair is too pretty to do that." He spoke quickly and then seemed to wonder if he'd said the wrong thing. "I mean if you want to do that, you could, you should. If you really want to."

Hannah laughed. "I'm not dying to color my hair. Maybe someday I'll try it though. If I could get it to look as good as Julia's."

"Hannah, I bet it would look amazing," Natalie said.

"I think the band is about to start again." Spencer changed the subject. He was obviously over the hair talk. Hannah was amused. She couldn't picture straitlaced Spencer ever dating someone with pink or blue hair. Though she couldn't really imagine she'd ever be daring enough to make such a dramatic change to her hair. She was artsy, but when it came to hair and clothing she tended more toward the Cape Cod preppy look or Lilly Pulitzer.

Hannah looked around. She hadn't seen Niall since they'd spoken with him inside. She wondered if he'd already left. But then she saw him on the deck, talking to a girl with pink hair, and she smiled. Niall probably had a few friends with hair like that, too.

The band started to play again and they called Jason up to sing a song. "We had a request for Pearl Jam, so we thought maybe we could get Jason to do this one," Tim said.

Caitlin and Jason were sitting at the picnic table next to theirs and she gave him an encouraging push to get up there. Jason walked up to the microphone and a moment later the first note of the song "Just Breathe" began to play. It was one of Hannah's favorites, a soft, slow song about slowing down to enjoy life. Jason had a great voice. Full and rich. He was just as good as the other guys in the band, maybe even better.

When the song was almost over, Hannah leaned over and whispered to Spencer, "He's so good. Too bad he doesn't play with the band more."

"Yeah. He could have gone professional with it maybe if he'd taken it seriously. But it was never his focus. Jason had a good job in finance before his father got sick and he took over the family business. He loves it though. He never liked working in the city, either. He likes being out and about, working with his hands."

"That's good. I suppose lots of people like to sing or to write. Most just do it for fun, not as a career."

"You'd have to really love it. They travel a ton and work nights and weekends. I'd hate that schedule," Spencer said.

Hannah laughed. "That's a good point. I like having nights and weekends free. Though I often work on weekends, too. But I don't have to and I can work around what I want to do."

When the band finished their second set, Hannah went inside to use the restroom. On her way back to the table, Niall saw her and waved her over. He was still in his spot on the deck, but the girl with the pink hair was gone and he was alone.

"Are you having fun?" he asked.

"Yes. It's a great night. I'm loving the band."

"They are good. Really good. You mentioned that you're from Chatham, right?"

She nodded. "I grew up here. I moved to Brooklyn when I graduated from college. I still get back when I can, mostly in the summer. My sister is still here and . . ." She'd been about to say that her mother was there, too. She sighed. "My mother was here. She passed a few months ago."

"Oh, I'm sorry to hear that. Were you very close?"

"Yes. She was young, too. Lung cancer. The only good thing is that it went fast, I suppose."

"It's an awful disease. I lost an uncle to it, too." They were both quiet for a moment. Niall took a sip of his drink. "If you're interested, I thought it might be fun for two authors to hang out one of these nights. Maybe you can show me one of your favorite places."

"Oh. Sure. That would be fun." Hannah felt suddenly flustered. It had been a long time since she'd been asked on a date and this sounded like a date.

"Great." Niall handed her his phone. "Can you put your number in and I'll give you a call to firm up a day?"

She punched in her cell number and handed the phone back to him.

"Here you go." It looked like the band was getting ready to start up again, for probably the last time. "I should probably head back to the table. You're welcome to join us," she offered.

He smiled. "Thanks. I actually have to get going. My parents are having a gathering tonight, too, and I should make an appearance. I'll talk to you soon."

Hannah was still smiling as she sat back down at the table. Spencer was deep in conversation with Chip and didn't look up as she sat down. Sara looked at her curiously. "Why are you looking so happy?"

"Niall Peterson just asked me out."

Natalie's ears perked up. "Did you just say that Niall Peterson asked you out?" Her voice was loud and excited and got everyone's attention at the table, including Spencer's.

"Yes, we were talking and he said we should get together since we're both authors and all. It's not a big deal."

"Well, I think it's a big deal. He sounds perfect for you," Natalie said.

"I agree. And he lives in New York City, too," her sister added.

"We'll see how it goes. I haven't been eager to date yet," Hannah reminded them.

"Just go and have fun," Natalie said. "Even if it's not a love connection, he might be good to know, since you're both authors and all."

"That's true. Is this the last set, do you think?" Hannah tried to change the subject. Spencer was still looking at her a bit strangely, almost as if he didn't approve of the date.

"Yeah, this is their last set. The crowd will probably start thinning out once they stop playing," Spencer said.

Sara glanced at her cell phone. Hannah knew she was probably checking the time. She looked, too, and it was almost ten.

"Do you want to head home soon?" Hannah asked her sister.

"Sure, if you don't mind. I don't want to be out too late. This has been really fun. It was great to get out."

The band played their final song and as predicted, people started saying their goodbyes, including Sara and Hannah. They made sure to thank Caitlin and Jason on their way out.

"I'm so glad both of you came. Hannah, I'm sure I'll see you soon in the cafe."

Hannah dropped Sara off at her house and waited until she was inside. She headed home and her aunt was watching TV in the living room. She looked up when Hannah walked in.

"Hi, honey, did you have fun?"

"I did. I think Sara did, too." She told her aunt all about the cookout and the band. "How was your dinner?"

"It was nice. I hadn't seen some of those friends in ages and we had a lot to catch up on. I just got home about a half hour ago myself."

Hannah told her about Niall and their plans to go out soon. Aunt Maddie looked happy for her. "Oh, that's great. Just what you need. Go on a date and have fun. Don't worry about where it's going, just enjoy the moment."

Hannah laughed. "That's what Natalie said, too."

"It's good advice."

Hannah agreed. She looked forward to going out with Niall and getting to know him better. They had the writing in common so it would be fun to talk about that. Even if it didn't go anywhere romantically, she liked that he also lived in the city. So, if it did turn into anything, she wouldn't have to worry about what would happen at the end of the summer. Not that she was thinking that far ahead; she really had no idea how things would go with Niall. But she was very happy that she'd taken Aunt Maddie up on her offer to spend the summer in Chatham.

Chapter 24

Mondays were always crazy busy for Maddie. This one was no exception. Her author Shelley had accepted the highest offer in the auction and called several times with detailed questions about the process. She'd been surprised when Maddie told her it would still be several months before they received the contract from the publisher. They'd agreed to terms in writing over email but now contracts had to be drawn up and gone over by the lawyers. It took time.

The author who wrote the Jack Reacher–like story that Maddie loved—about the female sheriff in the small town—also had other agents offering to represent her and needed more time to decide. Maddie made her best case and told the author truthfully that while she would send the story everywhere, she had one particular editor in mind for it. She had a good feeling that the author might choose her, but she'd thought that before and had been wrong. She'd just hung up with her when Kathryn called.

"How's your Monday going?" Kathryn asked. Maddie smiled, picturing her boss in her corner office at the agency, sitting behind her giant desk with her chair spun around the opposite way so she could look out the window at the Hudson River view while she talked. Kathryn always did that when she was on a call.

"Typical Monday. Full of surprises. How about you?"

Kathryn chuckled. "The same. We just had a publisher that we thought would up their bid and win an auction decide to stay put. Nothing makes sense today."

"Oh, that's frustrating."

"It's just perplexing. The author will be fine, two of the other houses are coming up quite a bit."

"Good. You just never know."

"No, you don't. Anything new with Richie?" There was a tone to Kathryn's voice that seemed off.

"New? No. I haven't talked to him since I came home to Chatham. We agreed to take the summer apart."

"Right. Awkward question, but does that mean the two of you are free to date other people?"

The question caught Maddie off guard. It hadn't crossed her mind to date or that Richie might want to. But she supposed maybe she should have considered it since she was the one who wanted more time apart.

"Honestly, I don't know. We didn't discuss that. I know I'm not even thinking about it. But I don't know what Richie is thinking."

"Okay. Well, I just thought maybe you should know this. I don't know if it's what it looked like or totally innocent, but I saw Richie out Friday night. We went to the same restaurant and he was at the bar having drinks and dinner with a woman. It didn't necessarily look romantic but it was just the two of them, and they seemed really comfortable together. Like they knew each other really well. There was a lot of laughing. Maybe it's just a coworker, but it was a Friday night, so I wasn't sure what to think."

Maddie tensed up. She was pretty sure she knew who it was. She described Laura, Richie's colleague.

"That sounds like her. Do you know her?"

"I think it is Richie's coworker. The one I told you about. She's married, but she and Richie totally connect. I think it's just work related, though. They both love their jobs. It can get a little intense at times."

"And it was a Friday night. I wonder how her husband feels about it?"

"He's pretty easygoing, but I can't imagine he'd like it if it happened often."

"Maybe you should give Richie a call and see how things are going with him?" Kathryn suggested.

"I probably should." They chatted for a few more minutes and then Maddie sat there and stewed, her mind going in a million different directions. Maybe she was a complete idiot, but she just didn't feel in her gut that there was anything inappropriate going on. She'd never worried before about Richie cheating. She knew this was most likely nothing. But it was a concern when it was starting to look like something else to other people, and it was a little embarrassing, too. Though Kathryn was a friend and Maddie knew she was just worried for her. She knew Kathryn would want to know if Maddie ever saw something like that.

Maddie made herself a cup of tea and tried to focus on work. She still had a pile of emails to go through and a Zoom call in a half hour. She'd call Richie later that evening when she knew he'd be home from work.

Maddie waited until after she and Hannah had eaten dinner and Hannah went off to take a bath before settling down for the night. She went into her bedroom to make sure she wasn't overheard and dialed Richie's number.

He picked up immediately and sounded surprised to hear from her.

"Maddie. How are you? Is everything okay?"

"I'm good. Everything's fine. How are you?"

"The same. Just busy working."

"Oh, did I interrupt you?" She thought he'd be done for the day by now.

"No, not at all. I just meant work has been busy. I just got home a half hour ago. I worked late at the office and then grabbed a bite with one of the guys."

"Did Laura go with you?"

"Laura? No. Why do you ask?"

Maddie sighed. "Kathryn saw you Friday night when she was out to dinner with her husband. You were at the same restaurant sitting at the bar with a blond woman."

"Oh, yeah, that was Laura. We worked late and decided to stop for an after-work drink and some food."

"She thought you two looked cozy together like it was maybe a date. Laura's husband doesn't mind if she goes out to dinner with other men on a Friday night?" Maddie sighed, then added, "Kathryn thought it was a little strange. And I was a bit embarrassed, to be honest, to get that call from my boss."

"Laura's husband didn't care. He was out with coworkers, too. It's nothing, Maddie. Really." Richie sounded frustrated and a little annoyed.

Maddie felt somewhat relieved to hear him confirm that there was nothing going on. "Okay. She also asked me if we have an agreement that we're able to date other people during the separation. We haven't discussed that so I didn't know if maybe that's what you wanted?"

There was a long silence before Richie spoke. "That's not what I want. Truthfully, Maddie, I'm lonely here and Laura is good company. That's all it was."

"Okay. I didn't think there was anything else to it. I do trust you. But the two of you have such a close connection, and I don't know her as well as I know you."

"Maddie. I'm really sick of this." He sounded angry with her.

"I'm not trying to fight with you, Richie," she said quickly.

He sighed. "I know you're not. I mean I'm sick of this. Of being here, while you're there. I want to come home."

His words took her by surprise.

"When?"

"This weekend. I want to take my wife on a date and I want to sleep in my own bed . . . or my own guest bed. My own house. I want to come home to Chatham. Let's see if we can make this work, what do you say?"

He sounded so sure that it made her pulse race. She thought he'd wanted the separation as much as she did. And she'd missed him, too. The thought of him dating someone else was too painful for her to consider. And she couldn't fathom dating anyone else. Maybe they could give it a try and see if they could get back to where they were.

"Okay. We can give it a try."

"Great. I'll book a flight to come back Thursday night. I'll never get a flight on Friday at this point. Even Thursday might be tight, but I'll find one."

"Let me know what time you'll land in Hyannis and I'll pick you up," she offered.

"I will. And Maddie, I can't wait to see you. I've missed you, missed us." She heard the emotion in his voice.

"I've missed you too," she said softly.

Chapter 25

Hannah went to the coffee shop earlier than usual on Monday. She arrived at noon and decided to have a bagel and cream cheese for lunch instead of her usual afternoon cookie and coffee. If she stayed long enough, she'd probably have that, too. She wanted to go in earlier because she had the writer group later that afternoon at three. Normally she ate lunch at home, but since she was going to be there longer, she decided to make it a bagel day.

Caitlin was behind the counter when Hannah arrived, ringing up an order, while Sally, one of the baristas, was making a latte. Hannah knew all of their names now and they knew hers and what she liked to have.

"You're here early. Is it an onion bagel day?" Caitlin asked.

Hannah laughed. "Yes, please."

"Toasted, with chive cream cheese and a tall black, no sugar?"

"Right. Thanks again for the party the other night. My sister and I had a great time."

Caitlin smiled. "It was a fun night. I'm glad you both could make it." She took Hannah's credit card, ran it through, and handed it back to her along with her coffee. "Here you go. If you want to have a seat, we will run the bagel out to you when it's ready."

Hannah settled at her usual corner table and opened her laptop.

The cafe was quiet for midday. Usually it was packed by now and on the drive over she'd worried that she might not get her usual spot, possibly not even a seat at all. A few times that had happened and she'd just taken her coffee to the bench outside until something opened up. Today, she had her pick of spots.

Caitlin brought her bagel over in a plastic basket and set it on the table. "Here you go."

"Thank you. Where is everyone today?" Hannah commented.

Caitlin looked around and frowned. "I know. It's dead. Mondays are weird, though, you never know. But it's usually busier than this at lunchtime." She glanced out the window. "A new coffee shop opened up down the street. Maybe that's where everyone is?"

Hannah hadn't known that. And Caitlin looked a bit worried about it. She kicked herself for saying anything. "If it is, it's just people being curious. They'll be back."

The front door opened and a group of people walked in. "I'd better get back to it. Enjoy your bagel."

Hannah ate her lunch, and checked email and social media while eating. For some reason, she could never write while she ate. She also people-watched as more people streamed in after that initial group. It was starting to look like a normal lunch rush, just a little later than usual. She was glad for Caitlin's sake. And she didn't think Caitlin really had to worry. There were often coffee shops near each other and they both did well.

She thought of how many times she'd seen a Dunkin' Donuts and a Starbucks on the same block. She almost felt guilty thinking it, but she was curious to check out the new coffee shop, too. It would be nice to have a backup for the times it was too busy here. If she liked the other place she could split her time between the two. She liked Caitlin, though, and sitting at this table had become part of her daily routine.

"I'm not interrupting your writing, am I?" Sara walked over from the bookshop on her lunch break.

"No, I haven't started yet. Join me."

Sara ordered, then brought her bagel and coffee over a moment later and sat down. She didn't like hers toasted, so it was ready faster. She checked the time, then unwrapped her bagel and took a bite.

"How was your Sunday?" Hannah asked her.

"Good. Tom took us all out on a boat for the afternoon and the boys fished. I read a book and relaxed in the sun. It was a great day."

"I didn't know you guys bought a boat. When did you get it?"

Sara laughed. "We didn't. I thought Tom was crazy when he first mentioned this idea to me, but it's actually pretty interesting. He joined Freedom Boat Club, it's a membership, and it's less expensive than owning a boat. And you don't have any of the headaches of maintaining it. You just sign up for the day you want to take one out and it's ready and waiting for you at the marina."

"Oh, that sounds pretty cool. Can you use it whenever you want?"

"Sort of. Not every day, of course, that's the tradeoff. If you want to be in your boat all the time, it's not ideal. But realistically we might use it a few times a month, if that. We could use it more often, but given how busy everyone is that seems about right. We'll take you out soon, if you want."

"I'd love that." Hannah hadn't been on a boat in ages. "Can you drive it, too?"

"Tom showed me how to do it when we went out, but I haven't gone through the class that they require so I can't go unless he's with me. Which is fine. I don't have time to take a boating class right now."

"How was Tom when you got home? He really didn't mind that you went out with me Saturday night?"

"He didn't seem to mind. He knew he'd had his turn, and an even later night, so what could he say?" Sara grinned.

"I have a little gossip for you," Hannah said. "Aunt Maddie told me last night that Uncle Richie is coming home Thursday night."

"Really? That's great. Is it just for Memorial Day weekend?" It was a huge weekend on Cape Cod, the official kickoff to the summer season.

"She didn't say anything more than that. Just that he was flying in and she was picking him up in Hyannis."

"Well, that is interesting. I really hope it works out for them. She mentioned having a cookout over the holiday weekend. I wonder if that's still on?"

Hannah nodded. "I'm pretty sure that it is. She mentioned Sunday might be the best day weather-wise. But she'll confirm as it gets closer."

"That sounds good. Other than your book signing on Saturday, we have no other plans so any day works." Sara finished her bagel and checked the time again. "I should get back, and let you get going on your writing, too."

Sara left and Hannah opened her manuscript and read through what she'd written the day before, made a few changes, and then started writing. She was at a fun part of the story and the writing went well for the next ninety minutes or so. She'd barely touched her coffee and it had grown cold. But she didn't care. She'd been deep in the writing zone where the story almost seemed to write itself and she was typing as fast as she could to keep up with her thoughts. But she'd reached a point where she wasn't sure what needed to happen next. It was time for a break.

She got up and ordered a new coffee, a fancy one this time, a caramel almond milk macchiato with extra foam. She liked the foam the best and would probably only drink half of the coffee, but it was a fun treat now and then. She got the coffee, settled back at her table, and read through what she'd just written. A few minutes later, she heard footsteps and looked up. It was Niall Peterson, holding a tall coffee in a paper cup.

"So, this is where the magic happens?" he asked, with a twinkle in his eye.

Hannah laughed. "Sometimes."

"Right. Was it a good session?"

"So far. I just finished a few scenes and am not entirely sure what I want to have happen next, so I'm just reading through to spark some ideas."

He nodded. "Yep. That's usually how it goes for me, too. Unless it's one of those days where it won't flow at all. I have my share of those, too. Had one this morning actually. So, I decided to come downtown and clear my head. I was also curious if I might find you here."

Hannah was flattered that he remembered she'd mentioned she liked to write at the cafe. And she found it comforting that a huge author like Niall sometimes got stuck with his writing, too.

"Do you want to sit down?"

He hesitated. "No, I don't want to take you from your writing. I need to get back to it myself. I just wanted to say a quick hello. And I had a thought for our first date, if you're still interested?'

She smiled. "What did you have in mind?"

"I thought it might be fun to play tourist and go on one of those Monomoy excursions. They used to focus on seal sightings but now it's great white sharks, too. And the weather looks great for the weekend. I was thinking maybe we could go on Friday, if that works. We could grab a bite to eat, too."

"That sounds fun. You know, I've never actually done that. I've often wondered what it's like."

"Good, let's find out. I'll make a reservation for us and touch base before then." He smiled and his dimple popped in his left cheek, giving him an impish and very cute look. His blond hair looked even lighter against his newly acquired tan—he must have spent most of the weekend at the beach. It made his green eyes pop, too. Hannah found herself looking forward to their date even more.

"Perfect."

"I'm off, then. Good luck with the writing."

"Thanks. You, too."

Hannah smiled to herself as she turned her attention back to her story. For a Monday, it had already been a productive day—in more ways than one.

❖

"Blast it!" Ben muttered with frustration as one of his crutches hit a bookcase as he walked by, sending a book crashing onto the floor. Joy jumped up to put it back on the shelf.

"How is your leg feeling?" Hannah asked. She'd stayed after the writing group to have a cup of tea with Joy and catch up.

"My leg feels fine. Will feel a lot better when I can get this cast off and stop using these useless things!" Ben was in an unusually grumpy mood. He was normally cheerful and upbeat.

"Why don't you go read for a while?" Joy suggested. "Supper's not for another hour. I'll come get you when it's ready."

"Fine." Ben shuffled off to the den.

As soon as he was out of earshot, Joy spoke softly. "He misses spending time in his workshop, doing his woodworking. It's too dangerous to go down those spiral steps, and until he's off his crutches, I don't like him down there, anyway."

"How much longer will it be?"

Joy sighed. "Three more weeks. But enough about that. Tell me what fun things you've been up to?"

Hannah filled her in on the cookout, the band, and her visit earlier that day from Niall.

"So, you have an official date this weekend? Good. It's time for you to get out there."

Hannah laughed. "That's what my sister and Natalie said, too. I'm just not anxious to jump into anything serious."

"And you shouldn't be. You young people put too much pressure on yourselves. Dating should be fun, it's all about meeting new people and getting to know them."

"That's true." Hannah knew most of her friends did that, immediately sizing up long-term potential before the first date, which did put a lot of pressure on the process.

"If you date more people, even go out with the ones that you'd never think would be right, you might learn that first impressions aren't always accurate when it comes to romantic potential."

Hannah smiled, thinking of one of her college roommates. "That's true. I knew a girl who ended up getting engaged to someone she thought she hated. They were in the same class in college and he annoyed her immensely. Until he didn't."

"See? It helps to be open. You never know where love will find you." Joy chuckled. "I certainly never expected to find it that weekend my friend dragged me to the mountain. I almost didn't go."

"I am looking forward to the date with Niall. Even if there's nothing romantic there, we have so much in common."

Joy looked thoughtful. "I dated another writer once. I was excited about it at first, but all we did was talk about writing. The romance fizzled out fast, but he turned into a good friend. And that's a good thing, too."

Hannah nodded. Joy didn't seem all that enthusiastic about this date, but Hannah suspected she knew the reason why.

"Did you see Spencer at that cookout? He mentioned he was going to one over the weekend," Joy asked.

"He was there. He sat with us. Natalie from the office came as well."

Joy smiled at the mention of Natalie's name. "I like that girl. I tried to convince Spencer he should ask her out, but he said it wasn't a good idea because they work together. She has a boyfriend, too. But they're not engaged. Until there's a ring, people are still available."

Hannah laughed. "I think Natalie is pretty serious. She can't wait for her boyfriend to come home from Dubai."

"Hmm. Well, even if she was single, it sounded like Spencer

wouldn't consider it because they work together. It is a very small office, so he may have a point there," she admitted. "When is your date with Niall?"

"This Friday afternoon."

"Well, keep me posted how it goes." Joy picked up her knitting and began clacking needles together as she continued to talk. "The fellow lives in New York City, too?"

Hannah nodded. "Yes. He's just here for the summer as well."

Joy looked up from her knitting and smiled. "Pity you have to go back. If you stayed in Chatham, Spencer might be perfect for you."

Hannah laughed. "You're assuming he'd even want to date me."

"Why wouldn't he? I think you'd make a great match. Though he never asks me for my opinion on things like that."

"Spencer is a catch for the right girl. I don't think it's me, though."

Joy was quiet for a moment before changing the subject.

"So, tell me, what are you reading and loving lately? I need to find something new."

Chapter 26

Wednesdays were always busy at the bookshop. It was almost two and several people were in line to pay for their purchases. There was no sign yet of Brooklyn. She usually arrived at least ten minutes early. Sara didn't think anything of it, though, and figured she was just running behind. She knew Brooklyn was coming straight from her last class at Cape Cod Community College in Hyannis. Maybe traffic was heavier than usual.

The office phone rang and Alison went out back to answer it. She returned a moment later looking concerned. Sara finished ringing up the last customer and turned to Alison.

"That was Brooklyn. She's not going to be able to make her shift today. Someone rear-ended her car as she was leaving school. She's not hurt, but she has to wait for the police to come file an accident report and get her car towed. Is there any possibility you can stay until six today? If not, I'll just work by myself. I already called Andrea to see if she can come in earlier—her shift starts at six—but she can't make it."

Sara thought for a moment. Tom worked from home on Wednesdays, so unless he had meetings scheduled, he might be able to pick up the boys and watch them so she could stay. "Let me call home and see." She went into the office where she kept her purse and cell phone and called Tom. He answered on the first ring.

"Hey there, what's up?"

"Do you have any client meetings this afternoon?"

"No, it's a light day. I'm just making follow-up calls and going through my inbox. Why?"

"Good. Do you mind picking up the boys after school today? We had someone call out and Alison needs me to stay and cover her shift. I'd like to help, if I can."

Tom hesitated. "What time will you be home?"

"A little after six. There's a lasagna I prepped this morning. All you have to do is pop it in the oven around five. It cooks for an hour. We can eat when I get home."

"Okay. See you then."

"Thanks, Tom." Sara hung up and gave Alison the good news that she could stay.

"Thanks a million. I really appreciate it." Alison handed her two colorful flyers with Hannah's photo and details about the signing on Saturday. "Do you want to tape these up just outside the door and inside, too, so people will see it as they come in and on their way out?"

"Sure." Sara put the flyers up and updated the Facebook page with a new post. There was already one up, but she knew that frequent posting helped spread the word.

An older gentleman walked up to the counter. "I'm looking for a book on lobsters. Can you help me?" He smiled as he looked around the store. "I tried to find it, but I don't think I looked in the right place."

"I'm happy to help. What kind of book are you looking for? A cookbook or more informational, about lobsters in general?"

"I'm looking to replace a book I had years ago. I lost it when I moved. It was a wonderful book, all about the history of the lobster. There might have been some information on how to cook it, but I wouldn't say it was a cookbook."

Sara thought for a moment, then led him over to the section where a book like that would be, if they had it. She looked through the shelves until she found something that seemed like what he described. She pulled the book out and handed it to him. He flipped it over and read the back cover. Then he nodded.

"It's not the same book, but it looks close enough. This one looks pretty good, actually. I'll take it."

"Can I help you find anything else?" Sara offered.

"Well, there is one more thing. My granddaughter is coming to visit this weekend and it's her birthday. She loves to read, but I don't know what to get for her. She's about your age."

"Do you know what kinds of books she likes? Mysteries or romance or something else?"

"She's always reading those romance books. And I know she likes a little humor."

Sara smiled. "I know just the thing." She led him to a stack of Hannah's books at the front of the store. "This author is popular and she's having a signing here this weekend, on Saturday. It's a romantic comedy so it has romance and some humor. I've read it and it's a fun book. I should probably also tell you that my sister is the author, so I may be a little biased."

He laughed. "Well, at least you're honest. I like that. I'll take a copy."

Sara rang up the books and when she handed him his bag and receipt, she added, "If your granddaughter is around on Saturday and you're looking for something to do, pop by the signing and bring the book, and Hannah would be happy to sign it for her."

"Oh! We just might do that. Thank you so much."

The shop stayed busy right up until six when Andrea came on. Alison thanked Sara again for staying.

"It was no problem at all," Sara assured her. "I'll see you in the morning."

It had been a good day. It was interesting to see what people were buying and what was popular in the newly released books. Sara was happy to see that Hannah's book sold steadily and of course she recommended it often.

When she got home, Tom was in his office with his door shut and the boys were fighting over what to watch on TV. They looked up when she walked in.

"Where have you been?" Cody asked.

"What's for dinner? I'm starving," Dylan said.

Sara noticed that she didn't smell anything delicious. Her mouth had been watering for the lasagna on the drive home. She opened the refrigerator. The uncooked lasagna sat there on the bottom shelf, waiting to go into the oven. She sighed and pulled a stack of cold cuts out of a drawer.

"Who wants turkey and who wants roast beef on their sandwiches?"

She took orders and made the sandwiches, including a turkey sandwich for herself. She set out a bag of chips for everyone to help themselves and then she knocked on Tom's door.

"Come on in."

She opened the door. Tom was typing out an email. He finished it, then looked up.

"You made it home," he joked.

"Very funny. Did you forget to put the lasagna in the oven?"

"Oh, crap. Yes, I totally forgot. I'm sorry." Tom sounded more frustrated and annoyed than sorry though.

Sara sighed. "I just made sandwiches for the boys. There's turkey and roast beef; help yourself when you're ready."

He nodded. "Will do." He immediately turned his attention back to his computer and Sara felt like she was bothering him.

She closed the door and ate her sandwich, then put the lasagna in the oven so all they had to do was reheat it the next day. It usually tasted better after it sat overnight anyway. It was just a little irritating that Tom couldn't remember to put the lasagna in the oven. Was that so much to ask? She realized that it was likely because he never had to do it, so it was easy to forget.

Once everyone was settled watching a movie, Sara retreated to her bedroom and shut the door. She turned on her TV and put it on the music station and curled up on the cozy armchair by her bedroom's bay window. Alison had given her an ARC to bring home and Sara was eager to dive into it. When she'd started at the bookshop, Brooklyn had told her that one of the perks of the job was that publishers sometimes sent them advance reader copies of upcoming books with the hope that they'd read it, love it, and recommend it to their customers.

This one was a psychological thriller, and the premise, a woman who suspects her husband is not the same man she married, was intriguing. Sara started reading and was halfway through the book by the time Tom opened the door to come to bed. She was startled to see that it was almost eleven. She'd lost all track of time, and she had a feeling this book was going to be very popular. The story had her on the edge of her seat, with each chapter propelling her to the next and one unexpected twist after another.

"Are the boys in bed?" she asked. She'd taken a break an hour or so ago to tuck the two youngest ones in.

He nodded. "They're all set. Are you ready to call it a night? I'm beat."

Sara yawned. "I am." It had been a long day and a good one for the most part. Except for Tom forgetting to put the lasagna in the oven. It was annoying that he couldn't be bothered to remember to do that. But she reminded herself that he also hadn't been expecting her to work until six, either. She sighed and wished he'd make a little more of an effort. Even though he had the higher paying job, Sara did so much more around the house, and now that she was working, too, the balance really felt off to her. Hopefully that would change at some point.

Chapter 27

"So, what's going on with your aunt tonight that you didn't want to be there?" Natalie asked. It was Thursday night and Hannah was sitting at the Chatham Squire bar with Natalie and Spencer. She'd texted Natalie earlier in the week and asked if she wanted to meet for after-work drinks on Thursday. And she'd suggested asking Spencer to join them if he wanted. Natalie had quickly agreed and then texted a moment later saying Spencer was in, too.

"My uncle is coming back tonight. My aunt is getting him at the airport." Hannah explained that they'd been separated for a few months. "I don't know what it means. If he's back for good or just the weekend, but I wanted to give them some privacy if they decided to head straight home."

"I hope it works out for them," Natalie said.

Everyone seemed to be in a good mood at the Squire. It was a Thursday night but there was more of a Friday vacation vibe because of the long weekend. Hannah knew that many people came down on Thursday nights to avoid the heavy weekend traffic. The weather was gorgeous and summer was just around the corner. A warm breeze washed over them as someone opened the front door and a big group of people came in laughing and talking loudly. They sounded like they'd already been celebrating.

The bartender looked a little concerned as the rowdy group made their way to the bar.

"How long for a table?" one of the guys hollered at the bartender. He was the biggest in the group, and seemed to be the leader. All the tables in the restaurant were filled and every seat at the bar, too, with people standing nearby. It was crowded and Hannah guessed that the wait might be a long one.

"Stacy, can you help this gentleman?" the bartender said. "He wants to know how long the wait is?"

The hostess came right over with her clipboard. "How many are in your party?"

"Eleven, no, twelve."

She looked over her list of people waiting for a table.

"I can add you to the list, but it might be an hour or maybe a bit longer. We won't have anything for a while, I'm afraid."

The guy looked at his friends. "She says at least an hour. Whaddya want to do?"

"I'm hungry now," someone in the group said loudly.

"I can't wait that long. Let's go somewhere else," the guy next to him said.

"All right, we're off." The big guy turned and headed toward the door and his group followed.

The bartender breathed a sigh of relief when the door shut behind them.

"They looked like trouble," he said. He'd just been about to take their appetizer order. "So, what can I get for you?" They put an order in for nachos, fried calamari, and buffalo chicken wings.

"So, tomorrow's your big date with the famous author?" Natalie said.

Hannah grinned. "He confirmed today."

"Where's he taking you? Impudent Oyster?" Spencer asked. It was the nicest restaurant in the area. A good choice for a date night.

"We're going on one of those harbor cruises to see if we can spot any great white sharks or seals. Have you guys ever gone on one?"

They both shook their heads. "That's such a touristy thing to do," Spencer said.

"I think it's cute," Natalie said.

"Neither one of us have ever been. I thought it sounded fun." She liked that it was a more casual first date, too.

"What are you up to this weekend, Spencer?" Natalie asked.

"No specific plans yet. I'd like to get to the beach maybe. Chip mentioned maybe taking a ride to the Beachcomber."

"This is their opening weekend, right? I haven't been there for a few years," Natalie said.

"Yeah, they always open Memorial Day weekend. You have to get there early, though, to get a parking spot. Especially now that they've lost the front lot to erosion."

"I have my signing on Saturday and I think my aunt is having a family cookout on Sunday. That should be fun . . . assuming things go well with Uncle Richie," Hannah said.

"Yeah, might not be so fun, if there's tension in the house," Natalie said.

"I had an interesting text message from Michelle," Spencer said casually.

Natalie pounced and gave him her full attention. "Michelle? As in your ex?"

He nodded. "Yeah, I'm not sure what's up, but she asked if we could meet for coffee sometime over the weekend."

"What do you think she wants?" Hannah asked.

"I have no idea," Spencer said.

"Maybe she wants you back?" Natalie suggested.

Spencer laughed. "I highly doubt that."

"Well, we will expect a full report," Natalie demanded.

"Definitely," Hannah said. She was very curious to hear an update on this as well.

The bartender set their appetizers down a few minutes later and they dug in. The wings and nachos were fine, good standard bar appetizers, but the fried calamari was Hannah's favorite. They were so tender, and lightly battered with a spicy aioli sauce for dipping.

They were just finishing up with the food when Natalie's phone rang. She glanced at it, saw who was calling, and answered.

"Hi, Mom, what's up?" She was quiet for a moment, listening. "I'll be there in a few minutes. No, it's no problem. I'll see you soon."

"Is your mom okay?" Hannah asked after Natalie ended the call.

"She's fine. She grabbed the wrong set of keys when she went to the store and now she's locked out of her house. I have a spare, so I can go let her in." She opened her wallet and put some money down on the bar. "That should cover me. You guys stay. No need to rush off because of me."

Hannah's glass of wine was almost empty and it was still early. She didn't want to go home yet. She looked at Spencer. "I'm up for another if you are?" Spencer's beer was almost gone, too.

"I'm in no hurry. If the band is good, we could stay and listen for a while. I know you aren't in a rush to get home."

"Sounds good to me." They got the bartender's attention and ordered another round.

"So, you really have no idea what Michelle wants?" Hannah asked. The bartender set down their new drinks and she took a sip of chardonnay.

"I really don't. I haven't talked to her since we saw her briefly at the wine dinner. And we hadn't talked at all before that."

"What if she wants to get back together with you? Would you consider it?"

Spencer's expression was hard to read. He stared out the window for a long moment before answering. "I don't know. It's hard to imagine it. I've moved on since then. I guess I just need to hear what she has to say. What about you? Would you get back together with your ex if he asked you?"

"He did ask me. Right before I came here. I ran into him at a party that I was sure he wasn't going to be at. It was awkward. He was all for giving it another try, but nothing had changed for me. I was the one that broke up with him, though. I told him I needed some time. I don't think I was clear enough initially so I did feel bad about that."

She wondered if it might be different for Spencer since it was Michelle who had ended things. She wasn't sure if Michelle had cheated or not. That would be a deal-breaker for her.

"Maybe she has come to her senses and realized that George isn't right for her." Spencer took a sip of his beer. "She swears that she didn't cheat. Just that she met him, was hugely attracted, and wanted to pursue it. It still didn't feel good though."

Hannah hated that Michelle had done that to Spencer.

The band started to play, and they stopped talking to listen. The music was upbeat, a good selection of popular hits. They chatted a bit in between songs when it was easier to hear each other talk.

"I saw your grandfather earlier this week. I think he's sick of those crutches," Hannah said.

Spencer laughed. "He is. I stopped in there yesterday and he's quite the grump. I think everyone will be happy when he gets that cast off."

"My aunt is having her cookout on Sunday and was going to mention it to Ben and Joy. That means you're included, too, if you're around."

"I'll definitely stop by. Unless we go to the Beachcomber that day. I'm not sure which day Chip is able to go. Might be Saturday or Sunday."

"Do you surf there?" Hannah remembered that area often had big waves and a dangerous undertow. She tended to avoid going into water like that.

Spencer looked at her funny. "When was the last time you went to the Beachcomber?"

"It's been ages. Ten years, probably. I haven't been since I was in college. Why?"

"The great white shark sightings have increased and that's one of their favorite areas. There was a young guy killed a few years ago by a shark in Wellfleet. He was close to shore, on a boogie board. But there had been a sighting earlier. People still went in the water. I won't be one of them."

"I remember hearing something about a shark attack. I didn't realize someone was killed."

"Too bad you have your signing on Saturday. You could go with us," Spencer teased.

"And swim with great white sharks?" Hannah made a face. "Actually, I hope we see a shark on Friday. That would be interesting."

Spencer laughed. "Well, hopefully you won't need a bigger boat."

Hannah laughed at the reference to the movie *Jaws*.

The band started up again and they stayed and listened to their second set. It was after nine when they took a break again and by then Hannah was ready to head home. They settled the bill and walked outside. Spencer was parked right near her in the lot behind the bookshop. It was a clear night and the stars were more visible than usual in the dark sky. Hannah stopped walking for a minute to get a better look. Spencer followed her gaze.

"Wow, do you see that constellation?" he asked.

Hannah smiled. "You mean Virgo?"

"I'm impressed that you know that," Spencer said.

"My mother used to be really into the stars. She had a big telescope and she loved to show us all the different constellations at the best time of year to see them. She made it all seem so magical."

"That's a nice memory." Spencer stared up into the sky. "She's right. It is pretty magical."

Their cars were straight ahead and they walked along in silence until they reached them.

"See you later. Have fun at the Beachcomber," Hannah said as she opened her car door.

"Good night, Hannah. See you on Sunday."

Hannah thought about Spencer as she drove home. She wondered what Michelle wanted to talk to him about. And she hoped that she wasn't looking for a second chance. In Hannah's opinion, she didn't deserve one and she felt somewhat protective of Spencer. She didn't want Michelle to hurt him again. She knew that Spencer didn't think Michelle had cheated, but she wasn't so sure. She'd always read that with people who cheated, the first time was the hardest—and once they opened that door, the odds were good that it could happen again.

Chapter 28

Richie's plane was due to arrive in Hyannis a little after five. Maddie found it hard to concentrate all day. She was feeling both nervous and unsettled, unsure and excited at the same time. She didn't know how this weekend was going to go. How she was going to feel when she saw Richie again. Knowing that he wanted to make things work was a step in the right direction though.

She changed outfits several times, not sure what felt right. She finally went with a black sweater, faded jeans, and dark brown cowboy boots he'd given her a few years ago for Christmas. She loved them and they looked good with everything.

Hannah had told her earlier that she was going out with friends after work so Maddie thought it might be nice to just get takeout and eat at home on the deck. They could have a drink or two and enjoy the view and talk.

She got to the airport early and went inside to wait for Richie's plane to arrive. She checked her messages while she waited and was thrilled to find that an author she'd offered to represent—the suspense author that Sara had loved so much and that Maddie did, too, when she read the book in one sitting—had emailed to accept. She wanted Maddie to be her agent. It made her day and Maddie immediately emailed her back and suggested they talk next week about next steps. She began to mentally make a list of all the editors she knew who might love the book.

She saw a small plane coming in and checked her watch. It was most likely Richie's flight. Sure enough, a few minutes later, people got off the plane and walked toward the terminal and Richie was one of them. He smiled and waved when he saw her. When he reached Maddie, he pulled her in for a hug.

"It's so good to see you." He smelled of woodsy cologne and home.

"You, too. Did you have a good flight?" Maddie asked as they walked toward the car. "Is that all you have for luggage?" He was just carrying a duffel bag.

"It was fine. Crowded. Every seat was filled on both flights. I didn't have that much to bring. I left my suits behind, for now. Most of what I need is in Chatham."

They reached the car and climbed in. Richie threw his bag in the back seat.

"What do you want to do for dinner?" Richie asked.

"Every place is going to be so crowded this weekend. What about getting some Chinese takeout and eating on the back deck? We can relax and unwind."

"That works for me. Do you want me to call in our usual order?"

"Sure, that would be great."

Richie placed the call and they made small talk for the rest of the drive. She told him about her recent sales and the author she'd just signed. He told her how things were going with his job. They talked about the weather and how the forecast looked great for the long weekend.

"I thought we'd have a cookout on Sunday and have Sara and the kids over and Ben and Joy. I thought it would be fun for them. Poor Ben is miserable with his crutches." She told him all about his accident and recent grumpiness.

Richie sympathized. "I'd be pretty grumpy, too, if I had to wear a cast and deal with crutches for weeks."

"And I feel for Joy. She's had to put up with it."

"That, too," he agreed.

When they reached the Chinese restaurant in East Harwich, which was their favorite local spot, Maddie pulled up to the door and Richie went inside to pick up the food. Twenty minutes later they were home and eating on the deck.

Maddie took a sip of wine as she nibbled on an egg roll and looked out at the ocean. In the distance a barge was going by, heading toward the Cape Cod Canal. The water was still, unusually calm. A soft breeze ruffled her hair. It was a gorgeous night to sit outside.

When they'd had their fill, Maddie packed everything up and put the leftovers in the refrigerator. Richie got another beer and refilled her wineglass. They settled back into their seats and Maddie took a deep breath. It was time to have that talk.

"So, you said you want to try again. Are you sure about that?" Maddie asked.

"Maddie, I've never not wanted to be with you. I know things felt off with us this past year but I thought it was just something people go through. The ebb and flow of a relationship. When you said you thought we should take some time apart, it threw me. But it also made me wonder if you were right. So, I agreed. I went to Manhattan. But it's not the same there without you."

"It hurt me when I saw how you were with Laura. The times when she's come here or we saw her in the city, there was something there that just didn't sit right with me. I never worried that you were cheating, but I just didn't get a good feeling about her. She was too familiar with you. You never saw it though. And I think we did kind of drift apart. My sister's death just made it worse. I withdrew from everything. It's been hard." Her voice broke as her emotions took over and she felt her eyes grow damp. She willed the tears back.

"When Kathryn called and said she saw the two of you, that

just brought it all up again. Imagine how you'd feel if you saw some guy like that with me?"

Richie sighed. "I'm sorry, Maddie. I didn't see it at all. Didn't see that it was inappropriate. Frankly, I liked the attention, especially these past few months in Manhattan. I thought you were overreacting a little. But you may have been onto something."

Maddie felt a sudden chill and shivered. "What do you mean?" She stood and took her glass of wine with her. She walked a few steps away and leaned against the deck railing and stared out at the ocean. There was a long moment of silence before Richie continued talking. When he spoke, she turned to face him and placed one hand on the railing, for support.

"So, like I said, I never picked up on any kind of a vibe from Laura before. But after you and I talked and we decided I was coming home today, I told the office I was heading back to Chatham. Laura wanted to go for a goodbye drink Tuesday night after work."

"Just the two of you?" Maddie asked.

"Not at first. Several others came with us. But after a few drinks, everyone was ready to head home. Laura insisted I stay for one more, said she needed my advice on a personal matter. So I agreed to stay."

"What was the personal matter?" Maddie sipped her wine and waited.

Richie sighed. "I'm an idiot. Kathryn was right; you were right. Not that there was ever anything going on, but Laura told me that she was thinking about leaving her husband. And that she didn't want me to go back to Chatham."

Maddie tightened her grip on her wineglass. "She was interested in you."

Richie nodded. "Apparently so. I sat there in shock while she went on about how we were meant to be together. She felt that we were soulmates or some nonsense like that. I couldn't listen to it all. It didn't make any sense to me." He looked sheepish and truly surprised that he'd had no idea how Laura felt.

"What did you tell her?" Maddie lifted her wineglass to take a sip but kept her eyes on Richie the whole time.

"I told her that I was very sorry, but I didn't feel the same way. I told her that I still love my wife."

"And what did she say to that?" Maddie shivered. And felt anger grow that Laura would make a move on her husband. What gave her the right to do that?

"She seemed perplexed. I think she was convinced that I would give it a go with her. Oddly enough." Richie shook his head at the ridiculousness of it.

"You never picked up on her signals, but she kept sending them and assumed you knew how she felt, and that you must feel the same. So, all she had to do was tell you to stay and that would be the end of it." For some reason, Laura had believed that her feelings were reciprocated.

Richie looked at her and his eyes widened. "You know, I think you're exactly right."

"Well, that settles it then. You're not going back to Manhattan," Maddie said. It wasn't that she didn't trust Richie, she just didn't want Laura trying to spend time with her husband.

Richie stood and walked over to her. He wrapped his arms around her waist and pulled her to him. "No, I'm not." He leaned in and his lips touched hers, gently at first and then more firmly.

Maddie felt the anxiety she'd been carrying with her for months begin to ease. She pulled back and spoke softly, "Welcome home."

Chapter 29

Hannah arrived at the marina on Friday at a quarter of twelve. Niall had said to meet in front of the shark boats. There were several that offered tours, so it was easy to find them. Niall was there, waiting for her. But she noticed that this area of the marina was unusually quiet. There were no signs of life on any of the shark boats—and no one waiting to board.

But Niall was all smiles as she walked up. He looked cute, too, in Ralph Lauren shorts, a white T-shirt, and a Nantucket sweatshirt in the unique shade that Hannah loved. It was called Nantucket Red and was a soft washed-out red, very popular on the island.

Hannah wore shorts as well and a white tank top with a warm cotton crewneck sweater over it. It was like a sweatshirt, but a little dressier. She wanted layers that were easy to take off if it got hot out there. She'd brought sunscreen as well, and had applied some all over when she got out of the shower.

She looked around again as she reached Niall. There were no other people at all on that dock. "Where is everyone?" she asked.

He laughed. "Well, that's a funny story. So, I have some good news and some bad news. Which do you want first?"

"Bad news, I guess?" Hannah smiled, wondering where he was going with this.

"When I called to reserve the shark tour I discovered that it doesn't normally run in May. Shark season in Chatham doesn't start until July—the first sharks are usually spotted around the fourth. Although sometimes it can happen in late May or June, just not enough to guarantee sightings."

"Oh. I had no idea."

"I didn't, either. But I came up with another idea—I knew it was going to be ideal boating weather today. So, I hired a different boat!"

Hannah stared at him, perplexed. Were they going on a seal watch then? Or whales?

"And this is even better. We'll have the boat to ourselves, other than the crew, of course. Someone has to drive it."

"Where will we be going?"

He grinned. "We have it for three hours, so all over. We might not see sharks, but we'll see seals and whales. It's guaranteed."

Hannah smiled. His enthusiasm was contagious. "How do they guarantee it?"

"It's very cool. They do the same thing for some of the high-end shark tours. There's a dedicated small plane that flies ahead and spots them for us."

Hannah was impressed. "I had no idea that was possible."

"Our boat is around the corner on a different dock." Niall led the way down the empty dock to one with a bit more activity. There were several deep-sea fishing boats that were getting ready to head out. And just beyond that was a more luxurious boat. It also looked set up for deep-sea fishing, but there was a roomy deck area and comfortable-looking chairs and a table that was beautifully set with plates and cups, and a bottle of Veuve Clicquot champagne on ice.

The captain welcomed them onto the boat and introduced himself and his crew. "I'm Dave, and I'm going to be driving you around today. Jim and Andy are here to serve you, whatever you need. Your lunch is ready whenever you want it, just let them know. Our spotter plane is already up in the air looking for sharks, whales, and seals. That's Mac and he's the best. If they're out there, he'll find them. Make yourselves comfortable and we'll get underway." Andy jumped out of the boat and untied the moorings, then climbed back aboard and the boat began to slowly move away from the dock.

They sat at the table and Jim opened the bottle of champagne and filled Hannah's glass first and then Niall's. He went into the galley of the boat and returned a moment later with a plate of sliced strawberries, crackers, and cheese and set it in the middle of the table. Hannah took a small sip of the champagne and reached for a strawberry. She looked back at the dock, which quickly grew smaller as they headed out on the water.

"What do you think? This is pretty cool, huh?" Niall helped himself to the cheese and crackers.

Hannah lifted her face and let the sun beam down upon her skin. Its warmth and the slight coolness of the salt air as they picked up speed felt intoxicating.

"I love this. It's been ages since I've been on a boat. I haven't spent much time in Chatham in recent years." Hannah realized she'd been missing out and wished she'd come back more often.

"You're here now. You can make up for lost time this summer. That's what I'm doing."

"You haven't spent much time here, either? Your parents bought their house a few years ago, didn't they?" Hannah wondered why he was just now spending time on the Cape.

He shook his head. "I was a bit estranged with them for a while. They didn't approve of some of my choices so it didn't make me want to be here for any length of time."

"Oh. Things are better now?"

He nodded. "It's because the books took off a little over a year ago. They were not super supportive before that. My father wanted me to follow in his footsteps and work at his company. But that felt like death to me. I couldn't do it. I spent one summer there and that was enough."

"What does your father do?"

"All kinds of things in the world of finance. But he's known for private equity. Buying companies and selling them later at a huge profit. Math was never my strong suit and that is a numbers job."

"They didn't approve of your writing?"

"Not at first. Especially when they read my first published book." He grinned. "The first thing they tell a writer is to 'write what you know.'"

Hannah thought about his first book, which she'd loved. It featured a highly dysfunctional family and a son who always disappointed them as he tried to carve his own path.

"It was autobiographical?" she asked.

He nodded. "Very much so. Though ironically, neither of them realized it until other people pointed it out to them. They were not amused."

"What did you do for work before you got published?"

Niall raised an eyebrow. "I've actually never had a real job. I have a trust fund. A sizable one. And after the first blowup when I told my father I wanted to be a writer and I wasn't going to join his company, he threatened to cut me off. Shut the trust fund down."

"So what did you do?"

Niall leaned back and grinned. "I spoke his language. I made a deal with him. He would agree to give me five years to write something publishable, that would generate a real income. If I failed to do that, I had two choices. I would either work for him, or continue writing—without the support of the trust fund."

Hannah was fascinated. She couldn't imagine having the luxury of a trust fund so she could just write, without having to work a job. She wondered if Niall realized how privileged he was. "How long did it take you?" she asked.

He grinned. "Four and a half years. I went to Europe for a year and lived high, staying in all the best hotels, going to all the 'in' bars, looking for inspiration everywhere. And I found it. I fell in love in Paris. It was a whirlwind affair. Literally an affair.

"She was married. I didn't know that at first. By the time I did, it was too late for it to matter. I was head over heels. But she tired of me and ended it. And that's when I started the book that I sold. I'd written a few others before it, but nothing stood out. I didn't even send those books out because I knew they weren't worthy. They weren't going to save me from my father's company."

Niall was spoiled and cocky and somehow still endearing. Hannah actually felt for him, not knowing that the woman he fell for was married. "So, heartbreak was your inspiration?"

He nodded. "I spent a week in bed at first, utterly devastated. She wouldn't even take my calls. I tried to resurrect it, but she was done with me. And of course it was for the best. What saved me was starting the book. It honestly seemed to write itself. I channeled all the pain and frustration I felt and told my story."

"And it sold right away?"

He laughed. "Not exactly. It took another year to get an agent. Most passed on the book. They didn't think the market wanted a dysfunctional family saga. But Byron got it. He said it reminded him of Bret Easton Ellis's *Less than Zero* or Jay McInerney's *Bright Lights, Big City* and he said books like that never go out of style. He thought the timing could be good as there hadn't been anything similar in decades."

"You sold at auction, if I remember?" It had been in all the trade publications. A staggering seven-figure advance for a debut novelist. Hannah had read it with envy. And to think he didn't even really need the money.

Niall nodded. "We did. It was a ten-way auction, which I guess is unusual according to Byron. He sold the film rights first, and word got out, so once he submitted the novel to editors, things happened very quickly."

"How did your parents take it?"

"Not well, at first. My father never makes a deal that doesn't benefit him. He thought he had me and there was no way I'd meet the terms as he'd laid them out. He knows most writers don't make a living, even if they do get published. But once he saw the size of the deal and then the accolades when the book was released, he came around. Now they both like to brag about me." He smiled and reached for his champagne.

Hannah was interested in everything Niall had to say but couldn't help but notice that he did most of the talking and it was all about himself.

Jim came over and asked if they were ready for lunch. "We have lobster rolls or chicken salad."

Niall looked at Hannah. "I wasn't sure what you'd prefer so I made sure we had a few options."

Hannah smiled. "I'd love a lobster roll, thanks."

"And I'll have the chicken salad. Thanks, Jim."

"You don't like lobster?" Hannah was surprised.

He shook his head. "I can't stand it. I'm not really into any seafood actually. My parents pushed it hard on me growing up and I did try it all. Raw oysters, shrimp, caviar." He shuddered. "They love caviar. Nasty stuff if you ask me."

Hannah laughed. "I've never actually tried it, but it doesn't look all that appealing."

Niall lifted his glass and sipped his champagne. "Enough about me. Tell me all your secrets, Hannah."

She smiled. "I don't think I have any. My life isn't as glamorous as yours."

"Glamour is definitely overrated." Niall looked lost in thought as if remembering something unpleasant. He snapped out of it quickly, though, as Jim returned with their sandwiches and set them down, along with two cups of steaming clam chowder and a bowl of potato chips.

"You hate seafood but you'll eat clam chowder?"

Niall grinned. "I know. Doesn't make a lot of sense. I like tuna out of a can, too . . . go figure. That's it, though."

Hannah took a bite of her lobster roll. There were big chunks of sweet fresh lobster, tails, knuckles, and claws all lightly tossed in mayonnaise and stuffed into a buttered and grilled hot dog bun. It was perfection.

They were just about done eating when Andy came over to them with good news.

"The plane spotted seals in a harbor nearby. We're going in for a closer look."

Ten minutes later they pulled into a harbor and Dave slowed the motor a bit so they could glide in more quietly. They walked to the edge of the boat for a better look and as they got closer, Hannah could see dozens of seals sunning themselves on a jetty. She pulled her phone out to take a picture and zoomed in to get a close-up of their faces. They looked totally blissed out and sleepy in the warm sunshine.

They stayed in the harbor for a bit, idling the motor and moving around for better views, before heading back out into the open ocean. They went out a bit farther this time instead of just hugging the coastline. And a half hour later, the spotter plane radioed Dave that two humpback whales were in the area.

Dave slowed to an idle when they reached the location given by the pilot. They sat there for another twenty minutes, waiting for a whale to appear. Hannah took her sweater off and Niall did the same with his sweatshirt. When the boat wasn't moving, they felt the heat of the sun more and it was hot. It felt good, though.

Hannah reapplied sunscreen to her face and shoulders. Her fair skin had a tendency to burn easily if she wasn't careful. She offered the sunscreen to Niall but he shook his head.

"I never burn. Thanks, though." His skin was darker so she imagined he tanned easily.

"Look to your right!" Andy got their attention and they looked off the right side of the boat. About twenty feet away, a stream of water shot into the air and a moment later a whale surfaced slightly and then its huge tail flipped out of the water and down again.

"Did you see that?" Niall asked.

"I did. Oh wow . . ." Hannah clicked record on her phone and shot a video of a whale jumping out of the water almost entirely and then coming down hard with a loud splash. For the next fifteen minutes the whales surfaced over and over again and then the show was over.

"That was incredible. I've only been on one other whale watch before. It was in Provincetown and I went with my mother and aunt. They were handing out Dramamine when we boarded and I took one, just in case, for seasickness. That was a mistake. It made me so sleepy I had to go lie down and missed most of the cruise. I did wake up in time to see one whale though."

Niall laughed. "I bet you never took Dramamine again after that?"

"No. I should have known better. I don't even get seasick!"

The boat continued on for another hour before turning to head back into the Chatham harbor. The time went by so fast. Hannah put her sweater on as the air grew chilly as they picked up speed. It had been such a fun afternoon. Niall was easy to talk to and complicated. She'd learned a lot about his background and it was so different from anyone else she'd ever known.

As they neared the spot where they'd seen the seals earlier, Andy came over to them excitedly. "This is crazy, but we're heading back in for a closer look by that jetty. The plane spotted Heath Ledger. We almost never see them in May."

Hannah was confused. "Heath Ledger?" The only Heath Ledger she knew was a famous talented actor who'd tragically passed away several years earlier.

"Scientists that study the great white sharks tag them so they can track them by radar. Heath Ledger is one of the sharks. One of over two hundred and seventy tagged so far."

"No kidding?" Niall picked up the binoculars that the boat supplied and scanned the water, looking for signs of the shark.

"We probably won't see anything until we get much closer," Andy said.

A few minutes later, Jim hollered back, "Fin spotted by the tip of the jetty."

"Must be feeding time," Niall said as he picked up the binoculars again and then handed them to Hannah to take a look. Andy had explained earlier that sharks were often found where there were seals as the sharks liked to feed on them.

They drew closer to the jetty and Dave cut the motor completely and the big boat swayed back and forth. They sat like that for ten minutes before Andy excitedly told them to go to the left side of the boat and look in the water. They did and saw the biggest fish Hannah had ever seen about ten feet below the surface. It swam by slowly, flicking its tail as it went, and it was terrifyingly large.

Niall whistled softly. "That has to be twelve or maybe fifteen feet long?"

"He's close to fifteen, I think," Andy said.

The shark swam by them again and then vanished into the ocean's depths.

Dave turned the boat around and headed back toward the marina. They arrived twenty minutes later and once they were docked and tied up, Dave came out to bid them farewell.

"I hope you enjoyed the day?"

Niall shook his hand. "It was outstanding. The trifecta of sightings. I didn't expect to see more than seals, to be honest."

"It was wonderful, thank you so much." Hannah shook the captain's hand as well and then Niall handed cash tips to all three men. They thanked him gratefully and said their goodbyes.

They walked down the dock and back to the parking lot. When they reached Hannah's car, she stopped and thanked Niall again. "This was one of the most fun first dates I've ever had. Thank you so much."

He smiled. "You're welcome. Does that mean my chances for a second date are pretty good?"

She laughed. "I'd say so."

"Good. I look forward to it then. I'll be in touch soon." He gave her a hug and a quick kiss on the cheek before heading off to his own car, a Range Rover, which was parked nearby. Hannah appreciated that he'd kept things casual all around. It had been a fun day and it left her intrigued to spend more time with him.

Chapter 30

Hannah felt a familiar case of nerves as she got ready for her signing the next day. She'd been terrified at her first signing ever, and then mortified when she hadn't sold a single book. That signing was at a tiny independent bookshop in Brooklyn and it had been pouring rain all afternoon, so there was no foot traffic and Lucy was away that weekend, so the one familiar face she could always count on couldn't be there. She hadn't told any of her other friends because she'd secretly worried that if they came, no one would be there. She'd dreaded it and it had lived up to her fears.

But it got much better after that. She'd taken a breath and put the word out on social media and figured no matter how bad it was, it couldn't possibly be worse than that first signing. So her expectations were low on future signings and she was pleasantly surprised. With each signing, more people came and more people read her book and seemed to like it.

So, given that she knew people in Chatham and her sister even worked at the bookshop and promoted her constantly, Hannah was only a little worried. It was just nerves. She knew now that once it got underway, the signing would probably be fun.

And it was. Sara met her there at twelve thirty and they chatted with Brooklyn and Alison until the official start time of one. Alison had put out a pretty, cloth-covered table with an assortment of her famous gluten- and dairy-free black brownies, which were so good no one could tell the difference. There were also raspberry jam–filled shortbread cookies and chocolate-chip, as well as a platter of ripe strawberries and grapes.

Hannah settled at the designated author table, with Brooklyn on one side to ring up sales and Sara on the other with her phone to take pictures for the shop. She'd also use customers' cameras if they wanted their own snapshots. Hannah had thought it was presumptuous to suggest that anyone would want a picture with her, but she'd learned from prior signings that most did and they loved to share on social media, which was a very good thing.

There was a small line right when they started at one, and while she didn't draw anywhere near the size of the crowd that Niall had, there was a steady stream of people who wanted a signed book. A few of them had already bought the book earlier and brought it with them. Sara pointed out an older man with a younger woman. She introduced him when he reached Hannah and explained that he'd been in earlier that week.

"This is my sister, Hannah. And that must be your granddaughter? Happy birthday."

"Thank you."

"This is Jamie, my pride and joy. She's already read your book, Hannah. I gave it to her yesterday and she stayed up till the wee hours."

"It was so good! I couldn't put it down," Jamie said.

Hannah was touched. She still wasn't used to comments like that about her books. It felt surreal.

"Thank you so much. I really appreciate it." Hannah signed the book and then Sara took a picture of Jamie and her grandfather with Hannah in the middle.

The two hours flew by and Brooklyn told them that they'd almost sold out of her book. "It's a good thing that we didn't sell all of them, as we will probably have people coming by the rest of the weekend that couldn't make it in today or got the date wrong. Happens every time."

The crowd thinned a little before three and they started to pack up. But then Hannah heard a familiar voice. "Can you squeeze one more in?"

She looked up and saw Niall standing there, a cheeky grin on his face. "I tried to get down earlier but time got away from me."

"I think we can fit one more in," Hannah said.

"Definitely." Brooklyn rang up the sale and Hannah signed the book. She didn't know what to write and finally went with, *Thanks so much for the support, you are an inspiration.* It was a little formal, but it fit how she felt. She was inspired by his success and she loved his books.

Sara took a picture of the two of them together and he asked for one for his phone, too, and she obliged.

"Is there any chance we could grab a drink to celebrate a successful signing? I'm sure you have plans later." Hannah did not have any plans later, but she wasn't about to admit it.

"I could go for a quick drink." She turned to Sara. "Would you like to join us?"

Sara shook her head. "I have to get home. I'll see you tomorrow at Aunt Maddie's though. The kids are looking forward to it."

They all walked out together and said goodbye to Sara.

"How about the Beach House at Chatham Bars?" Niall suggested. "We can sit outside and look at the ocean." Hannah loved that idea. It was right down the street from Aunt Maddie's house, too.

"Perfect. I'll see you there."

She arrived at the Chatham Bars Inn fifteen minutes later. The traffic was heavy because of the holiday weekend. Niall pulled in right after her and they walked in together and were seated right away. The hotel was busy but it was a beautiful day and at almost three thirty, it was late for lunch and early for dinner, so there were plenty of open tables.

"I feel like a vacation drink," Niall said when the server, a young girl who Hannah guessed was probably on break from college, came to take their order.

"What are you having?" he asked Hannah.

She had been thinking wine until he mentioned wanting a vacation drink and she thought of her favorite frozen fruity cocktail. "I'll have a frozen strawberry daiquiri made with Myers's dark rum."

"Nice! I'll go with a rum runner."

Because it wasn't busy, it didn't take long for their drinks to arrive. Hannah took a sip of hers and sighed. "This tastes like summer."

Niall laughed. They chatted for a bit about the boat trip the day before and how much fun they'd had.

"I got some great pictures and a video of the whale jumping. My nephews will be so impressed when I show them tomorrow at the cookout."

"Your sister mentioned you're all going to your aunt's?"

She nodded. "My aunt throws one every year, usually on Memorial Day weekend, sometimes the Fourth of July. It's nice to get the whole family together."

"My family isn't exactly the cookout type." Hannah noticed a slightly bitter tone to his voice.

"What are they doing this weekend?"

"They have company visiting. My mother's sister and her new husband." Hannah thought it was curious that he didn't refer to her as his aunt. "They'll spend most of the weekend at the club, of course. Dad will golf and Mother will play tennis, and they'll all meet up for drinks and dinner after. And everything will be done for them. I don't think my father has ever grilled. We have one, of course, but their cook handles that."

"That sounds fun though. Do you golf, too?" Hannah asked.

Niall laughed. "Poorly. It is fun though. I don't do it often enough to improve. But I do enjoy the after-golf festivities."

"So that's what you'll be up to tomorrow?"

"No doubt. I'll have to make an appearance. It's usually a good time though. A little stuffier than a cookout. I may be a bit jealous."

Hannah smiled. She agreed with him. There was nothing like cooking outdoors on a holiday weekend and watching the kids swim in the ocean.

Niall changed the subject and launched into the usual question that came up these days. Hannah hated it, as it always felt like an interview question that she was doomed to fail.

"So, how is it that you're still single? Have you had any long-term relationships?" Niall asked.

Hannah knew this was code for "What kind of baggage are you carrying?" She smiled and answered honestly. "Maybe I'm too picky. I just ended an almost two-year relationship because I didn't want to take it to the next step, and he did. What about you?"

Niall flashed her the cheeky grin that she suspected came out when he was trying to distract from something uncomfortable.

"I've actually never had a long-term relationship. Nothing longer than six months, usually it's less than that, though. I just haven't found the right person yet. But I'm having a lot of fun looking." His words sent up a red flag of sorts. With his looks and family wealth, Niall would have no shortage of women attracted to him. She could see how it might be hard to resist the temptation. She wasn't sure if she would be able to hold his attention longer than that. Or if she wanted to deal with worrying if her time was due to expire.

She thought of Joy's words and stopping assessing Niall's potential for permanence and decided to just enjoy the moment and go with the flow.

She changed the subject and brought it back to books that

they both admired, and they spent another hour comparing notes and laughing. He was good company. He insisted on buying their drinks and regretted that he had to leave. "I wish I could stay longer. I'm actually playing golf with a few friends. One of my rare outings on the course," he said.

"Thanks for the drink and for stopping by the signing."

"Of course."

They walked to their cars and once again, he gave her a quick hug, but this time he kissed her on the lips. Just for a moment, but it was nice and she liked the feel of his lips on hers. He might not be her long-term person, but she liked him.

"Maybe we can do something next week, if you're up for it?" he suggested.

"I'd like that."

Chapter 31

met Michelle for coffee earlier today," Spencer casually said to his grandmother.

They were all sitting outside at Aunt Maddie's house for her cookout. Joy had brought a big bowl of her macaroni salad, which looked delicious. Ben was sitting in a padded chair with his leg propped up on a stool and his crutches by his side. Hannah and Sara were sitting nearby, and Tom and the kids were on the beach. Lady and Tramp were lying in the shade and keeping an eye on everyone.

"What did she want?" Joy asked. She didn't seem thrilled at the mention of Michelle and Hannah knew that she hadn't been a big fan of Spencer's ex.

"Basically to tell me that George dumped her, she made a huge mistake, and wants to know if I can ever forgive her and can we try again." Spencer cracked open a can of Sam Adams IPA and took a sip.

"Well, what did you tell her?" Joy asked.

Spencer smiled. "What do you think? No, of course. She asked if I would at least think about it, sleep on it, and I said I would, just to be nice. But the answer is no. I don't think there's any going back when something like that happens."

"No, I wouldn't think so," Joy agreed. "I have to admit, I'm glad. I never liked her for you."

Spencer laughed. "I know. You knew."

Hannah wondered if Spencer might feel differently after he did what Michelle had suggested and slept on the idea. He'd wanted to propose to her, after all. Were those feelings gone completely?

"Okay, food's ready, everyone head to the grill and help yourselves," Aunt Maddie said.

Uncle Richie manned the grill and had steak tips and hot dogs ready as well as some chicken breasts.

Tom walked up but the kids weren't with him. Sara raised her eyebrows and before she could ask, he said, "They went into the basement to get the cornhole game. They'll be here in a minute."

"I love that game," Spencer said.

It was a fun game where players tossed small beanbags into open holes on a game board. People often brought it to the beach or it turned up at cookouts like this.

"I bet you're good at it," Hannah said.

He grinned. "Not too bad. We should play later."

"Somehow I think I'll regret that, but sure."

Spencer made a plate for his grandfather. He knew just how he liked his hot dogs: mustard, relish, and extra ketchup. He made two of them, piled on the pasta salad and chips, and brought it to his grandfather, who gave him a thumbs-up. "Just the way I like it. Thank you."

Hannah and Spencer helped themselves to the food and sat by his grandparents. There were several oval tables on the deck and plenty of chairs so there was room for everyone.

"How did your signing go yesterday?" Spencer asked.

"It was fun. We had a good turnout. Nothing like Niall's, of course, but I think Alison was happy. She said that we almost sold out of the books."

"That's great, honey," Joy said.

"Yeah, that's really good. Did you see any sharks on your excursion?" Spencer said.

"We did actually." She told him all about the boat and the seals, whales, and Heath Ledger.

"Who the heck is Heath Ledger?" Ben asked.

"He was a movie star," Joy said.

"And now he's a shark." Hannah explained about the tags.

Joy shook her head. "More importantly, what did you think of Niall? Will you go out with him again?" she asked.

Hannah hesitated a moment before answering. "I think so. He came to the signing yesterday and took me for a drink after. We went right up the street to the Beach House at Chatham Bars Inn."

"Oh, that's lovely. Nicest outdoor dining in Chatham."

"It is pretty. We didn't eat though. It was around three thirty, so we just had a quick drink. He was going golfing after that. His parents are members of the club."

"Really? That place is swanky. I've never been but I've heard it's outrageously expensive. Like over a million dollars just to join."

Ben laughed. "I'll stick to woodworking."

"He definitely lives in a different world than mine," Hannah agreed. "He told me that his parents never have cookouts. The closest they come is going to the club and eating and drinking there."

"Spencer, come play with us!" Two of Sara's boys called for him to join the game. They'd already eaten and were setting up the cornhole game on the back lawn.

Spencer looked at Hannah. She was done eating, too. "I'll play if you will?"

She laughed. "Sure, let's go."

They walked down the back steps of the deck onto the rolling lawn that led down to the ocean. The boys had the cornhole game all set up.

"You two can play the winners," Cody, the oldest, said.

"Sounds good," Spencer agreed.

They watched as the boys tossed the soft palm-sized beanbags and tried to get them through the holes on the board that stood at a slant about twenty or thirty feet away. It looked easy, but looks could be deceiving.

Hannah tossed her first beanbag and didn't even hit the playing board. She laughed and looked at Spencer. "So Michelle does want you back. How do you feel about that?" Hannah hadn't wanted to ask earlier in front of his grandparents.

"Annoyed. Confused. Flattered. Mostly annoyed."

"So that's it then?"

"Pretty much. As I said, she insisted that I think about it and we'll talk again in a week or two."

"Ugh."

He laughed. "Exactly. What do you really think of that Niall guy? Do you like him?"

"I do like him. Your grandmother gave me good advice actually. She told me to be more open. To just have fun and not make any decisions too soon. Take the time to really get to know someone and see where it goes."

He nodded. "My grandmother is pretty smart."

Hannah felt for Spencer. He talked like he was definitely not going back to Michelle but she sensed that it wasn't easy for him. It had to be confusing for him to hear that she wanted him back. Hannah didn't see how he could ever trust her again and was pretty sure he felt the same. But Michelle was smart to ask him to think about it. Maybe he would feel differently once he'd thought it over.

She played one round of cornhole, then excused herself to go chat with Sara. Spencer was clearly having a blast, so she encouraged him to stay and play with the boys. Tom was chatting with Uncle Richie by the grill and Sara and Aunt Maddie looked deep in discussion about something. They both looked up when Hannah walked over.

"How was cornhole?" Sara asked.

Hannah laughed. "It's fun, but the boys love it. All of them." Spencer hollered and high-fived Cody as they won a round.

"I was just filling Sara in on how things are going with your uncle," Aunt Maddie said.

"I'm so glad you two worked it out," Sara said.

"Me, too," Hannah agreed.

"How is it going with you, Sara? How are Tom and the boys adjusting to you working? How are you adjusting?" Aunt Maddie asked.

"The boys haven't noticed anything different. I'm still there to pick them up. Well, except for the first week when I almost forgot to collect Dylan." She smiled. "It's a bit more of an adjustment for Tom. He's used to doing nothing and me doing everything."

"Is he getting better about it?" Hannah asked.

Sara looked stressed just thinking about it. "Not really. I stayed late one day last week, so he had to get the kids and dinner was made—all he had to do was put the lasagna in the oven to cook an hour before I got home. And he couldn't be bothered. He said he forgot. But the reality is that he's just used to me doing everything. It didn't even occur to him to remember. It's not a priority." Her frustration was evident.

"And don't even get me started on the last-minute client dinners. We almost never go out, just the two of us. I'm tired of it."

Aunt Maddie frowned. "You need to talk to him."

"I've tried. I really have, but he just yeses me. I don't think he's really listening."

Aunt Maddie glanced at the ocean for a moment and seemed deep in thought for a moment before speaking. "It sounds like he takes you for granted. If he won't listen, maybe you need to show him?" Her tone was calm and measured but there was a mischievous gleam in her eye. Hannah wondered what she was thinking.

"What do you mean?" Sara asked.

"Take a week off from being a mom and a wife. Stay with me

and Hannah. We have plenty of room. There's another guest bedroom right next to Hannah's. You can still go to work, but come home here every day."

"Oh, I could never do that," Sara protested.

"Why not? Tom has the ability to work from home, right?" Aunt Maddie asked. "And his schedule is flexible? There's no reason why he can't pick up his own kids for a week and feed them."

"She's right. It would really show Tom all that you do," Hannah said.

Sara bit her lower lip and glanced at Tom, who was helping himself to a second beer. "It's tempting, but I don't know. I'll have to think about that."

"Well, the offer's always out there. You're always welcome," Aunt Maddie said.

Chapter 32

"You're working today? Seriously?" Tom looked at Sara in annoyance as she said goodbye to him Monday morning. He was sitting at the kitchen table, reading the paper and drinking coffee. "I have a tee time at noon."

"Well, see if you can push it to later. I'll be home by two thirty."

Tom laughed and rolled his eyes. "I can't do that. It's Memorial Day, the course is totally booked. I only got this time because there was a cancellation."

Sara tried to keep her voice calm. She was completely annoyed that he'd forgotten—though the truth was that he'd probably never really listened in the first place. "Tom, I reminded you last week that I was working today. It's a holiday but it's a Monday and the shop will be busy."

Tom stood and paced the room, running his hand through his hair. He was clearly not happy. "Well, this just stinks. This job of yours is not making things better for us. It's not like we need the money."

Sara felt frustration rise and the tears build. She would not cry. "Tom, I have to go. I can't talk about this now. Figure something out."

She left and as soon as she was in her car, the tears came. She took a moment to catch her breath and wipe them away before pulling out of the driveway.

Her mood improved when she walked into the bookshop at a quarter past nine. Alison was already there and smiled when she saw her.

"It should be a busy day," she said. "Are you ready for it?"

Sara felt herself relax. "I'm ready." The busier the better, as it would get her mind off her annoying husband.

Main Street was packed with tourists strolling and shopping in the bookshop. By the afternoon it slowed a little. Sara knew that many of the people in town for the weekend had started the trip home. She wondered if Tom had managed to move his tee time. She expected to see his car in the driveway and was surprised that it wasn't there when she got home. She assumed he'd gone somewhere with the boys, maybe to the beach or out for ice cream.

She opened the front door and heard a sound that stopped her in her tracks. Her boys were home and one of them was crying. She walked into the living room and saw Cody on the floor with his eyes closed. Her son Dylan was holding the phone and crying. The younger two were sitting by Cody, one of them holding his hand, and they all looked upset.

"Dylan, what happened to Cody?"

He looked up in a daze, and when he saw Sara he started crying again. "It's my fault. We were wrestling and we fell off the sofa and Cody hit his head. He hasn't moved since. I called you first but you didn't answer, so I called 911."

Sara pulled her phone out of her purse and sure enough, there was a missed call. She hadn't thought to check it because she'd thought the boys were with Tom.

"Where's your father?"

"He went golfing. He said Cody was in charge. I'm so sorry, Mom."

"It's okay, honey, it's not your fault." She kneeled down and spoke to her oldest son. "Cody, wake up. Cody, can you hear us?" He didn't respond at all and she felt a chill wash over her. She heard the sirens then as the ambulance came down their street. A moment later there was a knock on the door.

The paramedics came in and Sara told them what had happened. They tried to revive Cody but he was still unresponsive.

"His breathing is fine and his vitals are good. We're going to transport him to the hospital. Do you want to ride with us or follow behind?"

Sara had to take all the boys with her, so she opted to drive her car. She piled the boys in and they followed the ambulance to the hospital in Hyannis. She called Tom to let him know what was going on but her call went to voice mail. She left a terse message just letting him know they were at the hospital and that Cody was unconscious. She fought back tears again as she left the message but she refused to cry in front of the kids. She didn't want to scare them. And she was scared. Horrible things raced through her mind. What if Cody had a brain bleed or something even worse?

Cody was taken right in for evaluation. He'd come to in the ambulance and was groggy and disoriented. He was relieved when he saw Sara and he started crying.

"My head hurts. What happened?" He didn't remember hitting his head.

The doctor came in briefly and talked to Cody, and Dylan told him what happened. "I think he hit his head on the corner of the coffee table." There was a lump there now and they took him right in for a CAT scan.

"He likely has a concussion. It may be nothing, but we need to rule out anything more serious like internal bleeding," the doctor said. They ran some blood work as well and asked Cody some basic questions like what year it was and who was the president. Cody answered all the questions easily and the doctor said that was a good sign.

Two hours went by before they had the results of the blood work and the CAT scan. And there was still no call from Tom. Sara guessed that if he'd seen that she called, he hadn't listened to the message yet. He'd probably gone for a few drinks with the guys after golfing and didn't want to ruin his buzz. He had to know she wasn't happy that he had left the kids alone and likely just didn't want to hear it.

They had good news, though, when the doctor finally returned with the results. "The blood work is fine. Cody passed our screening questions and the CAT scan looked normal. There's no signs of swelling. He does have a concussion, though, so he'll need to avoid physical activity and video games for several weeks. Reading is fine, television in small amounts. If he starts to feel a headache he should rest and take Advil. He'll probably feel back to normal in a week or two. Kids usually bounce back fast. But follow up with your doctor if things get worse."

Sara signed the discharge papers and they headed home. They were just leaving the hospital when Tom called. He sounded equally guilty and concerned. "How's Cody? Are you still at the hospital? I just got your message now."

"We're on our way home. He has a concussion. He's okay. We'll see you at home." Sara ended the call and felt exhausted. Her adrenaline had been running high since she'd walked in and saw Cody unconscious on the floor. She hadn't relaxed until they got the results from the doctor.

It was almost six now. "Are you guys hungry? We can get take-out from Kream 'N Kone, burgers or fried seafood?"

Everyone voted for burgers, so Sara called the order in and picked it up on the way home. Tom was there when they arrived and looked contrite. He pulled Cody in for a hug. "Hey, buddy, I'm glad you're okay."

"Thanks, Dad. Did you win?"

"No, we lost. The other team killed us." He looked at Sara and smiled but she was so furious she could barely speak.

"We picked up Kream 'N Kone for dinner. There's a burger for you in the bag."

She put the food on the kitchen table and headed to her bedroom to change. She needed a moment to herself. She washed her face and changed into her oldest and softest sweats and matching sweatshirt—her comfy clothes.

She went back to the kitchen to help herself to a cheeseburger and some fries. The boys were done eating and were scattered between the family room and the den. Cody was lying on the family room sofa with a blanket over him and his eyes closed. She stopped there first and gently pushed his hair off his face, leaned over, and dropped a kiss on his forehead. "Would you rather go to your bedroom, honey? It's probably quieter there."

"No, I'm good here, Mom. I'm just resting and I like listening to the TV a little."

"Okay. Let me know if you need anything."

"I will."

Sarah continued on to the kitchen. Tom sat at the table, a half-eaten burger in front of him. He watched her but said nothing as she unwrapped a burger and grabbed a handful of lukewarm fries. She wasn't ready to talk to him, so she ate in silence, dipping her fries in ketchup and taking her time. Finally, when she'd finished, he spoke softly. "Sara, I'm so sorry. I thought it would be fine to leave Cody. He's twelve."

She glared at him. "We agreed that he's too young to be left alone with the others. It's too much at his age. It would be different if he was by himself."

"You're right. I'm sorry."

"You didn't listen to your message right away, did you?" Sara asked.

Tom said nothing, but a red flush crept across his cheeks and she knew that's exactly what happened. "You thought I was just calling to give you grief and you didn't want to hear it. It never occurred to you that something might have happened to one of your children. Because you are too self-absorbed to think about that."

He glared back at her. "I booked this tee time a week ago. It's not my fault your stupid little job got in the way again."

Sara stood. "That is unforgivable, Tom. I'm going to bed."

♦

Sara's mind was made up. But she couldn't act right away. She waited a week, to make sure that Cody was really okay. He was fine. A few days later, he wanted to play video games and go back to sports. She said no to both, per the doctor's orders, but she was glad he was feeling better.

She also wanted to see how Tom behaved. If the scare with Cody had any impact and if his overall behavior improved. But it didn't. She stayed late again the following Monday when Alison needed help covering a shift. Tom was grumpy about it and once again, couldn't be bothered to put any food in the oven. Sara had to do it all when she got home. And she'd had enough. She called Aunt Maddie first to make sure the offer was still on and then she went into Tom's office and closed the door. It was almost six thirty and he was sitting at this desk sipping a cold beer.

"Tom, all you had to do was put the casserole in the oven to warm it up." It had even been precooked this time. An American chop suey, and she always added mozzarella cheese and heated it in the oven for fifteen minutes before serving.

"I made myself a sandwich, so I didn't think of it."

"What about the boys, Tom?"

"They're fine. They're playing video games. I figured you'd take care of them when you got home."

"What about me? I've been working all day. All you had to do was put the tray in the oven, so it would be ready when I got home. I'm exhausted, Tom, and I'm hungry." She was frustrated beyond belief.

"If it's too much for you, just quit. Like I said before, it's not like we need the money."

Sara left the office and slammed the door behind her. She put the casserole in the oven after adding extra cheese on top. Then she went to her bedroom to pack while it heated up. When it was ready, she called the kids to come eat and they all gathered around the kitchen table. And then she told them she was going away.

"I'll be gone for a week. But your dad will be here. Cody, you can keep an eye on the others, too."

"Where are you going?"

"I won't be far. I'm going to stay with Auntie Hannah and Auntie Maddie. It's a girls' vacation and your mommy needs one."

"I'll watch them," Cody said seriously. The others nodded. Her youngest seemed the most concerned. "You'll be back soon, promise?" he asked.

"Of course, I promise."

After she cleaned up the kitchen, she went to the bedroom and wheeled out her suitcase. She wheeled it right into Tom's office. He was still on the computer, chuckling at something on the screen. He looked up when she walked in without knocking and he raised his eyebrows at the suitcase.

"What's going on?"

"I'm done, Tom. I'm sick of it and I won't stand for it anymore. You have no respect for what I do and you don't appreciate how important my job at the bookshop is to me. You're selfish and self-absorbed and it's time you thought of someone besides yourself for a while."

"Okay . . . but where are you going?"

"I'm taking a break. A one-week me vacation. Long overdue. I'm staying with Hannah and Aunt Maddie and I'm not coming back until next Monday. And what happens after that depends on you."

"You're leaving?" He was still trying to process what that meant.

She nodded. "Yes. So, for the next week you're going to fill my shoes as well as your own. You'll work from home in the afternoons, and pick up the kids, make dinner, and breakfast, do laundry, and shuttle them wherever they need to go. You'll put them first for a change. And when I come back, we'll talk. Things need to change, Tom. This isn't fair and I'm not happy."

"I have to work," he protested.

"You're a VP and your schedule is flexible. Plan your week and schedule your meetings while the kids are in school. I left you a sheet of paper that has their sports activities for the week and what time each boy needs to be picked up. You might want to go grocery shopping. I usually do that on Tuesdays and we're getting low on things." She smiled. "Have a good week, and don't call me unless someone is in the hospital." The parting remark stuck and Tom's jaw dropped. It finally registered that she was serious.

"See you in a week," she said as she wheeled her suitcase toward the door.

Chapter 33

It was great having Sara stay with them. Hannah was sorry that her sister and her husband were going through a stressful time, but she was glad that Sara was getting a break. They treated it like a real vacation, even though Sara went in to work each morning. Aunt Maddie had breakfast waiting for her when she woke up and every night they had dinner with her and Uncle Richie on the deck.

Thursday night, Hannah and Sara headed back into town to meet Natalie and Spencer at the Squire after work. Natalie's boyfriend was finally back from Dubai and was joining them as well. Niall had called and wanted to do something over the weekend, but Hannah explained about Sara and said she wanted to wait until she went home. She wanted to enjoy this time with her sister.

Sara drove and as they pulled into the lot her phone rang. She answered and it was connected to her car, so Hannah heard Tom's voice come over the speakerphone. He sounded defeated. "Sara, you win. Can you please just come home tonight? I promise I'll be more understanding."

"Hi, Tom," Sara said cheerfully. "How's everything going?"

"Well, let's see. I forgot to pick up Dylan yesterday. He called me and was waiting there alone because his father didn't get him on time. I remembered to put one of your frozen lasagnas in the oven, but I forgot to turn the oven on. I went back an hour later and it was still frozen solid. I ruined a load of laundry. My best white work shirt is now pink. And that's only the start of it. You deserve a raise."

Sara laughed. "I'm sorry."

"It's okay. Just say you'll come home. You made your point. We can't get by without you. Come home tonight. The kids all miss you." He sighed. "I miss you."

Sara chewed her bottom lip and Hannah could tell Tom was getting to her. She caught her sister's eye and shook her head, willing her to stay strong.

"Thanks for calling, Tom. I can't come home yet. I'm enjoying my vacation. Hannah and I are on our way out to meet her friends for drinks. I'll see you Monday after work."

"Oh, I'm on speakerphone? Hi, Hannah."

"Hi, Tom." Hannah tried to keep the laughter out of her voice.

"All right. I'll see you on Monday, Sara. Love you."

"You, too. Bye, Tom."

Sara ended the call and glanced at Hannah. "Am I a terrible person for not going home? He sounds miserable."

"You're not a terrible person. It's good for him. He'll appreciate you all the more when you go home on Monday. And hopefully things will change for the better."

Sara sighed. "I hope so."

❀

The Squire was busy as usual. Natalie, Spencer, and a tall man with dark brown hair and an easy smile who had his arm wrapped around Natalie's shoulders were by the wall because there were no open seats at the bar. Natalie introduced her boyfriend, Adam, and he insisted on buying the first round.

Three seats opened up at the bar and Natalie, Hannah, and Sara slid into them. They had a fun night. Natalie's boyfriend was the life of the party and knew so many people. They kept coming up to him and saying hello. "You're like the mayor of Chatham," Natalie teased him.

"It's just that I've been away and haven't seen people in a while. It's good to be back," Adam said.

Sara excused herself to use the restroom and Spencer came closer to chat with Hannah while she was gone. The band had started to play so it was loud and hard to hear. "How's she doing?" he asked.

"It's been good for her to take this break. And it's been nice for both of us. I feel like I'm on vacation, too. We are going to take a drive down to Provincetown on Saturday and we thought we might stay in Wellfleet that night and maybe have dinner at Mac's and drop into the Beachcomber to hear some music."

Spencer smiled. "That sounds fun." His smile disappeared and he tensed up suddenly and Hannah saw the reason why. Michelle had sidled up next to him and put her hand on his arm.

"Spencer, it's so nice to run into you!" She glanced Hannah's way for all of two seconds before turning her attention back to Spencer. She looked very pretty. Her hair was longer and curled into soft waves and her cheeks were pink from the sun. She looked as though she'd been working out. She was wearing a sleeveless bright aqua dress that showed off her tanned, toned arms. Hannah noticed that several men nearby were looking at her.

"Hi, Michelle. How are you?" Spencer didn't look pleased to see her.

"I'm good. Can we talk for a minute?"

"Now?" Spencer seemed uncomfortable, irritated even.

"Let's walk outside for a minute. The band is taking a break. You won't miss anything."

"All right."

Sara came back just as Spencer disappeared with Michelle.

"Did Spencer leave?" Sara asked.

"Michelle showed up. They went outside to talk."

Spencer made his way back into the Squire. Hannah's and Sara's eyes were full of questions when he reached them, but neither of them said a word. They waited for him to speak.

"I agreed to go on one date. She's upset that she was dumped and she's insistent that she wants to be with me. I don't really think she does. But it seemed easier to just go and then we can both say we tried."

"I think it's a good idea, actually," Hannah said. Spencer looked surprised to hear it.

"At least you'll know better once you go on an actual date with her, if you want to do it again. People do get through things like this. Remember what your grandmother said—just take it one date at a time." Hannah didn't love the idea of Spencer dating Michelle again, but she thought it might give him closure.

۞

Hannah was sorry to see Sara go on Monday. They lingered over coffee with Aunt Maddie in the sunroom and Sara admitted she was looking forward to going home.

"This week has been incredible. Thank you both so much. I am looking forward to seeing the kids later today and I'm even looking forward to seeing Tom, too."

They both laughed. Sara seemed more relaxed and lighter than Hannah had seen her in a long time. The week had been good for her. They'd had a great time Saturday in Provincetown. They'd had lunch at the Lobster Pot and strolled around all afternoon, walking up and down Commercial Street and stopping in shops that looked interesting.

Hannah bought a new pair of boots and Sara picked up a small, pretty painting of the ocean by a local artist. She planned to put it in her bedroom so she'd see it first thing every morning. They'd had sushi at Mac's Shack in Wellfleet, danced to live music at the Beachcomber, and stayed at an old but very clean motel just off the highway. It had been the perfect getaway.

"I'm going to miss you," Hannah said. "It's been nice having you here."

"It has," Aunt Maddie agreed. "You know you're always welcome here, Sara. Both of you."

✿

Sara rushed home after her shift ended at the bookshop. The kids were still at school, but Tom was home, working in his office. He came out to the kitchen a minute after she walked in the door.

"Hey there," she said as he walked over to her.

He wrapped his arms around her, pulled her close, and gave her a meaningful kiss. And then he said, "Thank god you're home. Promise me you'll never leave me again?"

Sara laughed. "That bad, huh?"

"Seriously, I'm so sorry, Sara. I had no idea. I've just always taken for granted what you do. You make it look easy. It's not."

She smiled. "Now you know why I needed to go back to work?"

He nodded. "I love our boys, but I couldn't be home all day, just taking care of the house and running around driving them here and there and cooking and shopping. Don't even get me started on the hell that is grocery shopping!"

Sara laughed again. "I don't actually mind that."

He looked into her eyes and she felt his sincerity. "I'll never suggest that you give up your job again. I get it now. And I'll try to pull my weight more and help out. Oh, and we're going out Friday night. Just me and you, for a date night. I already booked Emma."

That was music to Sara's ears. "Thank you. I approve of that plan."

He pulled her close again and kissed her, and she kissed him back. It was good to be home.

Chapter 34

A week later, Niall took Hannah out for their third date. They went for dinner and drinks at the country club that his parents belonged to. Hannah was curious to see the place. She'd never been and had always heard it whispered about. She didn't know anyone other than Niall who had been there. It was that exclusive.

"Just wear whatever you like. I'm sure you'll look great," he'd said when she asked him about the attire.

Natalie was more helpful when she called in a panic an hour before the date. "So, I've never been, either, but you can't go wrong with a little black dress."

That turned out to be good advice. Hannah wore a classic sleeveless dress with pink sandals and a black leather clutch. Niall picked her up and he looked handsome in a navy blazer and a crisp white shirt and light green tie.

Throughout the evening Hannah took many mental notes to keep in mind for future novels. She'd never been to a place quite like this. Where there were Maseratis, Lamborghinis, multiple Teslas, and other cars that she didn't recognize but suspected were way out of her price range. There was a door attendant outside and she felt like she was about to enter a grand hotel instead of a country club.

The attendant was gray-haired and stood tall in his navy-and-gold uniform. He recognized Niall and welcomed him with a smile.

"It's good to see you, Mr. Peterson. Enjoy your evening."

Niall grinned. "Thank you, Carl. Good to see you, too."

They stepped inside and Hannah was initially surprised by how ordinary it looked. She'd expected something fancier, but it was just a lobby that led to the locker rooms, tee shop, and the restaurant.

Once they were seated in the club restaurant, though, Hannah felt the air of luxury she'd expected from the soaring ceiling, with polished wood beams that ran the length of the room, to the plush black leather chairs, the thick white linens, gleaming hardwood floors, and the servers, all men, who glided efficiently from one table to another, clad in black pants, matching black vests, crisp white button-down shirts, and black ties.

She was surprised by the simplicity of the menu. It was not extensive or experimental in any way. Nor was it trendy—if anything, it was dated. Entrées like baked scrod, roast chicken, or filet mignon were served with a choice of baked or Delmonico potatoes. Appetizers were limited to shrimp cocktail, oysters on the half shell, and clam chowder.

They decided to split a shrimp cocktail and both ordered the filet. Niall picked out a bottle of wine, a Caymus reserve cabernet. Hannah had once had a regular Caymus cabernet with Lucy on her birthday. It was a very special-occasion kind of wine, and had been a gift from Lucy's father. And this was a reserve.

The server poured a small amount into their glasses, after Niall tasted and approved it. As expected, it was amazing, and as the bottle sat it opened up even more. By the time their steaks arrived, it was richer and silky smooth and made the food taste even better.

Throughout the meal, Niall was constantly greeted by members as they passed by. He seemed to know everyone, friends of his parents and people his own age. Hannah didn't recognize a single person. She didn't exactly move in the same social circles, but she'd thought having grown up in Chatham that she might see at least one familiar face. She also realized that while Chatham was one of the wealthier areas of the Cape, it was doubtful that all the people dining were actually residents.

"I wonder how many people live here year-round?" she asked.

Niall thought for a moment. "I think the majority are from somewhere else. Chatham is where they have a second home."

That made her feel a little sad. To think that the majority of people in town would never be able to afford to come here. Spencer, for example—it could be a great networking place for him. But he'd never be able to afford it, and she knew he wasn't all that keen on networking anyway. Still, it bothered her a little, the unfairness of it all. She'd also heard that there were long waiting lists—people often waited years to be accepted to country clubs like this. And you had to know someone to even be considered.

"How long has your family been members here?"

"Since they bought the place in Chatham a few years ago. My father knows someone on the board and he moved him to the front of the line." Of course.

They lingered over coffee and dessert, a baked Alaska that Niall insisted they order when Hannah said she was too full for dessert. "We'll share it. Bring her a spoon. She won't be able to resist taking a few bites," he told their server.

And he was right. The dessert was magnificent, and a relic from another era. Hannah remembered reading about it in old novels set in the fifties and sixties. It had a layer of cake topped with ice cream, covered with meringue, and baked until the meringue turned golden.

Niall was an entertaining dinner companion. He made her laugh with his many stories of his adventures and she enjoyed the peek into his world. When she asked if he liked living in the East Village, he told her about his apartment there.

"It's a two-bedroom in the Nathaniel building. I just moved in a year ago. It's a great spot. Kind of an artsy area but convenient, too. There's a nice grocery store on the ground level. I could easily go weeks without leaving the building." He grinned. "I only do that, though, when I'm at the finish line of a book or trying to meet a deadline."

Hannah could relate. If there was a grocery store in her building it would be tempting to hunker down and be a hermit, too.

"I'm actually heading back to the city tomorrow for a few weeks. I have some meetings with my publisher and there's a conference they want me to speak at."

Hannah imagined he was invited to speak often at writing conferences. She hadn't been, yet. And wasn't sure it was something she looked forward to. She'd never enjoyed public speaking. But still, it would be nice to be invited. She guessed she was several books away from that possibility, though.

"Will you be back for the Fourth?" The first week of July was the biggest tourist week of the year for Cape Cod and there were fireworks at Veterans Field in Chatham and a parade.

"I wouldn't miss it."

Niall signed for the meal, putting it on his family's account. He stopped and chatted briefly with a few people on their way out and introduced Hannah to everyone, letting them all know that she was a writer, too. Everyone was friendly and she could sense their curiosity, wondering if she and Niall were an item.

It still felt very early-stage to her though. Although she was getting a glimpse of Niall's world, she still didn't feel like she really knew him all that well. She liked him, but there was a distance there. She wasn't sure how close she wanted to get and sensed that he felt the same.

He walked her to her front door, and gave her an enthusiastic good-night kiss. "I'll be in touch when I'm back in town."

Chapter 35

Lucy called a week after Niall went to New York for his publisher meetings to let Hannah know about an item she'd seen on Page Six, the gossip page.

"Did Niall mention anything to you about Goldie Barnes? There's a picture of the two of them going to an event at the Met and they were spotted a few times at area restaurants looking all cozy." Goldie Barnes was a twenty-two-year-old supermodel who was impossibly tall, thin, and stop-traffic gorgeous.

"Goldie Barnes? No." Hannah quickly looked it up online and sure enough, there was Niall with Goldie all glammed up and looking very into each other.

"Wow. I can't say I'm totally surprised though," Hannah admitted. "He's never dated anyone for more than six months and things never got at all serious with us. He actually seemed a bit distant the last time I saw him."

"Well, better to find out fast, right?" Lucy said.

"Yes, absolutely. On a different note, I'm so excited for you to come visit. Do you have your ticket yet?" Lucy was coming to Chatham the week of the Fourth. Hannah thought that would be a great time to play tourist on Cape Cod.

"I fly in on Friday. Can't wait!"

Hannah chatted with Lucy for another twenty minutes or so, then made herself a cup of cinnamon tea and took it out to the sunroom where her aunt was watching TV. She had a stack of manuscripts next to her and looked like she'd just stopped working. Hannah filled her aunt in on the news Lucy had shared.

"Oh, that's too bad. Now that I think of it, though, I have seen him in the paper a few times with different women, almost always models. I hope you're not too upset, honey?"

Hannah shook her head and took a sip of tea. Its spicy warmth soothed her. "No. I'm just a little disappointed. He was fun company, but I think I knew it was never going to go anywhere."

Hannah thought back to Joy's advice and smiled. She was so right that it was good to take things slow and get to really know someone before ruling them out or falling hard. That way it was easier to move on when they showed you who they were.

She was excited for Lucy to meet her friends and family. She was coming for ten days and Hannah was excited to play tourist with her. It was always fun to see her hometown through the eyes of someone who had never been there before. It reminded her of how special Chatham and Cape Cod were and she appreciated how lucky she was to have a home there.

❦

She picked Lucy up on Friday at the airport in Hyannis. Lucy was damp and sweaty but all smiles when she saw Hannah and gave her a big hug.

"It's so good to see you and we couldn't have picked a better weekend," Lucy said. "It's like a sauna in the city. Oppressively hot. It feels twenty degrees cooler here."

A salty cool breeze blew by them as they walked to the car. Lucy tossed her bag in the back seat and climbed in the front, next to Hannah. Hannah gave her a running commentary as they drove down Route 28, pointing out various landmarks along the way.

When they entered Chatham and Hannah saw her mother's house straight ahead on the right, she mentioned it. "That's where I grew up." They'd found someone to cut the grass and it looked healthy and lush.

"Oh, it's so cute. Such a pretty place to live," Lucy said enthusiastically.

She was even more enthusiastic when they stepped into Aunt Maddie's kitchen and Lucy caught a glimpse of the ocean view beyond it.

"I can see why you love it here," Lucy said. "This view is just beyond. I'd never want to leave the deck."

Aunt Maddie walked up then and laughed. "Welcome. We love it, too, and spend a lot of time there. Richie's out with his friends golfing and Sara should be here any minute. I thought we could sit outside and have some wine."

"Perfect." Hannah hadn't been sure if Sara could make it when she spoke to her earlier. Tom was out golfing, too, and she'd been waiting to hear back from Emma as to whether she could watch the boys for a few hours.

Sara arrived a few minutes later and joined them on the deck. Aunt Maddie poured chardonnay for everyone and set out a bowl of chips, guacamole, and salsa. Hannah introduced Lucy to Sara.

"I feel like I already know you," Lucy said. "Hannah talks about you so often."

Sara smiled. "I feel the same. It always sounds like the two of you are having so much fun in the city."

"We are. I've missed Hannah this summer. Can't wait for you to come home to Brooklyn."

Hannah felt a pang of homesickness thinking about Brooklyn and all the places she and Lucy liked to go. There was always something going on.

"How are things with Tom?" Aunt Maddie asked.

"So much better," Sara said. She looked happier, Hannah noticed, more relaxed.

"Hannah told me about your week off. It sounds like that helped?" Lucy asked.

Sara nodded. "Tom came around totally after that. He even admitted it was good for him to spend a week in my shoes. Things are much better between us now. He's more considerate and we're going out for regular date nights now. I think that has helped a lot, having that alone time together."

They had a relaxing evening, drank more wine, laughed, and ate the pizzas Aunt Maddie ordered. Finally, around ten, Sara went home and Aunt Maddie yawned a few times. Lucy joined her and they decided to call it a night.

✺

Hannah and Lucy slept in the next day and got up around nine. They decided to go for a long walk along Shore Road and Hannah pointed out the Chatham Bars Inn.

"It's so pretty, with those rolling lawns and all that white it looks like something out of *The Great Gatsby*," Lucy said.

"I thought the same thing. I thought we could maybe have dinner there later and sit outside. We're meeting up with Spencer, Natalie, and Adam at the Woodshed in Brewster after that to hear some live music."

"Sounds good to me. I'll go anywhere."

After their walk, they had coffee with Aunt Maddie and chatted in the sunroom. After they'd showered and dressed, Hannah took Lucy for a drive to Main Street and they strolled like tourists, stopping into the different shops, including the bookshop and Hannah's favorite boutique where they had the cutest shoes. Lucy couldn't resist and bought a new pair of dressy sandals.

After they were all shopped out, they stopped at the coffee shop and had bagels and coffee and said hello to Caitlin, who was behind the counter. Hannah introduced her to Lucy.

"You live in Brooklyn, too? That sounds so fun. I went to New York with my girlfriends a year or so ago and I loved the energy of the city. We had a blast. Though I have to admit, I prefer it here. The Cape is my happy place."

"I can see why," Lucy said. "It's beautiful here."

When they left the coffee shop, they headed back to Aunt Maddie's and spent the rest of the afternoon on her beach, sitting in beach chairs and reading trashy gossip magazines and sipping bottled waters.

"I'm not sure I'd want to come back to Brooklyn after spending the summer here," Lucy said. "How can you leave this?"

Hannah laughed. "Well, this is Aunt Maddie's house and I can't stay here indefinitely."

"What about your mother's house?" Lucy asked. "You could stay there whenever you wanted, right?"

Hannah had plans to go there the Sunday of Labor Day weekend, before heading back to Brooklyn. She and Sara and Aunt Maddie were going to go through the house, look through her mother's things, and make some decisions on what to do with everything. She'd put it off as long as she could, but it had to be done before she went home. They all needed to go there, for closure.

"Technically, I could. But none of us really want to stay there. It's my mother's house. And it would just be too sad."

Lucy nodded. "I get that. And I am glad that you're coming back soon. I did worry a bit that you might decide not to."

"Brooklyn is where I live now. Chatham is where I grew up. It's been nice spending time with Sara and Aunt Maddie this summer, though. I do need to make an effort to get here more often."

"Did you sign your new lease yet?" Lucy asked.

Hannah had forwarded her mail to Aunt Maddie's house and the new lease had arrived just a few days ago. Her current lease expired at the end of September and she needed to sign and get it back to her landlord soon. She was planning on just dropping it off when she got back, and her landlord was fine with that.

☙

"How are things going with Richie?" Kathryn asked. It was just past four on a Friday, three weeks after he'd come home, and Maddie was surprised it had taken her this long to ask. Kathryn had been straight out at work, though, trying to get things squared away before her yearly vacation, and she'd just been back for a few days.

"They're good. We're in a good place now. We kind of eased back into it and now it feels like things are the way they used to be. I needed to get used to having him here again, especially after what he told me about Laura." She filled Kathryn in and she was quiet for a minute.

"I'm not surprised. I definitely picked up that vibe from her. It's funny how things can look a certain way when only one person is feeling it. She was trying to will it to be real," Kathryn said.

"I told Richie the same thing. He questioned himself and his ability to read a room because he never saw it, at all."

"He probably just liked the attention and assumed since they were both married to other people that there was nothing to it."

"Right. I couldn't just jump right back into how things were, though. I needed to process that. He understood. He gave me the space and time that I needed."

"I always liked Richie. I'm glad you two worked it out. So, fill me in on what I missed while I was gone."

Maddie moved out onto the deck while still giving Kathryn an update. It was a warm, sunny day and it felt good to stretch her legs. After this call, she was going to call it quits and see if Richie wanted to get dinner somewhere. She felt like going out.

"Maddie, I'm actually going to be on the Cape this weekend, staying at the Chatham Bars Inn. If you have time on Sunday, I'd love to meet up there for brunch. I have something I'd like to run by you."

"Sure, I have no plans on Sunday. Brunch sounds great." Maddie wasn't sure what Kathryn wanted to talk to her about. She knew that they'd recently brought on two new agents; maybe it had something to do with that. Kathryn often bounced management ideas off of her as situations came up. And since Maddie had been there so long, she was always happy to share her thoughts.

She sipped from her water bottle as she leaned against the deck railing and looked out over the ocean. There were several sailboats in the distance and a fishing boat heading back into the harbor. She was just saying goodbye to Kathryn when she felt a pair of warm, familiar arms wrap around her from behind.

"Have a good weekend, Kathryn. I'll talk to you Sunday."

Richie nuzzled her neck and whispered in her ear, "Are we done working yet?"

She turned around and put her arms on his shoulders and pulled him closer.

"I'm all yours now."

His eyes lit up and he leaned in and kissed her. She felt a rush of happiness. Things were so much better now. It was like she and Richie were in the honeymoon stage again and she was in no hurry for that to change.

♦

Sunday was a gorgeous day, sunny and warm. Maddie met Kathryn at the Chatham Bars Inn and they sat inside at a table with a view of the water. They both ordered the lobster eggs Benedict and mimosas.

"How was your weekend?" Maddie asked. She'd never stayed at the Chatham Bars Inn but it was so elegant and comfortable at the same time.

"Relaxing. I can see why you love it here so much. It's a nice change of pace from the city. It's stifling there right now. You know how the summer heat is."

"I do. I have to admit I'd much rather be here this time of year especially."

Kathryn took a sip of her mimosa and smiled. "You miss the city a little, though, don't you? The energy of everyone working in the office, the great restaurants just a short walk away."

Maddie nodded. "I do always enjoy my trips into town."

"What if you could make those trips a little longer?" Kathryn paused dramatically and Maddie had no idea what she was about to suggest. She said nothing and waited for Kathryn to continue.

"As you may know, I'm no spring chicken. I just turned seventy-five this April and while I think I could keep going indefinitely, my husband and I had a serious discussion recently. He wants me to step back. If it was up to him, he'd have me retire completely, but I couldn't do that. He wants to travel more and spend time with our grandkids. I'd like to do those things, too."

"What are you proposing?" It made sense that Kathryn might want to slow down a bit. But Maddie wasn't sure how she fit in.

"I'd like you to consider stepping into a management role. I'd like to be in the office one day a week, probably on a Friday or a Monday and maybe once a month be in for the week. That would mean that I'd like you to be here two or three weeks out of the month—we could work that out. And it would just be four days a week, you could have Friday to travel home to Chatham."

The offer took Maddie by surprise. "I've honestly never thought about managing an office."

"I think you'd be very good at it. You're the most senior person working for me and you know the industry inside and out. And you've always been great with the junior agents, they think of you as a mentor." That was true. Maddie did enjoy helping the new agents and they often called to ask her advice on sticky client issues if Kathryn wasn't available.

"Would I still be able to keep my authors?" Maddie asked. She didn't want to give that up.

"Of course. I wouldn't take anything away from you. And you'd be paid a significant increase for the management duties. This is what I was thinking of . . ." She mentioned a number that almost made Maddie drop her drink. It was very significant. And it would be hard to turn down. But it meant a big change in her lifestyle, one that she wasn't sure she wanted. She loved her life in Chatham, working by the ocean.

"Thank you. I'm flattered that you have faith in me to take this on," Maddie began.

"It's a great opportunity for you. A new challenge and a chance to stretch yourself. But I know you weren't expecting this. And of course you'll have to discuss it with Richie as it will affect him, too."

Kathryn looked up as their food was set down. They were both quiet for a moment as they took a bite of their lobster and eggs. Maddie's head was spinning. She hadn't planned on ever going back to Manhattan again, other than the occasional work trip. She had very mixed feelings about this opportunity.

Kathryn reached for the salt and pepper shakers and added a bit more of each to her eggs. "Richie loves it in the city, doesn't he? Just think of how much fun the two of you could have. And you could still go home to Chatham on weekends and one or two full weeks a month. It could be the best of both worlds. What do you think?"

"It's tempting, of course. But I'm really not sure if this is the right move for me, or for us. I'm going to need some time to think about this and talk to Richie."

"Of course. Take all the time you need," Kathryn said. "But the sooner you can let me know the better. If you are not able to do this, then I'll have to make other arrangements." She smiled and cut into her eggs.

Maddie knew that Kathryn expected her to take the offer. It really was a fantastic opportunity all around. She'd be crazy not to take it. But was it really what she wanted? And what was best for her relationship with Richie?

☙

She told Richie about the offer over dinner that night. They had the house to themselves as Hannah was out with Lucy. They were sitting outside on the deck, and were eating grilled bluefish that Richie had caught that afternoon and cooked on the grill. Maddie had been thinking about the conversation all day and went back and forth about what she wanted to do.

"What do you think about it?" Richie asked, when Maddie finished relaying the conversation to him.

"I really am torn. It's a great opportunity, completely unexpected, and it's nothing I had been expecting or striving for. But now that it has fallen in my lap I'm not sure what to do about it. Part of me likes the idea of a new challenge and being more hands-on with everyone. The other part of me isn't sure I want to lose what we have here. I like my lifestyle in Chatham, working from home with you."

"Well, I'm fine either way. So whatever you want to do, I'll support. It might be fun to spend more time in the city." He looked out over the water, at the sun that was turning the sky pink as it slowly slipped off the horizon. "But then again, it is so beautiful here." He laughed. "I'm glad I don't have to make that decision."

He winked at her and Maddie laughed. And relaxed a bit. She had worried a little about what Richie would think of the idea and was glad that he really seemed open to the possibility of spending more time in the city. Now she just had to decide if that's what she really wanted to do.

☙

Maddie had three good friends over for drinks and appetizers a few nights later. She'd gone to high school with Alison, Jess, and

Beth, though Jess had lived in Charleston since graduating from college and only moved back to Chatham a year or so ago when her marriage ended. Alison and Jess owned the bookshop and coffee shop downtown now. Alison ran it with her daughter, Julia, and Jess had an office nearby where she practiced law. Beth owned an inn at the end of Main Street and the four of them often got together to catch up over dinner or drinks.

Maddie picked up a platter of shrimp cocktail, which was easy as the girls all loved shrimp. Beth brought an assortment of cheeses and salami, and Jess laughed when she set down her offering.

"Caitlin made this for us. It's a buffalo chicken dip. It's decadent and delicious."

Alison brought dessert: homemade brownies. They brought everything out to the deck and sipped chardonnay and ate everything while catching each other up.

"Well, I have big news," Alison said. "Julia and Tim got engaged over the weekend!"

"Oh, that's great news," Maddie said. "And you really like him? I know you weren't crazy about her last boyfriend."

Alison made a face. "That's an understatement. No, we love Tim. And I think it's cute that they've been friends forever, but never looked at each other that way until about a year ago."

"That's wonderful," Beth said.

"I have some news, too," Jess said. "Ryan and I are moving in together. In about thirty days. We found a house we both fell in love with. It's not on the ocean, but it is across the street and has great views and a huge yard."

"Congratulations," Maddie said. "Do you think the two of you will ever get married?" She thought she knew the answer, but she hadn't expected Jess to buy a house with Ryan so soon.

Jess laughed. "No. I'm not ruling it out completely but neither one of us is in a rush for that. We're happy just being together, and after one divorce that's not something I want to do again."

Maddie nodded. She understood that. She looked at Beth. "Any big news from you? How's Riley?"

Beth laughed. "Not a thing. Riley's good. Still loving living in the city. She's been dating that lawyer for a few years now, but hasn't mentioned getting engaged, so I don't want to put pressure on her. I have yet to meet him. He's always too busy to make the trip to the Cape." She laughed it off, but Maddie knew it bothered her. She'd mentioned before that her daughter's boyfriend was a workaholic. He was on the partner track at a Manhattan law firm. So that was to be expected.

"Well, I guess I have some news to share. Speaking of Manhattan . . ." She told the girls about her offer and for a moment there was silence as they took it in.

"Congratulations on the offer. That's fantastic news—if that is what you want?" Jess asked.

"Yes, congrats. If you do go, you know we'll miss you. But you'll be back and forth, right?" Alison said.

Maddie nodded. "Yes, I'll be able to get back here on weekends and for one or maybe two full weeks a month."

"That's a great offer. Do you know what you want to do?" Beth asked.

Maddie shook her head. "I'm so torn. I keep going back and forth."

Beth took a sip of wine, then said something that really struck Maddie. "When you think about all the pros and cons, be sure to think about how you would feel if you pass up the opportunity. Do you feel relief or regret?"

Maddie felt her eyes grow damp as she looked around the table at her friends. "That's great advice, Beth. I will think long and hard about that. And thanks to all of you for your support. If I do go, I will really miss you guys."

Jess raised her glass and the others followed her lead. "We're not going anywhere. We'll still be here, even if we only see you once a month. It's all good."

Hannah, Lucy, Natalie, and Adam sat on Spencer's back deck the Saturday after the Fourth of July weekend. He'd invited them over for drinks and pizza. After they finished eating, Natalie demanded an update on Michelle. "So, are you back together or what?"

Spencer reached for his beer, and took a sip before answering. "I gave it a try with Michelle. We went out a few times, but I just couldn't make it work. I thought maybe I could. We had a great first date and I remembered how much fun she could be. But at the end of the day, I can't be with someone that I can't trust. And she broke that trust when she left me for George." He sighed. "I told her that I didn't think it was going to work out, but it doesn't seem to have sunk in."

"She calls him constantly," Natalie said. "I recognize the ringtone."

"My grandmother says I need to have another conversation with her. She drops by all the time, too. Usually when I'm not in the mood for company," Spencer said.

"I dated someone like that once," Adam said. "Total lack of boundaries. She did the same thing when I called it quits. Kept dropping by unexpectedly to change my mind. She showed up at all the places I often went, too, which was even more annoying. I let it happen for a while, so that was on me."

"What's up with you and Niall, Hannah? You haven't mentioned him in a while." Spencer shifted the focus to Hannah.

"That didn't work out. We're too different."

"That's too bad. I thought he seemed really into you." Natalie sounded disappointed. Hannah hadn't had a chance to update her yet.

"I was never that sure of him. He was fun, but there was always something a little off to me. He's never had a long-term relationship. And I'm not sure he really wants one."

The conversation shifted and they all spent the rest of the evening laughing and telling stories. Hannah thought she noticed Spencer looking her way more often, but didn't think much of it. Lucy got along well with everyone, as Hannah expected she would. It was a fun night.

Later that evening, they stayed up watching movies and eating ice cream with Aunt Maddie. It had been such a great week. Hannah had felt like she was on vacation, too, yet she'd still managed to get some writing done in the early mornings while Lucy slept in. The book was rolling along now, finally, so Hannah didn't feel guilty about playing tourist with Lucy. Hannah showed her all her favorite places and Lucy loved them all.

Aunt Maddie headed to bed a little before eleven. Hannah and Lucy stayed up an hour or so longer, watching a few episodes of *Friends*. They were both reluctant to end the vacation. Lucy was heading back to New York the next day.

"I can see why you love it so much here," Lucy said.

"It's a beautiful place," Hannah agreed. "I always appreciate it more when I play tourist and see it through someone else's eyes."

"So, now that Niall is out of the picture . . . what about Spencer?" Lucy asked.

"I like Spencer too much to date him," Hannah said quickly.

Lucy raised her eyebrows. "What on earth does that mean?"

"Just that I don't want to start something that I can't finish. I'm heading back to Manhattan in a few months and, assuming there was even any interest, I don't think I'd like a long-distance relationship. And I don't want to hurt anyone."

"Didn't you say Spencer's own grandmother gave you some good dating advice? Something about not overthinking it and just enjoying each date as it comes?"

"She did say something like that," Hannah admitted.

Lucy smiled. "I thought so."

Hannah dropped Lucy off at the airport the next day and thought of what she'd said, when Spencer called that afternoon and wanted to see if she felt like seeing a movie. "I texted Natalie, too, to see if she and Adam wanted to join us, but I haven't heard back. It just opened at the Orpheum and I'm dying to see it." She didn't think it qualified as a date since he'd asked two of their friends along.

The movie was an action-suspense starring Ryan Reynolds, and Hannah had seen the trailer and thought it looked good, too. She'd also been meaning to get to the Orpheum since she'd been back in Chatham and hadn't gotten around to it. The movie theater was right at the start of Main Street and had been restored in recent years to her full glory. It was a beautiful building and felt a bit like going back in time when you stepped inside.

"Sure, I'll go." They made plans to meet outside the theater just before four.

Spencer was waiting by the door when she arrived.

"Natalie and Adam couldn't make it. They have dinner plans with her parents."

Hannah noticed that Spencer was wearing a shirt she hadn't seen before, in a deep blue green that made his eyes pop. He was smiling and she suddenly felt a different vibe from him.

They went inside and Spencer paid for their tickets. Hannah insisted on buying the popcorn. The movie wasn't too crowded and they found good seats in the middle of the theater.

The movie was entertaining and Hannah was on the edge of her seat the whole time. There were a few suspenseful moments where she actually jerked back in her chair, she was so into the story and startled. The second time it happened, Spencer laughed out loud.

When the movie finished and they walked outside, she laugh-ingly apologized.

"I do that. I get jumpy in movies like that. If it was a horror movie I probably would have grabbed your arm."

Spencer laughed. "I thought it was cute. You were so into it."

"That's how it is when I watch a movie or when I write a story. It's like it's totally real."

They were too full for dinner after having the popcorn but get-ting an ice cream seemed like a good idea. And it was a warm night, perfect for strolling Main Street. They walked to Buffy's Ice Cream shop and Spencer got a brownie sundae with hot fudge and Hannah got a big scoop of coffee Heath bar on an old-fashioned sugar cone. Spencer insisted on paying for the ice cream and Han-nah accepted and said she'd get it the next time.

They took their desserts to a wooden bench that overlooked Main Street and people-watched while they ate.

Hannah didn't ask, but Spencer brought up Michelle.

"She popped by right after we spoke this afternoon and wanted to do something. I told her that I already had plans with you."

Hannah noticed that he didn't mention Natalie and Adam. Maybe he worried she would invite herself along if it was a friend group going.

"How did that go over?" she asked.

"She didn't seem to listen to me, at first. When I said I was busy, she quickly said she wanted to make a plan to do something on another day, but I shut it down. I told her she couldn't keep stop-ping by and that she needed to move on. She didn't take it well." Spencer looked frustrated.

"She's upset now that the tables have turned. Do you think she will really stay away now?" Hannah hoped so.

"Yeah, I don't think she'll drop by again. I made it clear that she can't do that." His mood shifted as he smiled at Hannah. "I had fun tonight. I hope that we can hang out more this summer."

"I'd like that." Hannah felt relief that Spencer truly seemed to be over Michelle. And she definitely liked the thought of spending more time with him.

❦

A week later, Maddie woke up on a Monday morning and knew what she wanted to do. She felt a bounce in her step and she walked to the kitchen and made a cup of coffee for herself and for Richie, who was already in the shower. She handed him his coffee when he walked into the sunroom a few minutes later. His hair was still damp and tousled and he was wearing a crisp button-down shirt and his favorite seersucker shorts. He loved that he could wear shorts in his home office and be on Zoom video calls and no one would be the wiser.

"You look like you're in a good mood. Did you sleep well?" he asked.

Maddie was sitting on the soft love seat that faced the ocean, sipping her coffee and smiling as Richie walked toward her.

"I made a decision. Finally."

He sat down next to her. "Oh? And what did you decide?"

"Something Beth said resonated with me. She told me to imagine how I'd feel if I didn't take the job, would I feel relief or regret. And I wasn't sure at first. So, I needed to sit with the idea for a while. And as each day has gone by, I keep thinking about it and picturing myself doing the job. And instead of dreading it, I've been feeling excited about it. I think I want to try it. I don't want to regret passing an opportunity like this up. But only if you really are okay with it? Are you sure that you don't mind spending more time in the city? Kathryn said it wouldn't have to start until the fall, so we can still enjoy the summer."

Richie set his cup of coffee down and grinned. "I'm sure. It's a new adventure for both of us. Let's do it."

Chapter 36

The rest of the summer raced by and before Hannah knew it, it was mid-August. She finished her book and the final quarter of it came out in a mad rush of ten-hour days where all her muscles ached as she hunched over in her chair, fingers flying on the keyboard as she tried to get all the words down as fast as they came to her. It was her favorite part of the writing process, that last downward slide where she picked up speed and clocked daily word counts she could only dream of at the start of a book.

Meditation tapes had become a part of her daily routine, too. By emptying her mind for a half hour at the beginning of the day, it seemed to turn on a creative tap and she got some great ideas for new storylines. By the time she finished the book, her mind was already whirling with a new plot and she was itching to get started on it.

She and Spencer spent quite a bit of time together, as well. They often went out as a foursome with Natalie and Adam and it felt comfortable and fun. They hadn't crossed the line from friendship to romance yet, though Hannah had been tempted, but they both knew she wasn't staying in Chatham and it didn't make sense to start something. She definitely sensed at times that Spencer wanted more. But neither of them were ready to go there. People often assumed they were a couple, which Hannah found interesting, just because they were together often. And they were familiar with each other.

She knew Joy was hopeful that their friendship might turn into something more. But Hannah knew Spencer was never leaving Chatham so whenever the thought flitted into her mind, she banished it and got on with her day.

One night after dinner at the Impudent Oyster with Spencer, Natalie, and Adam, they walked across the street to the Squire to hear some live music.

A few seats opened up at the bar and Natalie and Hannah sat. Spencer ordered a round of drinks for them and it wasn't long before two more seats opened up next to them. It was a band they all liked and they got there in time to catch the last two sets.

"How's your friend Lucy?" Natalie asked. "Will she be coming back to visit this summer?"

"She's great. I don't think she will. She was hoping to, but her work has gotten so busy."

"Well, it won't be long before you're back there, too," Natalie said. "I will miss you, though."

"I'll miss you guys, too." Hannah didn't want the summer to end. She loved the city, but she was dreading leaving Chatham and her new friends behind.

"I can see why she's your best friend," Spencer said. He and Lucy had really hit it off. Spencer tended to be the quieter one in the group, usually listening and taking it all in, but Lucy had gotten him to open up. "I bet the two of you have a lot of fun there," he added.

"We do. Meeting Lucy was the best thing about my first job there," Hannah said.

After the next song ended, Hannah excused herself to visit the ladies' room. When she was finished and washing her hands, a familiar face walked in and stopped short when she saw Hannah. It was Michelle. Spencer's Michelle. The look she gave Hannah was a vicious one and took her by surprise.

"You live in New York, don't you?" Her tone was cold and accusatory.

"Yes."

"Just so you know, as soon as you leave, we're getting back together. He was going to ask me to marry him." Michelle stood with her hands on her hips, glaring at Hannah. It was disconcerting and annoying to say the least. Especially as there was nothing going on with her and Spencer.

"We're just friends, Michelle. Not that it's any of your business."

Michelle looked furious and hissed, "The sooner you leave, the better."

Hannah had had more than enough. "Excuse me." She walked by Michelle and opened the bathroom door. She couldn't get away from her fast enough.

When she sat back down at the table, Natalie saw her face and immediately asked what was wrong.

"I just ran into Spencer's Michelle in the bathroom."

He frowned. "She's not my Michelle."

"Well, she thinks she is or that she should be." She told them what Michelle had said and they all agreed that she was out of her mind.

"I'm so sorry, Hannah. I don't know what she was thinking," Spencer said.

"It's okay. It was just bizarre. I'm leaving soon, so I doubt I'll run into her again."

"Actually, she is heading toward this table," Natalie said.

Spencer turned to look and narrowed his eyes when he saw Michelle. Hannah had never seen him look so angry. Michelle saw it, too, and stopped in her tracks. The expression on her face shifted from determined to uncertain. She looked away and changed direction, walking out the door a minute later.

They all breathed a sigh of relief, especially Spencer. The band came back on for their last few songs and they ordered a final round for the table and enjoyed the rest of the evening.

Chapter 37

It was almost time to go back to Brooklyn. The clock was ticking and Hannah had mixed feelings about leaving Chatham. It was bittersweet to say her goodbyes to all her new friends. She'd grown close to Natalie and Spencer especially. And she'd miss seeing Caitlin every afternoon at the coffee shop and at cookouts now and then. But she was also looking forward to being back in Brooklyn and hanging out with Lucy again. She missed her best friend and looked forward to getting together with her again soon and going to their favorite local spots in the city.

Spencer invited her over Saturday night for a cookout at his place. Natalie and Adam were coming as well to say their goodbyes. Spencer said he had all the food covered, and to just bring whatever she wanted to drink, so she picked up a bottle of wine, a cabernet to go with his steak tips. She was feeling restless that afternoon, though, and decided to bake a batch of chocolate-chip cookies with extra chocolate and chopped nuts. They were still warm when she packed them into a cookie tin and brought them over to Spencer's house.

His eyes immediately went to the tin of cookies when she walked in the house.

"You baked?"

She nodded. "They're still warm. Want to try one—for quality control?"

"I can't say no to that." She opened the tin and they both had one.

"Those are too good. I might need one more, just to make sure . . ."

She laughed and handed him another cookie as Natalie and Adam arrived.

They went onto Spencer's back deck and Lady and Tramp immediately came over to investigate. Hannah was so impressed by how well behaved the dogs were. Tramp was such a big boy and Lady was so delicate with her long fur. They came around and said hello to everyone and then settled nearby on the deck.

Hannah thought that Spencer's house fit him perfectly. He'd had it built and it was a single-level open concept with a slanted roof that soared high in the main living area and had big wooden beams that went across the room. He had a finished basement, too, and there was a pool table and a two-car garage. The deck was a highlight though; it was big and wrapped around the side, which was where he put his grill.

Spencer fed the dogs first, and then they ate at a hightop table on his deck. He wasn't on the ocean, but he did have a view of a lake and the yard had lots of tall trees. It was a quiet neighborhood and the lots were big, which was nice.

The evening was so fun. They stayed on the deck all night, laughing and drinking wine, and later on, attacking the cookies. Finally, around eleven, Adam said he had to be up early the next day and Natalie yawned.

"I should probably head out, too," Hannah said as Natalie stood.

"If you don't mind staying a minute, Hannah, there's something I want to talk to you about."

"Sure." Hannah gave Natalie and Adam hugs goodbye and promised to keep in touch with Natalie.

"Anytime you want to come to the city, let me know," Hannah told her.

After they left, Hannah helped herself to another cookie and wondered what Spencer wanted to talk to her about. He'd seemed a little pensive all night. He'd laughed with the rest of them, but she sensed that something was on his mind.

"Let's go back outside. It's such a nice night," Spencer said.

Hannah followed him back outside. Instead of sitting at the table, he leaned against the deck railing. She walked over and stood next to him.

"So, what was it you wanted to talk to me about?"

"I just didn't want to let the whole summer go by without doing this at least once." Spencer smiled and leaned toward her and she realized what he was doing. It felt both unexpected and inevitable at the same time. He kissed her, tentatively at first, but when she responded back he pulled her close and kissed her with enthusiasm. The kiss lasted for a while and when it finally ended, Hannah felt dazed.

"Hannah, I wish you were staying in Chatham. I really hate to see you leave. I don't suppose there's any chance you might decide to stay?"

It was tempting. But she knew it wasn't possible. "I can't. Brooklyn is my home now—has been for years. I don't suppose you'd ever move to Brooklyn?" She knew he wouldn't. And he shook his head sadly.

"I can't. My life is here. My job. And my grandparents. They're like my parents and I can't leave them. I'd be miserable in Brooklyn."

"I'm sorry, Spencer. It's been so great getting to know you this summer. I wish things were different."

He nodded. "I know. But I couldn't let you go without letting you know how I feel. Just in case. If you change your mind about this, well, you know where to find me."

"I do. Goodbye, Spencer." She gave him a hug goodbye and he

squeezed her tight and then kissed her forehead gently. "Safe travels, Hannah. Come back and visit soon."

"I will." Hannah didn't expect it would be so hard to leave Chatham, and Spencer. She had very mixed feelings now about going back to Brooklyn. She was excited but also sad. She had a new appreciation now for Chatham and the people there. And she would miss them.

Chapter 38

Hannah woke early Sunday morning. Her head was still spinning from that kiss the night before. From the feeling of being in Spencer's arms and not wanting to leave. But she knew she had to. It just wouldn't work. Spencer couldn't leave Chatham and she was heading back to Brooklyn on Monday.

Sure, it had crossed her mind to move home and give it a go with Spencer, but that didn't feel right, either, to move home just because of a man—and with no guarantees that it would be something long-term. It was just a few months ago that she couldn't stand him. They'd become good friends and more since then, but still. Going back to Brooklyn and signing a new lease still felt like the right thing to do.

She went for a long walk, all the way to Chatham Bars Inn and back, listening to upbeat music the whole way and working up a sweat. It was only eight and it was already hotter than usual. The forecast was for the highest temps of the summer, close to a hundred, through Monday. She hoped the air-conditioning at her mother's house was still working. They were heading over there at eleven and planned to spend most of the day there.

She came home, showered, changed, and had two cups of coffee. Aunt Maddie and Uncle Richie were still in bed and it was only a quarter past nine. Hannah decided to get a head start on her packing and threw a load of laundry in as well.

By a quarter to eleven, her laundry was done and she was almost completely packed. She headed out to the kitchen and Aunt Maddie was sitting at the island, drinking coffee and checking the news on her iPad. She looked up when she heard Hannah's footsteps.

"Hi, honey, are you about ready to go?"

"As ready as I'll ever be." She'd been dreading this day all summer. Putting it off as long as she could. Her sister had been to the house a few times to check on any remaining mail and her aunt stopped in every few weeks just to make sure nothing needed attending to. Neither one of them had tackled going through her things yet. They were all dreading it.

Sara's car was in the driveway when they pulled up. She was still in it. She got out when she saw them.

"I wanted to wait for you to go in," she said. Hannah understood totally.

Aunt Maddie unlocked the front door and they stepped inside, into the living room. A heavy cloud of warmth enveloped them. Aunt Maddie turned the air-conditioning on and it whirred to life with a groan. But it worked and instantly began to cool the room.

What hit Hannah right away was that it looked like her mother still lived there. Like she'd just stepped out for a minute and would be right back. A book from one of her favorite authors was on the coffee table, a bookmark three quarters of the way through to mark the spot. Hannah felt a sharp pang of sadness to think that her mother never got to the ending—never knew how the book turned out.

She took a deep breath and looked around the living room at all the pictures on the wall. They were mostly family photos of Sara and Hannah at various ages and group family photos. There were none of her father. But there were quite a few of her mother's parents, the grandparents that she had only the faintest memory of. She was young when they passed. They'd both had health challenges and were older when they had their children. Their father's parents were still alive, but they lived in Arizona and rarely visited the East Coast.

It was the pictures of Sara, Hannah, and their mother that moved Hannah the most. It felt like it was always just the three of them against the world. They'd both been so close to their mother and she'd always been such a hard worker. It hadn't been easy to raise two children alone. Their father had sent child support but it wasn't much. More than once Hannah had wished it was their father who had gotten sick instead of their mother. She'd always felt horrible even thinking it, but Sara had confessed she'd had similar thoughts, too. It was just so unfair for someone as good as their mother to be taken at such a young age.

They made their way into their mother's bedroom and that's where Hannah lost it—when she saw the sweater she'd given her mother for Christmas hanging in the closet. Her mother had loved that sweater and now she'd never get to wear it again. The tears came fast and furious and she had to sit on the bed and try to get herself together. Aunt Maddie sat next to her and put her arm around her and wiped her own eyes with her other hand. Sara sat on her other side and gave her a hug.

"It's okay to cry, girls. Let it out," Aunt Maddie said. And they did. They were all three a blubbering mess for a good ten minutes. Sara got up at one point and came back with a box of tissues, which they all grabbed.

Once their tears dried up they spent the next hour just talking about their mother, remembering the happy times. And Hannah felt a change in the air, a sense of warmth and welcoming as if their mother was there wrapping her arms around them.

They gathered their strength and went through her closet and her drawers, organizing her clothes into piles and setting aside any items that they wanted for themselves, that had special meaning. Hannah took the sweater she'd given her mother and a few other sweaters and her mother's favorite old sweatshirt, a pale pink oversized one that simply said CHATHAM across the front. She'd bring it to Brooklyn and wear it in memory of her mom and on the days she missed Chatham, too.

They'd brought garbage bags with them and put most of the clothes into bags, sorted by type—pants, tops, etc. The plan was to donate the clothes to a local charity that helped families in need. Her mother would have liked that.

"Have you girls decided what you want to do about the house, if you want to sell it or keep it?" Aunt Maddie asked.

Hannah and Sara exchanged glances. "We haven't decided that yet," Hannah said.

"We thought we'd revisit after a year is up. I'm probably leaning toward selling it but it depends what Hannah wants to do," Sara said.

"I'll probably be fine with selling it, but not just yet," Hannah said. She knew neither one of them could imagine staying there with their mother gone.

They went through the kitchen next and cleared out the cupboards, tossing anything that had expired and setting aside any dried goods or cans that were unopened and still good. They could bring those to the local food pantry. Aunt Maddie had cleared the refrigerator months earlier of perishable stuff, but they did another sweep and emptied it totally and tossed everything in the freezer, too.

They did the books last. Their mother had been a big reader and that's where both Sara and Hannah's love of books came from. She had a nice collection and it was impossible to throw any of her books away. They each took the ones they wanted and left the rest there. Eventually they would do an estate sale and sell the books and anything else that the three of them didn't want.

Hannah thought she was all cried out but her eyes grew damp again when they went into the basement and she and Sara looked at the washer. They'd bought it for their mother just two years ago as a surprise when she complained that hers was acting up and it was going to cost almost as much to fix as it would to buy a new one.

And then again when they went out to her back patio and Hannah saw the cute patio set she'd bought for her mother's birthday one year. The one she'd had was rusted and she hadn't wanted to spend the money on a new one. Hannah had been so excited when she'd found this set on sale at a local furniture shop. It had a painted tile top with vivid blues and greens that swirled into an image of the ocean. Her mother had loved it.

"You have to take that," Sara said.

Hannah wondered if it would fit on the balcony of her Brooklyn apartment. It might be too big. She would have to measure. She hoped it would fit.

"Yeah, I can't give that up. It will be like having a little piece of Mom with me."

They did a final walk-through, put the bags of clothes in the back of Aunt Maddie's car, and called it a day.

"Who's ready for a glass of wine? I know I am," Aunt Maddie said as she locked the front door behind her.

"I am so ready," Sara said, and Hannah agreed.

They drove home to Aunt Maddie's house. Uncle Richie was there and he gave them all a hug, but sensed that they could do without his presence and went in the other room to watch a game on TV.

Aunt Maddie opened a bottle of Santa Margherita pinot grigio, which had been their mother's favorite wine.

"It seemed appropriate," she said as she handed them each a glass of wine and they toasted her memory.

They sat on the deck for hours, remembering their mother, talking about everything else under the sun, drinking wine, eating potato chips and eventually a frozen pizza that Aunt Maddie overcooked, but they ate it anyway.

Toward the end of the evening, it must have been ten or maybe eleven—Hannah had lost track of time—Sara stood and suddenly gave her a hug. "It's been so good seeing you this summer. Maybe you can make this a regular thing, spending your summers in Chatham."

"I think that's a great idea," Aunt Maddie said.

"You can live anywhere," Sara reminded her. "You could even move back here year-round if you wanted to. We'd all love that. But I know you don't want to do that." She sighed. "I know how much you love Brooklyn."

"Spencer kissed me last night." Hannah blurted it out. She hadn't intended on saying anything but the wine loosened her lips.

Sara and Aunt Maddie looked at her in shock.

"What does this mean then? Did you like it?" Sara asked.

Hannah laughed. "Yes, he's a very good kisser."

"So are you a couple now?" Sara pressed.

Hannah shook her head. "No. It took me by surprise. I like Spencer a lot, but I don't see how it could work. I'm heading back to Brooklyn tomorrow."

"You have to do what feels right, honey. I'd love to see you stay, but I know how much you love living in the city," Aunt Maddie said.

Hannah was grateful that she understood. "It's my home now. For almost ten years."

"I'm going to miss you," Sara said simply.

"I'll miss you, too. And now I'll bother you more often by phone."

Sara smiled. "I would hope so."

They went to bed soon after, exhausted from the long day. Sara stayed over and had coffee with them in the morning before heading home. Hannah gave her a final hug and promised to text as soon as she got home.

※

After Sara left, Hannah went for a final morning walk, showered and changed, and headed next door to say goodbye to Joy and Ben. Joy had coffee waiting and Ben came up from the basement to visit with her, too.

"We'll miss you at the weekly writers' group," Joy said.

"I'll miss all of you, too. I really loved the weekly meetings." She'd enjoyed listening to the different stories and hearing their feedback. It was a friendly group and she'd always stayed afterward for a cup of tea with Joy and occasionally for supper.

"Spencer is going to miss you, too," Joy said.

Hannah smiled. "I'll miss him, too. He's become a good friend, both him and Natalie."

"Well, you know how I feel about that. He could be more than a friend. My grandson thinks I don't see how he looks at you. I know you think it couldn't work and maybe you're right. It certainly won't work if he's here and you're there. That's all I have to say about that."

"My wife has strong opinions," Ben said.

Hannah laughed. "I know she does. I am really going to miss both of you."

"Be sure to stop in and say hello next time you come home for a visit," Joy said.

"I will," Hannah assured her. She hugged both of them goodbye and headed back to the house. It was time to go home.

Chapter 39

Aunt Maddie drove Hannah to the airport and Hannah gave her a big hug and thanked her for everything.

"We're family, honey. I told you, you're always welcome in my house. I'm glad it was a good summer. Uncle Richie and I are looking forward to seeing you in the city." Hannah was excited for her aunt and her new promotion. It would be nice to see them there.

Hannah gave her a final wave goodbye as she wheeled her suitcase inside.

Both flights were packed but ran on schedule and a little over three hours later, she jumped into an Uber at JFK airport and was home twenty minutes later.

Her apartment felt so empty and still when she stepped inside. It was also very hot and stuffy. She turned her air-conditioning on, dropped her suitcase in her bedroom, grabbed a cold bottled water from the refrigerator, and took it onto the balcony. She sat at her little bistro table, sipped her water, and listened to the sounds of the city around her. It was much quieter in Chatham. Brooklyn was loud and full of energy and she heard voices of people talking all around her as they walked by on the street below or in apartments that had their windows open. It was a holiday and there were still people celebrating.

As soon as her apartment cooled off, Hannah went back inside, unpacked, and collapsed on her living room sofa. It was good to be home and she was exhausted. It had been a long, emotional weekend and she looked forward to getting a good night's sleep in her own bed.

❦

She woke early the next day and was disoriented at first, expecting to hear the sound of the ocean and instead heard the blare of a car honking outside. It was the Tuesday after Labor Day and everyone was back to work. After a shower and breakfast, Hannah joined them. She took her laptop to her favorite coffee shop, ordered a latte, and settled in the corner. She didn't recognize the barista behind the counter, or anyone actually. She knew turnover was high in places like this. She missed Caitlin's smile and their daily chitchat as she took Hannah's order.

Her writing went slowly as she was working on a new story and wasn't in her usual Chatham surroundings. She figured it would take a few days to adjust, so she wasn't concerned. She had plans to see Lucy later that night for dinner and was looking forward to catching up.

❦

Lucy came over a little before six and suggested going somewhere new.

"I'm sick of all our usual spots around here. Someone at work mentioned a place in the East Village that they loved. Want to check it out?"

Hannah was up for it, so they ordered an Uber and arrived at the recommended restaurant in the East Village twenty minutes later.

It was a trendy spot and Lucy said people had been raving about it all over TikTok.

"They have some really unique cocktails, no food, though, so we should eat dinner elsewhere. It's more of a vibe type of place and there have been some celebrity sightings recently."

"Really? Like who?"

"Leonardo DiCaprio was there a week or two ago, and I forget who else."

Because it was a Tuesday night, they didn't have to wait for a table and were seated right away. Lucy was right, the cocktails were fantastic. They each ordered a specialty drink that their server recommended called the Handsome Devil, made with silver tequila, fresh lime, and lavender honey. It was smooth and different, and it was fun to sip.

Over dinner, Hannah filled Lucy in on her last weekend and the kiss.

"So interesting! I thought I picked up on a vibe. You guys looked good together. Will you do anything about it?"

Hannah shook her head. "It doesn't really change anything. I told you before, there's no point to it."

Lucy sipped her drink in silence for a long moment.

"Look, I love having you back here, I do. But what if Spencer is 'the one'? How did you feel when he kissed you?"

"It was good."

"Okay good or tingling-toes-and-butterflies-taking-flight good?"

"Hmm. Very good." There were definitely tingles and a few flutters.

"Better than Jeremy?"

Hannah laughed. "No comparison."

"Well, then. The answer seems obvious to me."

"You think I should uproot my life and move home to Chatham?"

Lucy shrugged. "Up to you. But why not take a chance? If it doesn't work out, Brooklyn will still be here."

"Hannah, is that you?" Hannah turned and saw Niall walking

toward her with a much younger and very beautiful woman by his side. She looked vaguely familiar, too.

"Niall, good to see you."

He gave her a hug. "Are you home for good now?" Was she?

She nodded. "I just got back yesterday."

"I came back a week ago. Great summer." Hannah introduced Lucy, and Niall introduced his companion. She was a famous Victoria's Secret swimsuit model. As soon as he said her name, Hannah recognized it.

"Well, we won't keep you," Niall said smoothly. "Enjoy your evening." They wandered off and Hannah smiled.

"He seems nice enough," Lucy said.

"Oh, he is. I wonder if he'll ever settle down?"

"He doesn't really need to, I suppose. Men like him, good-looking, with insane wealth, will always be in demand," Lucy said. "There's always someone new coming along."

"Maybe. He is a nice guy though. I hope he's happy." Hannah was feeling contemplative after Lucy's earlier comments.

"He looked happy to me. I'm starving, let's go eat."

The next week Hannah went to all her favorite local spots, found a new coffee shop, and got some writing done. But the nights that she didn't go out, when she stayed in, her apartment seemed so empty. It was fun seeing Lucy and her other friends again, but she couldn't stop thinking about Spencer. And she hadn't heard from him. She hadn't expected that she would, though, this soon.

She and Sara talked almost every day now. Usually in the morning before Sara headed into the bookshop. She was still loving it there and things were going well with Tom. Cody's thirteenth birthday was coming up in a few weeks and they'd decided he would be old enough to babysit the others. Cody was all for the idea, once they told him they'd pay him the going rate for babysitting.

"Tom didn't think we needed to pay him anything. That he should want to keep an eye on his siblings. But I'll feel better if we do—he'll have more of an incentive to pay attention to them. And it's good for him to start earning a little money," Sara had said.

The following Sunday, Hannah slept in, made herself a mug of black coffee, and opened her laptop to read the news. She made room on her small table first, moving a stack of mail out of the way. On top of the pile was her new lease, still unsigned. She needed to get that back to the landlord, but hadn't gotten around to doing it yet.

She sipped her coffee and scanned the local news, then pulled up the Chatham news. There was a new movie at the Orpheum that she wanted to see, a romantic comedy. She'd have to check with Lucy and see if it was playing anywhere near them.

She accidentally clicked a pop-up ad and landed on a real estate rental page. She was about to click off the page when a familiar house caught her eye. It was a cute A-frame style that was on the way to Spencer's house. And it was on the same lake. It felt like a sign of some sort. She clicked on the listing to take a closer look.

It was adorable inside. The description said it was newly painted, the walls were a pretty soft blue with white trim. The kitchen was small but had everything she needed. It was a two-bedroom and there was a gas fireplace in the living room and a deck that over-looked the lake. It was much smaller than Spencer's place, but twice the size of Hannah's apartment and half the rent.

But she was being silly. She clicked out of the listing, and de-cided to go for a long walk, hoping to clear her mind. Hannah walked for over an hour, all over Brooklyn, and she did clear her mind. She came home and before she could change her mind, she pulled the ad up again, and called the number listed. She expected to leave a message since it was a Sunday, but someone answered on the first ring.

"Chatham Realty, this is Susie. How can I help?"

"Oh, I wasn't sure you were open," Hannah stammered. "I'm interested in a rental." She told the woman the address and she looked it up.

"That's available, would you like to make an appointment to see it?"

Hannah had looked at the pictures again and knew the area. She didn't need to make an appointment.

"I'd like to rent it, please."

Chapter 40

A little over two weeks later, on a Wednesday, Hannah moved into the Chatham rental. Once the rental agreement was signed, everything moved quickly and she found a moving company to move her furniture. She didn't have a lot, so it wasn't a big job, and because she was flexible on the day of the week, they were able to squeeze her in sooner.

She went down the day before the movers were scheduled to deliver her furniture and spent the night at Aunt Maddie's. She met the movers at the rental at one. It didn't take them long to move everything in and she spent the rest of the day unpacking.

The house was even cuter in person. Whoever had lived there had taken good care of it. Hannah could turn her spare bedroom into an office and keep a pullout sofa there, too, for overnight guests. She'd never had a dedicated home office before. The price of New York real estate didn't allow for it. She knew she'd still want to go to the coffee shop though. But it would be nice to work in her home office, too.

She'd expected to be wrestling with doubts about her decision, but once it was made, she instead felt like a weight had been lifted. As much as she loved Brooklyn, she'd slowly come to the realization that home didn't have to be a physical place as much as where she felt most connected—where her people were.

Aside from Lucy, most of her family and friends and most importantly, Spencer, were in Chatham. And she thought of Lucy's wise words—that nothing had to be permanent. She could always move back to Brooklyn if she wanted to. But now that she was in Chatham, at her own place, Hannah couldn't imagine that she'd want to go back.

She knew that Spencer usually left work by five thirty, so she waited until six and then drove the short distance to his house.

She breathed a sigh of relief that his car was in the driveway and then felt a rush of butterflies in her stomach. She took a deep breath and pulled in behind him, turned the motor off, and walked to his front door.

Hannah was about to knock when the door flew open, surprising her. She heard the dogs barking and figured they'd heard her car.

"Hannah, what are you doing here?" Spencer looked confused but happy to see her.

She smiled nervously. "I hope you don't mind that I just dropped by. I know you hate that."

A slow smile spread across his face. "It depends who it is."

She felt a tingle in her toes as his eyes met hers. "I have a favor to ask . . ."

Spencer looked amused. "What's that?"

"I need some help moving a table from my mother's patio to my rental house."

It took a moment for her words to sink in and then his smile grew into a grin. "Where is your rental?"

She told him.

"That's right around the corner from here. What about your Brooklyn lease?"

"I didn't sign it. I found something better."

He pulled her close and kissed her hard. She wrapped her arms around his neck and felt a rush of happiness she hadn't felt in a long time. If ever.

When they stopped kissing Spencer looked at her in amazement. "I can't believe you're really here."

"I missed you. Missed my life here. Missed Chatham. But mostly, I missed you," she admitted.

"I missed you, too. I really didn't think you'd come back."

"I wasn't sure, either. But once I was back in Brooklyn, it just didn't feel the same. I wanted to be here. With you."

He kissed her again, then took her hand. "Let's go get that table."

Epilogue

Mid-December

Hannah was excited to host everyone for a holiday gathering a few weeks before Christmas. She had the Michael Bublé holiday station playing on Pandora radio and her small house was completely decorated for Christmas. She had a thick balsam fir tree in the corner of the living room, fully decked out with her favorite ornaments and lots of tiny white lights. Stockings hung on heavy polished reindeer that lined the fireplace mantel, which had silver tinsel garlands draped across it and pine-scented green pillar candles anchoring it in place.

And Hannah was completely settled into the new place now. She'd hung pictures on her walls and over the past few months had found a few more from local artists at the galleries on Main Street in downtown Chatham. She'd set up the spare bedroom as her office. The room faced the lake and had a nice big window with a view of the water. She'd found a glass-topped desk she loved at Pier 1. It was wrought iron in a seafoam-green shade and the combination with the clear glass was really pretty. It came with a matching chair with a white padded cushion. She also got a deal in the clearance section of Jordan's Furniture: a creamy white sofa covered in a crisp cotton fabric. It looked very beachy and it opened into a queen-size mattress.

Her whole family was there—Aunt Maddie and Uncle Richie were home from Manhattan for a long weekend, Sara and Tom and the kids. Joy and Ben, Natalie and Adam, and, of course, Spencer. And Lady and Tramp. They were sprawled out near the fireplace, preening as people kept giving them attention, and they loved every minute of it.

Aunt Maddie and Uncle Richie had surprised her the weekend she moved in with an awesome housewarming gift—a gas grill. She'd never had room for one in Brooklyn. They actually weren't allowed anyway as they were considered safety hazards in her building. It sat on her deck, and she'd used it constantly since it arrived. She had burgers and hot dogs on it now and some chicken and grilled vegetables. She also made sausage-stuffed mushrooms from a recipe that Joy had given her.

Sara had brought potato salad and Natalie had brought chips and soda. Aunt Maddie had brought a platter of shrimp cocktail and Joy had brought brownies. Spencer had brought cheese and crackers and a new IPA beer he'd been wanting to try, from a local brewery. The others had also brought wine and Hannah had some chilling as well. The weekend was beautiful, cold, but sunny and clear. Hannah opened a bottle of her favorite wine, Bread & Butter chardonnay, and poured glasses for everyone who wanted some.

"How's everything going with Spencer?" Natalie asked later after they'd all eaten and when it was just the girls gathered around. The guys and boys were outside, all bundled up and playing cornhole in the backyard. Joy looked especially interested in her answer.

Hannah smiled. "It's going really well." Better than well, actually. They'd seen each other almost every day and they lived so close that they were always at one house or the other.

Joy smiled. "You don't miss Brooklyn, then?"

"I expected that I would. But I haven't missed it at all." That had surprised her the most. From the first night she slept in her new home, she hadn't thought of Brooklyn at all, except for when Lucy called. And it wasn't Brooklyn Hannah missed, just Lucy. But as it turned out, on her last call, Lucy shared some big news.

Things had gotten more serious with the guy she'd been dating off and on for over a year, and they were moving in together on Long Island, which was a good hour and a half from Brooklyn. It just reinforced that Hannah had made the right decision. She would have been lonely in Brooklyn without Lucy around.

Later that evening, once everyone said their goodbyes and Hannah and Spencer cleaned up the deck and kitchen, they took the trash outside and paused for a moment to enjoy the night air. It was colder now and the air felt like it wanted to snow. Hannah had read that flurries were possible at some point.

They stood by the railing and Hannah leaned against Spencer's chest. He put his arm around her shoulders and pulled her close. The sky was still clear and they stared up at the stars and found the Big Dipper and the Little Dipper easily. Spencer pulled her toward him and wrapped his arms around her waist. She turned to face him and her arms automatically found the back of his neck and settled there.

"Have I mentioned how happy I am that you decided to come back?" he asked softly, and she smiled.

"Maybe once or twice."

"No regrets?"

"None. I love it here, Spencer." She took a deep breath as they hadn't yet said the words, but it felt like the right time. "I love you, Spencer."

His face lit up. "I love you, too, Hannah. So much." He kissed her then, to show her how he felt, and she definitely felt her toes tingle. They stopped for a moment when the dogs started barking. Someone at a nearby house had set off fireworks. They watched for a moment as streaks of color filled the sky. It was a perfect, festive way to end the evening.

They went inside and made sure the dogs were okay. They settled down once Spencer and Hannah went inside and curled up at their feet as they sat on the sofa. Spencer reached into his pocket and then got off the sofa and down on one knee. The dogs looked at him in confusion and Hannah was equally confused. Until he held up a small velvet box.

"Hannah, I know it hasn't been that long, but when you know, you know. And I know that you're it for me. And I hope you feel the same. Will you marry me?"

Hannah was speechless for a moment. She hadn't thought this far ahead, since like Spencer said, it hadn't been that long. But unlike Jeremy where she spent two years with him and knew she'd never want to take it further, it was different with Spencer. She knew it was fast, but it also felt right. She couldn't imagine her life without him in it.

"Of course I will."

He slipped the ring on her finger and kissed her. Hannah was so glad she'd waited for someone who made her toes tingle. And she agreed with Spencer—she didn't see a reason to wait any longer now that she'd found her person.

They talked for hours and made plans. They were both happy to be engaged for almost a year or so, until Hannah's lease was up. It took at least that long to properly plan a wedding anyway. Tomorrow she would call everyone and tell them the happy news. But tonight, she wanted to celebrate with the person who mattered most, in her new home. She glanced at her ring. She couldn't stop looking at it since Spencer had put it on her finger.

It was custom-made, a square-cut diamond on a gold band with more small diamonds and a hammered pattern on the gold that looked like waves. It was a piece of art, and Alison's daughter, Julia, had made it.

"I went to see her the day after you moved back," Spencer said. "You took a big leap, a risk moving back here, and so I took a leap, too."

Hannah leaned over and kissed him. "I'm so glad you did. And I'm so happy that I decided to move home. You are my home." Her heart felt even fuller as she glanced out the window and saw the first snowflakes of the season dancing in the light.

Spencer leaned in to kiss her again, and just before his lips met hers, he said, "And you're mine."

Acknowledgments

Thank you to author Judith Campbell and Chris Stokes, the best neighbors ever—to our many suppers together and for inviting me to join your writing group so many years ago.

A special thank-you to my sister Jane and my niece Taylor for their invaluable feedback in reading early drafts of this book. A huge thank-you to my editor, Alexandra Sehulster, for sharing the most helpful insights to make this book stronger. And to associate editor Cassidy Graham for your help in keeping track of everything! And to the wonderful foreign rights team—Sabrina Prestia, Maria Napolitano, and Tori Clayton. A huge thank-you as well to the incredible marketing and sales team—thank you so much for all that you do—Anne Marie Tallberg, Marissa Sangiacomo, Alyssa Gammello, Brant Janeway, and Kejana Ayala. Also a special thank-you to Danielle Christopher for designing such a beautiful cover.

Turn the page for an excerpt from the next book by **Pamela Kelley**

THE CHRISTMAS INN

Available Fall 2024!

***

Chapter One

Riley Sanders sipped a caramel latte as she walked back to her office. It was a little past three and all around her fat snowflakes swirled and danced on their way to the ground. The first snowfall of the year always gave her a thrill. It made her want to go home, curl up on the sofa, and watch a Hallmark Christmas movie.

But she couldn't do that tonight. She and Jack had dinner plans. They were going to their favorite neighborhood Italian restaurant, which was a good thing, because it was close to home. There was barely a dusting on the ground now, but it might get messy later.

Riley turned onto Madison Avenue and walked half a block to her building. She said hello to Gerry, at the security desk, and took the elevator to the fourth floor.

"Boost Marketing, please hold." Marissa, the normally bubbly front desk receptionist, paused when she saw Riley. "They're all in the conference room. Hank said to tell you to join them as soon as you returned." She looked serious, worried even.

Riley dropped her purse on her desk, then went to the conference room where the entire content team of eight people was gathered. In January, she had been promoted to a senior content manager role, which came with a nice raise. She'd loved the role so far, as her responsibilities were still writing-related—and included writing content for their website, social media, email, and print. They had also expanded to managing a small team and working more directly with several of their top clients. Hank looked up and nodded when he saw her. He wasn't smiling. Hank normally always smiled. He was the director of the group and was one of the most upbeat managers Riley had ever worked for.

"Riley, come on in. You haven't missed anything." Hank cleared his throat. "Well, I'll just come right out and say it. I'm afraid I don't have good news. We're laying the content team off, effective immediately. Myself included."

The room was silent. Riley was in shock. She glanced around, and everyone looked equally confused. Finally Sheila, the most senior-level person on the team, spoke. "I don't understand. I thought the company was doing so well. We just landed two big accounts."

"The company is doing better than ever. But apparently we are replaceable," Hank said shortly.

Sheila's jaw dropped. "AI?"

Hank nodded. "Yes. Half of the copywriting team is being laid off as well. Those who remain will oversee all content work done by the AI tools."

"Terrible timing, so close to Christmas," someone else said. It was barely December and normally it was Riley's favorite time of year. This put a huge damper on things.

"Please feel free to use me as a reference," Hank said. "I'm hopeful that we'll all easily find new jobs. I don't think every company is embracing AI the same way. We still have plenty of value to offer."

They all went back to their desks and started packing up their belongings. Riley was just about done when her phone rang and she breathed a sigh of relief when she saw who it was. "Hi, Jack."

She was looking forward to their dinner even more now. After such unexpected news, she welcomed the chance to get out and vent about it.

"Hey, Riley, I can't talk long. I need to cancel for tonight. This case is a killer. I won't get out of here until nine or ten." Jack was a senior associate on the partner track at a big law firm. He was smart and very successful, but he worked long hours. It wasn't unusual for him to cancel last minute like this. Riley understood, though it was a disappointment.

"No worries. Another night." She didn't want to talk about the layoff over the phone, especially since her cubicle was in an open area where others could overhear. Even though she knew they'd be sympathetic, she valued her privacy.

"Definitely. How's tomorrow? I'll be out early and we can have a nice long dinner, anywhere you like."

Riley smiled. "Sounds good. I'll see you then."

All of her personal belongings fit easily into the cardboard box that had appeared on all their desks while they were in the conference room. Marissa nodded sadly as Riley said goodbye as she walked past the reception desk on her way out.

She sighed as she stepped into the elevator and pushed the button for the ground level. It didn't seem real yet. Thankfully, she had enough savings to tide her over until she landed something new. Riley wondered how easy it would actually be to find another job. She enjoyed her work, which was mostly writing company blogs, newsletters, white papers, website content, and social media posts. She hoped that Hank was right and there would be plenty of companies that would still hire people to do the work.

Her one-bedroom apartment was a fifteen-minute walk from the office and she didn't even mind that it was cold and snowflakes kept falling on her face. Riley walked along in a daze. It didn't seem real that they'd all lost their jobs. It was just starting to sink in by the time she reached her apartment. She let herself in and dropped the box onto the kitchen table, hung her coat up, and rubbed her hands together to warm them.

"Meow!" Lily, her beautiful silver-and-brown Maine coon cat, hopped down from her favorite perch by the window that overlooked the busy street below and ambled over to say hello. She rubbed against Riley's leg, purring loudly. Riley bent down and scratched her behind her ears. Lily then threw herself onto the floor and rolled around so Riley could scratch her back and pet her belly. This was their daily routine. When Lily'd had enough, Riley fed her, then stared blankly at her empty refrigerator, wondering what to make herself for dinner.

She hadn't planned anything because she'd thought she was going out to eat. She found a can of pea soup in a cupboard, and while it heated on the stove, she toasted an English muffin and buttered it liberally. She ate in her small dining area and searched on her laptop for her resume. It had been five years since she'd last updated it. Riley sighed, dreading the start of a new job search. She felt numb with the shock and disappointment of the layoff. She'd finally earned her dream job only to have it snatched away too soon.

She stared at the old resume, which needed a major rewrite. She didn't have the energy to do that yet. She closed her laptop, and decided to deal with it all tomorrow. Tonight she was going to pretend that all was well and get lost in a cheerful Christmas movie.

She changed into comfy pajamas, made herself a cup of cinnamon tea, and settled on the sofa. Lily jumped up next to her and Riley picked up the remote as her cell phone rang. It was her sister. Which was odd, Amy almost never called Riley in the evening. They usually spoke in the morning, though it had been a few days since they'd talked.

"Hey, Amy, is everything okay?"

"It's Mom." Amy sounded stressed and a bit shaken. Not at all like her usual calm and annoyingly organized sister. "She broke her leg a few days ago. Is there any chance you could come home for a week or two? She won't ask you—but she really needs some help."

"What happened?"

"She fell off a ladder. She was trying to change the lightbulb in the foyer and lost her balance."

"Oh, no. She's okay, though, otherwise?"

"She is. But she can't put any weight on it for at least a month. So she's going to need help at the inn. I can help a little for a few days, but it's really impossible to do more than that with the girls—they need me at the same time Mom does."

Riley thought for a moment. "Lily and I can drive home tomorrow and stay for at least a few weeks, maybe longer."

"That's great. You can take that much time off work?"

Riley chuckled. "I can now." She told her sister about the layoff.

Amy sounded furious on her behalf. "That's just awful. Can they actually do that? It doesn't seem right."

"There's no law against it. I'm sure I'll be able to find something else. As Mom always says, everything happens for a reason."

"Well, I'm sorry it happened, but I'm so glad you can take the time to come home. It will be nice to hang out. It has been way too long." Riley had only made it home twice in the past year—at Christmas and for a long weekend over the Fourth of July. She'd meant to get back again but the weeks seemed to fly by.

"It really has. I can't wait to see the girls, too." Amy had twin girls that were four years old. Bethany and Emily were adorable and Riley looked forward to a reading session. The girls loved when Auntie Riley read to them. They'd snuggle together on the sofa, a girl on each side, and Riley would read book after book until the girls fell asleep.

She looked forward to seeing her sister in person, too. Amy was four years younger and they'd always been close. Though with Riley living in Manhattan and Amy and her family in Chatham, they didn't see each other often enough. And of course, Riley looked forward to seeing her mother, too. Her parents had divorced years ago, when Riley was twelve, and her father remarried a year later to someone less than half his age. Her father lived in Maine, and they didn't see him often, maybe once a year, if that.

But they had a much closer relationship with their mother. After the divorce, it had felt like the three of them against the world. Her father hadn't worked steadily back then because of a back injury, so child support was minimal. Her mother had worked for two different restaurants, waitressing the lunch shift and often the dinner shift, too, to make enough to pay the mounting bills. She always managed, but there wasn't much left over.

When her grandparents on her mother's side passed, they left everything to her. It wasn't a fortune, but it was enough that her mother was able to pay off her mortgage and buy a bed-and-breakfast that was in walking distance to her home. That was about five years ago, and her mother finally seemed happy and more relaxed.

Not that running the Chatham Coastal Inn was a relaxing job — it definitely had its stresses—but it was a different kind of stress. Her mother had explained that it was exciting to own the business and do everything her way. She'd always loved taking care of people and the guests enjoyed the extra attention to detail. There were only ten rooms, so it wasn't overwhelming. And she had help now to do the cleaning. She'd done it all herself at the beginning and that was definitely too much.

Riley called home as soon as she hung up with her sister. Her mother didn't mention the broken leg right away, and Riley didn't want it to seem like Amy had called to ask her to go home. She wanted to have it come up in conversation so she could just offer to and her mother wouldn't feel that she'd been forced into it. Her mother always worried about being a burden, which was the furthest thing from the truth. So instead Riley shared her news about the layoff.

"Oh, Riley, honey, I'm so sorry. I know how much you loved that job. And right before Christmas, too." Her mother sounded as disappointed as Riley felt and her supportive sympathy made Riley's eyes unexpectedly well up.

Riley took a deep breath. "The timing isn't the best," she agreed. "But I'm sure I'll find something else easily enough. I haven't taken any time off in ages, so I'm looking forward to a little break. I thought I might come and visit, if it's a good time?"

"Of course! It's always a good time to see my girls. Actually, I had a bit of an accident the other day." She told Riley about the fall and the broken leg.

"Oh no! Are you able to get around at all?"

"I'm on crutches. I can still get things done, I'm just slower. At least I have help for the cleaning. And Amy has popped over with the girls to visit. She's manned the front desk while I read to the girls. We're managing."

Riley smiled. Her mother always looked on the bright side even when things were challenging. "Well, I can help, too. I'll be looking for things to do to keep busy. I thought I'd head home tomorrow, if that works for you?"

"That's perfect. I'll see you then, honey."

Beth felt pensive as she ended the call with Riley. She was relieved that she hadn't had to ask Riley to help—she hated to do that as it wasn't like her daughter lived nearby. She didn't want to have her use vacation time to help out. She was excited to see her but also worried to hear about the layoff, especially at this time of year.

As she glanced at the clock, there was a knock at the door. It was exactly seven. She hollered for her best friend, Donna, to let herself in. Donna entered the room holding a big bag of takeout from their favorite Thai restaurant and a bottle of Pinot Noir.

"You didn't have to bring wine, too," Beth said as Donna set the bag on the counter and fished around in a drawer for a wine opener.

"We don't usually drink Pinot, but the guy at the wine shop said it goes well with Thai if you prefer red. So let's see." She poured them each a glass and Beth went to get up to help her with the food, but Donna shot her a look.

"Don't be silly. I've got this. I know where the paper plates are."

Beth laughed and sat back down as Donna handed her a glass of wine. She took a sip. It was smooth and light and a bit peppery. Donna returned a moment later with paper plates, napkins, and utensils, and she put all the boxes of Thai food on the coffee table, within easy reach for Beth. They loaded their plates with pad Thai, spring rolls, and Massaman curry with rice. As they ate, Beth told her that Riley was coming the next day. Donna looked thrilled to hear it.

"That's awful about the layoff. But great timing. I'm glad she's able to come and stay for a while. We don't see enough of Riley these days."

That was true. Riley was busy with her job and boyfriend in Manhattan and made it home just a few times a year and usually just for a long weekend. It would be nice to have her around a bit longer.

"She doesn't seem worried about finding a new job, but it seems like a tough time of year for that," Beth said.

"If she's not worried, I wouldn't be. Riley is good at what she does. She'll find something soon enough. And it will be nice for you to have company this time of year especially."

Beth nodded. Donna was right about that. She was one of the few people that knew that Beth suffered from mild depression, mostly around the holidays. Every year, ever since her marriage ended a week before Christmas, Beth had struggled with the blues at what should be one of the happiest times of the year. She hid it well and forced herself to go all out for the holidays. It kept her busy and she'd created some wonderful memories with Riley and Amy.

Beth had always tried to make sure that the girls never had any idea that this was a tough time of year for her. The heaviness usually lifted a few weeks after the New Year. And over time, it seemed to lessen some. But it was still there. When she broke her leg so suddenly, it was all she could do not to give in to the self-pity and wallow in it for a few days. But of course, she couldn't do that.

"How's Bill?" she asked. Donna's husband was traveling for work this week. Donna was an attorney and had a thriving practice right on Main Street. Many years ago, Bill had been one of her clients and they'd been attracted instantly. Once her work was finished for him, he asked her out to dinner and that was it for them. They married six months later. Beth liked Bill. He was fun to be around, and she often went out to dinner with the two of them.

"He's good. He's not crazy about the food in Louisiana, though. At least not the fried alligator. Says it does not taste like chicken!"

Beth laughed. "At least he tried it."

"True. Speaking of trying things—have you given any thought to putting a profile up and trying online dating? Don't you want someone fun like Bill to do things with?"

"I do. I'd love that," Beth said. "But I don't think I'm ready for online dating. I'm not sure I ever will be."

Donna sighed. "Well, I'm keeping an eye out for you as I always do. But you know all of our friends. I ask Bill all the time if he knows anyone but he says they are all married or people he wouldn't want his friend dating."

Beth smiled. "I appreciate that. I'm not even thinking about any of that right now . . . might be a little difficult to date at the moment anyway." She glanced at her leg, which was propped up on the ottoman. The cast was heavy and it itched occasionally. She couldn't wait to get it off. But until then, she knew she had to be careful so she didn't reinjure herself.

"True. It will be fun for you having Riley around at least. Do you two have anything planned?"

"Just the usual holiday things. It will be a huge help just having her with me at the inn during the day."

"And next weekend with the Christmas Stroll, I'm sure you'll be extra busy," Donna said.

Beth took a sip of her wine. "This is actually very good with the Thai food. We'll have to remember that." She took a bite of a spring roll. "I'm actually not as busy as I was last year at this time. I'm hoping Riley might have some marketing ideas for me."

Donna frowned. "You're not sold out for next weekend?"

"No. Not yet."

"Hmm. Well, hopefully you fill up at the last minute with people that couldn't get to the Nantucket Stroll the night before."

"Maybe. We'll see."

Donna looked at her quietly for a moment, then smiled and lifted her glass, tapping it lightly against Beth's. "Well, cheers to a happier holiday season than usual."

Beth grinned. She was looking forward to spending more time with her girls this year. "Cheers to that."

Riley got up early the next day and packed her biggest suitcase with a wide assortment of clothes—lots of layers as it was the time of year when the temperature in New England could be all over the place. She'd rented a car the night before. After breakfast she'd scoot back to her apartment, and as soon as her rental arrived, she'd grab her suitcase and Lily, and head to the Cape.

She met Jack at seven thirty sharp at their favorite bagel shop. She'd texted him the evening before to share the news about her mother and her trip to the Cape and suggested they meet for a quick breakfast before she left. He was there already when she walked in, which didn't surprise her. Jack was always early. He smiled, and she saw that he'd already ordered for both of them.

"Tall, black, no sugar, and an everything bagel toasted with chive cream cheese. How'd I do?" The flash of annoyance that he hadn't waited to see what she wanted faded when she realized that it was exactly what she would have ordered.

"Perfect, thanks."

"So, you're heading to the Cape today? The agency didn't mind a last-minute day off?" Jack asked.

Riley sighed and told him about the layoff.

His eyes radiated sympathy as she finished recounting the events of the day before. She noticed as usual that not one of his hairs was out of place. Jack was always dressed and groomed impeccably. Today's suit was black with pinstripes, a crisp white shirt, a charcoal-gray tie, and his thick, wavy black hair had just enough gel to give it a polished look and keep the waves under control.

"That's rough. It's not entirely surprising, though. We expect to see more of this now that AI can be used in so many ways. Have you thought about shifting gears a little and doing something slightly different, maybe more analytical or strategic? Something the AI can't easily take over?"

Riley nodded. "You're probably right. I thought I'd take some time to mull that over and see what other skills I have that might be a good complement to the writing. I'm looking forward to not thinking about it at all for a week or two and just helping out my mom and relaxing on the Cape."

Jack frowned. "Don't take too long. The sooner you get back out there, the easier it will be to find something new. You know companies hate gaps on resumes." Riley knew he was right. She also knew Jack had never had a gap to worry about.

She smiled. "Of course. This tends to be a slow time of year for hiring. Lots of hires are put on hold until after the holidays. It always picks up in January."

Jack didn't look convinced. "It's still a good idea to get the ball rolling."

Riley felt a rush of annoyance. She hated when he lectured her—especially when she knew he was probably right. "I need to update my resume. That's the first step."

Jack checked his watch as it beeped with a new text message.

"I need to run. I have a client call in fifteen minutes. That was just my reminder alert. Text me when you get to the Cape safely."

Riley stood. "I will. Good luck with your case." She gave him a quick kiss goodbye and they walked out together, then turned in opposite directions as she headed back to her apartment.

Her rental car was delivered at ten, so she could avoid rush-hour traffic. She quickly brought her suitcase and tote bag with cat food and her laptop down first and put it in the back of the small Honda SUV. Then she ran back upstairs for her purse and for Lily in her soft pink cat carrier. Lily was already not happy about the situation and was meowing in protest as Riley carried her down-stairs and settled her onto the passenger seat. Riley climbed in and turned on the ignition.

Riley's stress about the layoff eased up some as she stepped on the gas. In a few hours she'd be crossing the bridge to the Cape Cod Canal and that always brought a sense of peace, knowing that she was almost home. She was looking forward to relaxing and spending time with her mother and not thinking about her job search for at least a few days.

"Okay, Lily, we're off."

About the Author

Alison Thompson Photography

Pamela Kelley is a *USA Today* and *Wall Street Journal* bestselling author of women's fiction, family sagas, and suspense. Readers often describe her books as feel-good reads with people you'd want as friends. She lives in a historic seaside town near Cape Cod. She has always been an avid reader of women's fiction, romance, mysteries, thrillers, and cookbooks. There's also a good chance you might get hungry when you read her books as she is a foodie and occasionally shares a recipe or two.